Rose Wilkins had an idyllic childhood in the Welsh countryside before being sent off to an all-girls' boarding school. She survived the experience and started writing while studying Classics at university, as an escape from all the gloom and gore on her reading list. She now lives and works in London. Her first novel, *So Super Starry*, was published in 2004.

Rose Wilkins

So Super Stylish

MACMILLAN

First published 2005 by Macmillan Children's Books

This edition published 2006 by Macmillan Children's Books
a division of Macmillan Publishers Limited
20 New Wharf Road, London N1 9RR
Basingstoke and Oxford
www.panmacmillan.com

Associated companies throughout the world

ISBN-13: 978-0-330-43135-4
ISBN-10: 0-330-43135-8

Text copyright © Rose Wilkins 2005

1 3 5 7 9 8 6 4 2

A CIP catalogue record for this book is available from
the British Library.

Typeset by Intype Libra Ltd
Printed and bound in Great Britain by Mackays of Chatham plc, Kent

For my god-daughter, Amara Wilkins

With grateful thanks to Sarah Davies and all the wonderful people at Macmillan, to my agent, Sarah Molloy, and most of all to my parents, William and Lynne, for leading the cheers.

You know it's not going to be a good day when you trip up a paparazzo among the milk bottles. Actually, he was quite nice about it, considering he tumbled backwards down five steps and ended up sitting in a glass-strewn puddle of organic skimmed.

'Oh! I'm terribly sorry!' I said, somewhat flustered, and not feeling entirely respectable in my stripy night-shirt that had shrunk in the wash. I helped him up and tried to brush milk off his behind, wielding the doormat as a sort of giant mop-cum-scouring pad. Unfortunately, its bristles weren't all that clean to begin with and he ended up with little bits of dead leaf and grit in the wet patch. From the smell, I was beginning to suspect my mother had decided to try the deluxe goats' milk again. 'Oh God, I am sorry. It's just – well, I wasn't quite expecting to find anyone there—'

'That's all right . . . quite understand . . . not to worry.' He was backing off nervously. 'An accident. One of those things. Can't think how it happened.'

'As a matter of fact,' I said, 'I think it happened because I suddenly opened the door just as you had crouched down to look through our letterbox.'

'Ah – ahem. Really?'

 1

'Yes. And when you stepped back, you tripped. On the milk.' A thought occurred to me. 'Why *were* you looking through our letterbox, by the way?' (I'd only been awake five minutes, otherwise this question might have come up earlier.)

'Er . . . Lost cat. Wrong number. You know how it is. Anyhow, must be off—'

'Are you sure you're all right?' I'd heard a nasty crack as he'd gone down the steps, but realized that this must have been the camera. I'd only just noticed the camera.

'Oh, perfectly fine. Just perfect. Er, let me know if you find the cat.' He was already halfway down the street.

I picked up the one surviving milk bottle and went back into the house thoughtfully. My mother, clad in a baby-blue negligee and with flaxen tresses tumbling romantically about her shoulders, was sipping guava juice in the kitchen. Somehow she always manages to make the transition from bed to breakfast without ever being spotted with frizzy hair, blotchy cheeks and bleary eyes. A process of transformation must take place at some point, but during my sixteen years of living with her I've yet to see it.

'Good morning, sweetheart! Goodness, is that the only milk? I've already had words with the delivery man, you know. Premium service indeed! Last week we got two pints of filtered soya instead of the one pint GM-free soya and two pints skimmed Kashmiri goat I *specifically* requested. If this alternative dairy regime is going to work, proportion is all, you know . . . and, darling, I don't mean to criticize, but speaking of proportions, that nightshirt is getting just a *little* indecent.'

'Yeah, I know. Just as well I trashed his camera then,' I said, going over to find the Choco-Nut Flakes and my private stash of full-fat, mass-produced cow juice. Instantly, my mother sat up, Kashmiri goat forgotten.

'Camera? What camera? *Whose* camera? Octavia!'

'I don't know exactly, but I think he must have been a journalist,' I said through a mouthful of cereal. 'Lurking by the letterbox with some story about a lost cat. Then when I opened the door we both got a bit tangled up with the milk bottles.'

'Darling! No! What happened next?' she asked breathlessly, hand on heart, eyes wide (she's an actress).

'He fell down the steps and so did the camera. I tried to check he was OK (there was milk and glass everywhere), but he sort of ran away.'

'My goodness. Our very own paparazzi! Or is it paparazzo when it's in the singular?' She patted her hair rather self-consciously. '*What* a bore. It'll mean sneaking round by the back door for the next few days.'

'Do you think he'll be back then?'

'Darling, these people always come back. They're *relentless*.' Her voice throbbed tragically but there was a gleam in her eye. 'I know – what do you think about some sort of disguise? Maybe a *really big* hat is the answer. And huge, gorgeous dark glasses, of course. Like Jackie O.'

I stopped examining my flip-flops for bits of milk bottle and looked at her narrowly. 'Mum, do you know what this is about?'

She got up and started fiddling with the cappuccino machine. 'Whatever do you mean?'

'Well, why are the press interested in us – you – all of a sudden? Of course,' I added hastily, 'people *are* interested in you, being the star of *Lady Jane* and everything, but . . . being stalked outside your own front door, well, that's different. Like they're after something.'

'Now there's no need to be *dramatic*, Octavia. And isn't it about time you got a move on?' she added briskly. 'You wouldn't want to be late for school.'

I've been a member of Year Eleven at the local school, Jethro Park, for nearly a term now. Before that I was at this awful place called Darlinham House, where everyone was the son or daughter of somebody famous and so spent all their time competing for the biggest and best party invite/celebrity pal/gossip-column appearance. The boys went in for brooding looks, wandering eyes and designer stubble. The girls tended to be petite, pouty and bronzed: the Pygmy Blondes. As for the perma-pale, dark-haired and gangling variety . . . well, without even a third-rate modelling contract to my name, it was clear I was destined for life in the Z-list. I'm slightly less gangling these days and I'm learning to make the most of the 'pale and interesting' niche, but the sight of a red carpet still brings me out in a rash.

As far as the actual schooling went, we were very intensively coached in stuff like Contractual Law (Media & Film) and Elementary Buddhism but, unfortunately, our teachers weren't so hot on things like maths or German or biology. I had to have a lot of extra tuition to bring me in line with some quite basic bits of the national curriculum and even so there was an almighty fuss before they let me come to Jethro Park. I've been fine so far but I've still got some catching up to do.

Not that I miss anything about Darlinham House and its flock of Little Darlings. (Except the espresso bar in the library, perhaps. Or the fact that you could stroll into school mid-afternoon and get away with it. All right, so maybe the Vedic Astrology classes were quite fun . . .) Nor am I tempted to entertain my new school friends with tales of life among the rich and shameless. I did attract a bit of attention when I first started at Jethro Park, mainly because a film that Dad directed had recently premiered to quite a lot of fuss. And most people have seen my mother doing her ditzy aristocrat routine at some time or other, whether in her American sitcom, *Lady Jane,* or in her various spin-off activities. But after my first week there, when it was abundantly clear that I wasn't going to be artistic or theatrical or glamorous, everyone forgot to be impressed and more or less left me to get on with things. Which is exactly how I like it, and also why the scene at breakfast had left me with a very ominous feeling indeed.

I said as much to Viv as we were filing out of Double Maths. I've been friends with Viv for years (in fact, I probably wouldn't have survived the Darlings without her), so she is well aware of what At Home With Helena Clairbrook-Cleeve actually involves.

'What was he like then, this stalker of yours? Trench coat and goatee, sleazy grin?'

'No, he was just an ordinary bloke. Denim jacket. A bit balding. I mean, that's the point, isn't it? I only found out by accident. If I hadn't opened the door so suddenly . . .'

Viv gave her hair an impatient flick. She has very good hair for doing this – long and brown and shiny – but Viv's the only girl I've ever met who can toss her hair about and still look tough. 'He can't have been at the peak of his profession. I thought that if these people were after you they stake you out for days and then sort of blend in with the scenery so the first thing you know about it is when you buy a paper and see your cellulite magnified on the front page.'

'That's what I'm afraid of.'

'Cellulite?'

'Duh. No – more journalists. Ones who don't trip over the milk but sneak around looking for scandal . . . oh, Viv, it's just so *odd*. Mum's quite well known, popular even, but she's not . . . exciting. Not hot gossip. What would the paparazzi want with her?'

'Relax. She's hardly the type to be caught snorting cocaine at the Bang-Bang Club. It's mistaken identity or something.'

By now we'd nearly reached the girls' locker room. I drew Viv into the space between the chocolate machine and the caretaker's cupboard. 'That's what I'm worried about, you see.' I lowered my voice. 'Mistaken identity. Well, kind of. Maybe someone's been digging around her past, found out how she's not so posh after all. Maybe they're selling an exposé to the Americans about how she's not an English Rose born and bred, but just a working-class girl who got lucky.'

'Is all that a big secret?'

'Not exactly . . . she just doesn't mention it much.

In interviews and stuff she prefers to dwell on having Lord Clairbrook-Cleeve as her papa-in-law.' I sighed. 'Things are going really well for her at the moment, you know. She's just signed this amazing deal to be the face of Avilon cosmetics, then there's a big acting job lined up, a proper costume drama at last . . . even things between her and Bud seem to be working out. So I guess I'm paranoid that something's about to go wrong.'

Viv gave my shoulders a friendly shake. 'Don't stress. It won't. Anyway, did your mum seem worried?'

I shook my head. Quite the contrary, now I came to think about it.

'There you go, then. And I'm sure that the sight of you in your nightie first thing in the morning was more than enough to frighten one poor lone paparazzi away . . . or should that be paparazzo?'

It was very definitely paparazzi in the plural when I arrived home that afternoon. I was trailing round the corner of our street, lost in thoughts of English course-work, when I suddenly noticed that there was a gaggle of people milling around our front door. It was getting dark, but even from the end of the road I could make out the cameras and microphones. Our neighbours, with whom I've yet to exchange even a nod of greeting since we moved into this house three months ago, clearly weren't the type to indulge in a bit of discreet curtain-twitching – they'd flung open their curtains and shutters and were frankly staring instead. One or two had come out on to their front steps to get a better view of the fun.

Since I stand at the princely height of six feet tall,

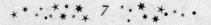

hiding behind a letterbox wasn't really an option, so I retreated round the corner to assess the situation. At that moment a big, shiny black car turned into the street and swept up to our front door. With a sinking feeling I poked my head round the wall again and saw Lady Jane emerge to the flash and whirr of cameras. She was wearing dark glasses, a tight cerise suit and her most dazzling smile. There was a surge of people around her and a babble of questions – none of which I could make out – and then my mother, having obligingly posed for a moment at the top of the steps, disappeared through the door. The car pulled away and slid past me with a soft purr.

Now what was I going to do? The press pack didn't show any signs of disbanding and there was no way I was going to fight through that lot just to get to my own front door. But I certainly couldn't skulk at the end of the street for much longer – what if one of these people recognized me and chased me round west London asking for my angle on . . . well, whatever it was they wanted? I could have gone round to Dad's, of course, but I was burning with curiosity as to what all this was about. At any rate, I reasoned, I'd prefer to find out from my mother rather than wait until the morning papers told me. I dithered for a moment or two, then decided to take a gamble that they hadn't staked out the back door in the garden wall.

The garden door wasn't under surveillance, just locked. Perfect. Cursing and panting, I somehow managed to haul myself over the wall, tearing my school blazer and several nails in the process. Miraculously, I got past the climbing rose without losing an eye and, having picked myself up from the iris bed – shedding bits of leaf and splinters of trellis in my wake – staggered over to the French windows. For a horrible moment I thought these were locked too. However, it turned out that the handle was only a bit stiff so I didn't have to hurl one of Mum's marble cherubs through the glass after all. Then I collapsed on the drawing-room sofa and closed my eyes. A moment later my mother came into the room and let out a piercing shriek.

'Oh my God, darling! What have they *done* to you?'

I tried to reassure her but found that a bit of bark had gone down the wrong way. She enfolded me in her arms, tears welling in her eyes.

'But these people are *animals*! You're covered in blood!'

'Not – animals – rose – bush –' I managed to get out in between the choking. 'HRRGAHMPH.' That was better. 'I had to climb over the garden wall, you see. It was a long way down.' I checked myself in the mirror for signs of bloodshed but was relieved to find only a scratch or three.

'Oh.' She breathed a sigh of relief. 'That's all right then.'

'All *right*? How can it be "all right" to come home and walk straight into a media feeding frenzy? Which, I might add, didn't seem to take *you* wholly by surprise if the short skirt and cheesy smile were anything to go by.' I glared at her accusingly.

'Ah.'

'Well?'

She lowered her eyes bashfully.

'Mum. Please. What exactly is this all about?' My conversation with Viv had come back to haunt me. 'It's not something . . . um . . . illegal, is it?'

'Darling! No! How could you *think* such a thing!' There was an uncomfortable silence. She got up and started pacing up and down the room, wringing her hands a bit. 'Please, Octavia, you have to understand. I really, truly was going to tell you – to *prepare* you. It's just that everything's blown up much quicker than I expected and . . . oh dear . . . I had what I was going to say all planned out and now I'm so flummoxed . . . you *will* forgive me, won't you?' Her voice trembled.

I was beginning to get seriously worried. And also seriously exasperated. 'Mum, just TELL ME.'

She sat down again, took a deep breath, and clasped my hand in hers. 'Actually, it concerns Bud.'

'*Bud*?' Budwin H. Carnaby is my mother's boyfriend. Partner. Paramour. Whatever. They've known each other for years but have only started seeing each other 'seriously' for the last few months. He's an executive in the US cable network company Tempest TV and is your clean-cut, all-American-hero type. I quite like him but, even if I didn't, I still couldn't imagine him getting mixed up with anything dodgy.

'Yes. Bud and his, er, wife.'

'But he's divorced . . . wait a minute . . . oh my God – are you trying to tell me he's still *married*?'

'Technically, yes, I suppose that's correct, but—'

'Either he's married or he isn't, Mum. And if he is, that makes you his *mistress*. The Other Woman.' My voice was starting to rise. 'A home-wrecker, that's what all the papers will call you tomorrow! And you were *posing* for them . . . dear Lord . . . in that tiny red suit . . . bloody hell—'

'It wasn't red. It was cerise.'

'Same difference. You're a scarlet woman now. Oh, Mum, don't you see how bad this is going to look?'

'Nonsense.' She said this very firmly. She seemed to have recovered from her hand-wringing fit. 'You're getting hysterical, Octavia. Just listen while I explain. Now, while Bud is still *technically* married to this woman, they've been living *completely* separate lives for years now. Goodness, they don't even live in the same *state*!'

'Separate lives? Ha! That's the oldest line in the book. I bet he also told you that his wife "didn't understand me". How could you fall for this kind of crap?'

'OCTAVIA. Wait. Think about it. I've been seeing Bud quite openly, as you know. We've been friends for years. All our friends and all our colleagues – yes, even those in the media – have known about our relationship *right from the start* and have never, ever treated it as an "affair". That's because everybody knows that Bud is negotiating a very *tricky* divorce settlement, and the only reason he's put it off for so long is for the sake of his son.'

'So why the fuss? His wife obviously sees things a little differently.'

'That's because she is a very bitter and very *disturbed* person,' said my mother sorrowfully. 'Now that divorce is finally on the horizon this woman is resorting to *desperate measures* to reach a settlement that is wholly in her favour.' She patted my hand reassuringly. 'So, you see, this attempt to set the media on us – it's not "personal", as such. A lot of money, a lot of *status*, is at stake.'

'Status? Mum, who is this woman?'

'Lola Salanova.'

That would explain it. Lola Salanova: hostess-with-the-mostest of American trash TV and now The Wronged Wife. I put my head in my hands.

'Sweetheart, I really don't want you worrying about this. I have always enjoyed *extremely* good relations with the press. Poor Lola needs the attention, you see, now that her new show's slipping down the ratings – not that that's *any* excuse, of course. Name and shame indeed! No, I think her attempt to blow this up as some sort of . . . scandal . . . well, it's going to backfire. Bud and I had a long talk today and we've decided that the best way to turn this situation to our advantage is to meet it head on.'

'And how are you going to do that, exactly?'

'Why, we'll confirm everything of course!' She smiled radiantly. 'Once everyone witnesses our commitment to each other, how open, how *genuine* we are, they'll realize that there is nothing in the least bit underhand or – or – *sordid* about our relationship. And to prove it, Bud has come up with the most marvellous idea!' She gave a dramatic pause. 'He's flying into London at the end of the week and rather than checking into a hotel, he and his son are going to come and stay with us instead. We're all going to stand firm and face this together. Isn't it *wonderful*?'

Oh yes – it was wonderful, all right. Fan-bloody-tastic. Absolutely *!#*!*# fabulous. How could Bud do this to us? How could my mother do this to me? Did they have no *shame*?

Well, I thought sourly, it just goes to show that you never truly know a person until you read about them in the tabloids. I thought of Bud's last trip to London, how he'd taken the two of us out to a swish restaurant for Mum's birthday and got some music students to serenade her with Freddy's love song from *My Fair Lady* when the waiters brought the cake in. OK, so it was mildly embarrassing and hugely cheesy, but Mum had loved every minute of it. The cake was wreathed in a garland of roses and Bud made Mum wear them in her hair the whole way back home, even though there were bits of pink icing in the leaves . . . I remembered how playful and giggly they'd been, like little kids. Whenever Bud's around, Mum forgets to pester me about the way I paint my nails/do my hair/eat my lunch or whatever, and she's also a lot nicer to Dad. More relaxed, I suppose. And as for Bud . . . I thought of his manly jaw and good-humoured grin, the way his honest grey eyes misted over whenever he looked at my mother . . .

Bud the love rat? The wicked seducer? The cad who carelessly abandoned his wife and child for a cute little blonde a whole time-zone away? My mother might be ditzy but she ain't dumb. No, I decided, if she thought Bud was a nice guy in an unfortunate fix I should probably give him the benefit of the doubt. After all, she knew him a lot better than I did. Fine. But what I *really* resented was the way she had sprung this on me without any warning – the lovebirds must have known that Lola couldn't be quietly stashed away like the mad-woman-in-the-attic. In fact, I was ninety-nine per cent sure that the press stampede hadn't come as much of a shock either to my mother or to Bud. The two of them had probably discussed the likelihood weeks, *months*, before. And what was their solution to this hold-the-front-page invasion of peace and privacy? Hunker down and wait until it all blew over? Keep a discreet distance from each other, at least until the divorce papers came through? No: it was cerise suits, group-hugs and – hey presto! – a ready-made nuclear family.

Which was another thing. Bud Junior. Who until now I'd kind of assumed was safely tucked away with the ex-Mrs Carnaby. I wondered, with growing unease, how he was reacting to the happy news that we were all about to Stand Firm and Face This Together.

'I thought you might be here.'

It was eight-thirty the next morning and Viv had found me grimly surveying a stack of *Daily Bellowers* – 'The LADY is a TRAMP!' – in the newsagent's opposite the school gates. I'd had some mad idea of coming in early and buying up every single newspaper in the shop, but was forced to face the fact that there was no way on earth I could raid every single newsagent's, doormat and breakfast table within a five-mile radius of Jethro Park.

'Look. This one's my favourite.' The *People's Snitch* had Lola Salanova's best-known catchphrase – 'Losers Can't Be Choosers' – emblazoned over a five-year-old picture of her, Bud and my mother all grinning tipsily at an awards do. 'But this is kind of catchy too.' I held up a *Comet* with Lady Jane blowing a kiss from the top of our steps in the infamous cerise suit. The caption read

'High-Class Looker Gets Lucky In Lurve.' *Lucky in Love* is the name of one of Lola's game shows.

'Such wit.' Viv eyed the headlines thoughtfully. 'Or maybe I mean shi—'

'Come on, let's go.' I dragged her out of the shop by the arm. A group of Year-Eight girls had just come in and were nudging each other and giggling by the chocolate counter. 'Care to share the joke?' I snarled at a spotty youth who was sniggering by the entrance to the science labs. 'Or are you just hoping for some inside information? You want to know my mother's seduction techniques? Cos from where I'm standing, you need the help.'

'*Octavia*.' Now it was Viv who took me by the arm. 'Ignore him – or do you actually *want* to draw more attention to yourself? Look: it'll be over by tomorrow. You know what these rags are like. The only reason your mum's on the front page is because there's nothing really going on in the news at the moment. Prince Richard hasn't been caught doing something he shouldn't for weeks now.'

'Nothing going on? Only the usual worldwide collection of death, disease and disaster, you mean. And you know what? Death and disaster just about sums up the rest of my school career.'

'Don't be such a drama queen.'

'I am not exaggerating. Everyone, and I mean *every-one* – from dinner ladies to Deputy Head – is going to know *everything*. It'll all be rehashed and raked over . . . the bust-up she had with Lord Clairbrook-Cleeve, Dad leaving Mum for another man, her bodice-ripper days, that advert she did as a dancing yogurt pot . . . every crappy thing that's ever happened, just in case they missed it the first time around.'

'This is about your mother, not about you, and anyone with half a brain will know it. Anyway, it's nearly the end of term, so people will have the whole Christmas holiday to forget about it . . . and, talking of disaster, we're already late for registration. Come on, girl – stiffen that upper lip and let's get it over with.'

Registration wasn't disastrous but it wasn't much fun either. Mr Pemberton, our form teacher, bears a grudge against the world in general and anything connected to showbiz in particular. Viv's theory is that he was a failed actor or musician in his youth, which might explain all those cute little mottos along the lines of 'Only a lowlife thrives in the limelight' or 'As long as celebrity's a ticket to the top, talent's the road to nowhere' or 'Tight connections and loose morals – that's what you need to join the fame-game club.' I would love to be able to tell him that I actually agree with him on much of this but my own showbiz connections, small as they are, seem to particularly irritate him and he's been on the lookout for diva-like behaviour from me ever since I condescended to join 'our humble community' (as he likes to put it). So far I've been careful to keep my head down and look suitably shy and retiring in his presence but now, thanks to Lady Jane's antics, he had the perfect opportunity to make one of his feeble digs. 'Ah, the Right Honourable Clairbrook-Cleeve! How gracious of you to join us. I'd be very sorry to *miss and tell* – ha ha – when I got to your name in the register.'

After assembly Vicky and Meera scampered up to

me in the corridor. Vicky and Meera are diehard celebrity groupies and at one time had great hopes that I would put them in the path of film stars and pop idols. So far they'd been sadly disappointed, but my mother's appearance in the papers had put new heart in them. A spot of high-profile adultery is nearly as exciting as an Oscar nomination or fashionable eating disorder, after all.

'Hi, Octavia,' said Vicky, goggle-eyed and oozing sympathy. 'How are you feeling?'

'Fine, thanks.' I flashed them a cheery smile and tried to move on, only to find Meera blocking my way.

'You're very *brave*,' she said. 'I would have *died*, seeing my mother like that.'

'Like what, exactly?'

'Well, her private life stripped bare for all the world to see. I hadn't realized that she's had such a *turbulent* past. Not that she's done anything wrong, of course,' she added hastily.

'I think it's really romantic,' put in Vicky. 'Star-crossed lovers and all that.'

'Let's just hope I don't get home to find her and Bud lying dead in the family vault, then. Now, I'm already late for—'

'Bud looks very *manly* in those photos,' said Meera, hot on my heels. 'He works in a TV company, doesn't he? I bet with a job like that he must know lots of stars.'

'So is he going to be your stepfather, then?' Vicky called after me as I fled into the girls' toilets.

The rest of my classmates were fairly tactful, although Viv had to physically restrain me after one of the lads from the year above called out, 'Wha-hey, Octavia, your mum looks a bit of a goer!' as I crossed the playground between lessons. Someone else shouted out – to a chorus of whistles and catcalls – that if Lady J felt the urge for a younger man she could give him a call any day of the week. Even so, I almost preferred this kind of thing to all those people who made a point of being extra specially super-nice. My teachers used a gentle, sickroom voice whenever they talked to me that only made me feel more enraged. It was almost as if someone in the family had *died*. I couldn't help but think, wistfully, of how much easier this would have been at Darlinham House, where every other week somebody's next of kin was embroiled in a high-profile sex scandal or court case or drug/alcohol addiction claim. Nobody ever bothered to pass comment because it was entirely possible that it would be your turn for the named-and-shamed relative next week.

Lunchtime saw me avoiding the cafeteria in favour of eating sandwiches with Viv and Hannah in a quiet corner of our form room. Hannah joined Jethro Park the same time as me and is one of those slightly irritating people who agrees with everything anybody ever says. This can have its advantages when you're in need of a good rant, however.

In spite of a half-hearted attempt to move the conversation on to general topics such as Freddie Lions's new single or the boy in Year Nine with the Mohican haircut, Viv had just launched into a lecture on sexism and double standards in the media.

'It's shocking, really – look how Bud hardly gets a mention even though he's the one doing the cheating,' she said, 'and yet we get to know all the dirt on your mum and, to a lesser extent, Lola.'

'Oooh, I know. It's really unfair, isn't it?' said Hannah.

'Yes, but Mum and Lola are in the public eye. Not many people outside the industry would recognize Bud until now,' I pointed out.

'That's very true,' chimed in Hannah.

'Even so, it's still women who get criticized for not being faithful or chaste or whatever, while men are applauded for acting like studs. And it's not just in the media, either, that men can get away with it. It's the same in school – look at Jack.' Jack is one of the most admired guys in our year and is just as popular with boys as with girls. He also happens to be a grade-A slapper.

'You are so right,' said Hannah, nodding her head wisely.

'No she's not. Jack's a very *genuine* and *caring* person,' said Jack's latest fling, Katie, who had come over to pin a poster for Jack's band on to the noticeboard.

'Oh, absolutely,' agreed Hannah.

'Forget about Jack,' said Viv impatiently. 'My point is that Helena's reputation is especially vulnerable because she's a successful and attractive woman. And as far as the press is concerned, that makes her an obvious candidate for temptress-of-the-month.'

'Poor old Lady Jane,' I sighed. 'I don't think she realizes quite what she's getting into.'

'For the only child of media darlings, you're very naive.' This was from Ben, who had wandered over with Katie. Ben is the only person at school who I really don't get on with. Like Mr Pemberton, he assumes that I think I'm doing everybody a massive favour by giving up the young, posh 'n' loaded lifestyle to slum it with the yobbos of Jethro Park. He's supposed to be very clever but, as far as I can see, he doesn't do anything but slope around looking sort of sarcastic. 'Of *course* she knew exactly what she was getting into.'

'What are you trying to say?'

'Well,' he said, sprawling comfortably in a chair opposite, 'doesn't it strike you as odd that all this has come out just as she's taken a break from that sitcom of hers? I'll make a bet that every article about her fling with Bim or Butt or whoever he is mentions her new role in the *Gone With the Wind* remake.'

'So?'

'Quite convenient, isn't it, that all this attention comes as she's relaunching her career as a straight actress?'

'He's got a point,' said the horrible Hannah.

'He doesn't know what he's talking about.' I flushed angrily. 'If my mother was going to sleep her way to an Oscar nomination she'd choose someone a hell of a lot more super-starry than poor old Bud. Mum didn't fix this. It was Lola, trying to get the sympathy vote because her new quiz show's on the blink and she wants to screw Bud over in the divorce settlement.'

'Calm down,' said Ben patronizingly. 'Maybe you're right. But whether it was your mother or this Lola woman who first contacted the press, my point's the same. You lot use the media whenever it suits you and then when something comes out that you don't like you start making Bambi eyes and bleating about invasion of privacy or discrimination or whatever. Then you expect the rest of the world to feel sorry for you.'

'What do you mean by "you lot"?' 'What would *you* know about discrimination?' said Viv and I at the same time in mutual outrage. But Ben had already got up and wandered away, giving me a funny lopsided smile as he went.

'Bastard,' said Viv.

'A *complete* bastard,' said Hannah.

'Look, will you please stop slagging off Jack?' said Katie, with a truly stupendous glare.

I went home by a different route than normal and approached our street with unusual caution. I'd even packed a baseball cap and dark glasses when I'd sneaked out of the back of the house that morning, just in case. As it turned out, there were a few journalists loitering by the front steps but nothing like the mob of the day before. They still hadn't wised up to the door in the garden wall and now that I was equipped with the right key I was able to let myself in without difficulty. Even so, I went into the house rather nervously. I hadn't a clue how Mum would react to her write-up in the papers. I half expected to find her collapsed on the chaise longue in flowing black robes, dabbing her eyes with a scented handkerchief. As it happened, she was sitting at the dining-room table with her lawyer, agent and publicist, all of whom were drinking rosé and laughing. An assortment of newspapers was spread out before them.

'Hello, darling! Good day at school?'

'I've had better . . . how was yours?'

'Simply *brutal*.' My mother failed to look brutalized. In fact, she was glowing. 'Come and have a glass of wine with us, sweetheart. Malcolm, Frisbee, Euphoria and I are just toasting the end of a very exhausting couple of days.'

'You really think the worst is over then? Er, no thanks.' I waved away Frisbee, Mum's agent, who was sloshing the wine bottle about. The second wine bottle, I noticed.

'Absolutely.' This was Euphoria, the publicist, who in spite of an unfortunate taste for wild grey curls, bangles and billowing purple drapes manages to be both smooth as butter and hard as nails. 'Helena and Bud's joint statement struck *exactly* the right note. Of course, as soon as he gets here the paparazzi will probably come out to play again, but once we've organized an official interview or two things should be well and truly under control.'

'So you see, darling,' my mother put in, 'you really mustn't worry about me. I've already received all these wonderful, wonderful messages of support. *Very* touching. I can always count on my fans, of course, but you know who sent me a little message of encouragement today? Can you guess?'

I shook my head.

'Tigerlily Clements!' My mother was triumphant. 'She said she had *every sympathy* for what I was going through. That sad business of her and the Uzbekistani oil baron if you remember . . . it just goes to show doesn't it?'

'Show what?'

'That even millionaire ex-supermodels suffer from

heartache, of course! I've only met Tigerlily once,' she explained to the others, 'but her daughter, India, used to go to school with Octavia so I suppose she feels we have a certain *bond*.'

I laughed a short and bitter laugh. India is the pygmy-blonde spawn of Tigerlily Clements and wrinkly rock star Sir Rich Withers and the only bond we ever shared was one of mutual loathing. This intensified after I became involved with her brother Alexis: an inexplicable and shameful lapse of taste on his part, as far as she was concerned. To be honest, it was pretty inexplicable on my part too. Tall, Dark and Handsome was not enough to compensate for sharing a gene pool with Short, Blonde and Poisonous. I decided it was time to change the subject. 'But what about the stuff in the papers?'

'Not bad at all,' my mother beamed. '*All* of them mentioned that I'll be playing Scarlett's mother in the *Gone With the Wind* miniseries! And despite their horrid headline, the *Bellower* was *very* complimentary about that dress I wore to your father's premiere! Of course, the American press has been the *teeniest* little bit more hostile because, well, Lola's quite an institution over there but, what with the Prince Richard punch-up in Las Vegas last night, she won't get a *tenth* of the coverage she's hoping for.'

'She will be *mad*,' said Euphoria with relish, bangles jangling away. 'You know, if she really wants to boost her ratings she should stop trying to play the tragedy queen and concentrate on revamping that God-awful show of hers. What's it called?'

'*Losers Can't Be Choosers*,' said Frisbee.

'No, that's just her catchphrase. More wine, anyone?' said my mother.

'Are we talking about the show with the Last Chance Carousel?' asked Malcolm gravely, holding out his glass for a top-up. 'Because I quite like that one.'

At this point I left. They looked as if they were settling in for the evening and I'd had more than enough tabloid tittle-tattle for one day. I was also feeling slightly uneasy about Ben's remarks on media manipulation. Of course, he was totally wrong about Mum setting up her relationship with Bud as some kind of twisted publicity stunt. That was just the mean-minded, cynical way that Ben's mind worked as he looked down his superior nose at everyone and everything. But even so, it was fairly obvious that the press onslaught hadn't taken her completely by surprise . . . and all the attention *had* given her profile a boost . . .

I decided to go round to Dad and Michael's since, judging from the unruly laughter now coming from the dining room, there wasn't much chance of getting any work done at home. Dad wasn't yet back from rehearsals at the National Theatre when I arrived but Michael, his boyfriend, had already started on supper and sat me down in the kitchen with a pile of potatoes to peel. There are some times in life when peeling potatoes is very good for the soul. Then I made a special potato-face carving for Dad, which Michael said bore a spooky resemblance to his current leading lady, Dame Tilda Sweeney. Michael had just started on a potato-portrait of me when Dad came in.

'Hello, hello.' He gave Michael and me a kiss. 'How lovely to see you.' He took another look at the potato.

'Goodness me, if I'd known that Dame Tilda was dining with us tonight I would have put on a tie. And, er, speaking of grandes dames, how's Helena bearing up?'

'Nobly. In fact, being in the midst of a sex-scandal seems to suit her.'

'Ah.'

We didn't discuss it any further until after supper. I went into Michael's study to make a start on my history essay but had only got as far as my opening paragraph when Dad came in with a cup of tea. 'Is your mother really all right? I haven't been following the story, of course, but I gather that this Salanova woman is a force to be reckoned with.'

'Oh, Mum seems to be holding her own . . . even though Lola's done her best to make her out to be a posh, man-stealing bitch.'

'So, presumably, it won't suit Lola's purposes to bring up Lady Jane's past life as Helen Slater?'

'The plucky little lady from the wrong side of the tracks? No, I gather that's Lola's pitch. Apparently she put herself through college by working nights at a Vegas casino, then got talent-spotted making calls at a bingo hall. She's the American Dream. Mum's the evil English aristocrat.'

Dad sighed and rubbed his face. 'This kind of situation can so quickly get out of hand . . . I hope she's got people looking out for her?'

'Oh yes. I left her knocking back the rosé with the usual gang – Malcolm and Frisbee and Euphoria. They're having a right old time. And Bud, of course, arrives on Saturday. With Bud Junior in tow. We're all going to Face This Together, apparently.'

'I see. And how do you feel about that? You get on well with Bud, don't you?'

'Yeah . . . I guess. I just didn't . . . well . . . I suppose I didn't realize how serious they were. It's all a bit sudden. I mean, he's moving *in* with us for the next couple of weeks. And his son too . . . I've never met the son.' As a matter of fact, it was only now that the implications of this were really hitting home. Vicky's remark about star-crossed stepfathers was also beginning to prey on my mind. 'I hadn't expected to be playing happy families this soon, that's for sure.'

'It's certainly very sudden. But sometimes these things need a bit of pressure to resolve themselves, to move on to the next stage, as it were, so that everybody knows where they stand.'

'The thing is, I've been so busy stressing about the stuff in the papers – and how people will react in school and everything – I haven't had a chance to think about the whole Clairbrook-Cleeve-Carnaby scenario.' I fidgeted with my pencil case. 'But what I do know is that Mum's been so happy lately. And it's not just the fact her career's on the up. Bud's her first boyfriend in *ages*. I think she really likes him and I don't want anything to spoil that.'

'Good girl.' Dad gave me a hug. 'Good girl. Helena's very lucky to have you rooting for her. I'm sure that everything will work out just fine.'

The Friday night before Bud's arrival I decided to do a little preparatory research. Even now, it was hard to believe that I could have been so blissfully ignorant of the not-so-ex-Mrs Carnaby's day job. So I channel-hopped until I found a Lola Salanova game show, watching it in my room with the volume turned down so that Mum wouldn't know what I was up to. I hit on a repeat of one of the earlier series called *Twist of Fate*, in which Lola was dressed up in some kind of Arabian belly dancer/gypsy costume. It was basically like charades in that the contestants had to guess a well-known phrase or film or song title or whatever, but the clues were all disguised as fortune-telling tricks. There was a smoke-filled crystal ball that lit up with random images, and playing cards whose sequence of numbers had a special meaning, and tea leaves that formed patterns in a giant teacup. And all the while Lola pranced around in her headdress and bangles, tossing her long red hair, wiggling her sequin-encrusted breasts and bottom, and casting mysterious looks at the camera. At the end of the show, the winner picked a prize out of a jar presented by a sulky-looking kid in a gold turban and Lola disappeared in a puff of glitter.

How on earth did Bud fit in with all this? Perhaps he was the tall blond stranger whom Lola had foreseen in her crystal ball and then seduced under a cascade of steaming tea leaves . . . Still curious, I decided to go online and check out the show's official website. Before I found the Lola Salanova link, however, my eye was caught by a shout-line on the Tempest TV homepage: 'Tempest Launches Production Arm in London.' This, I knew, was why Bud had been over in the UK such a lot recently; although I usually switched off as soon as he and Mum started to drone on about boring business stuff, it occurred to me that now would be a good time to start paying attention to what Bud and Co. were officially doing over here.

'Spurred by the recent boom in the British film industry,' I read, 'Tempest Films UK was set up in London four months ago to develop, produce or acquire low-budget British films with box office potential. Although in the US the Tempest TV films label is primarily associated with teen features such as the hugely successful *American Cherry* franchise, the London offshoot will focus on bringing cutting-edge, quality British drama to a wider market.' There followed a list of the key players, including 'Budwin H. Carnaby, Director of Marketing'. Hmmm. So ole Buddy Boy's little trips to London were the beginning of something more permanent.

I suppose I should be relieved that he wasn't about to whisk Mum off to a new life of domestic bliss in America, especially as she already spends most of the summer there filming *Lady Jane* while I stay in London with Dad and Michael. It's nice going to visit Mum when she's working in the States, but it's even nicer to come home again. The only person I got on with at Darlinham House, a girl called Jezebel but known as Jess, had to move over to LA in the summer when her mother became the personal trainer to TV starlet Bambi Luxmore. She occasionally sends me homesick emails requesting emergency parcels of Marmite and PG Tips and complaining that people keep telling her what a super-cute accent she has.

I was just investigating one of Lola's multiple fansites when my mother knocked on the door. I disconnected guiltily, but not before the screen had filled with a portrait of a vampy sort of woman, all big shiny hair and teeth and nails. She was photographed hugging a puppy but, in spite of the smile and the soft-focus glow, there was something about her eyes that suggested she'd be just as likely to kick the poor beast as cuddle it.

'Sorry to disturb you, sweetheart, I know how hard this new school of yours likes to work you.'

'Don't worry, I was just, er, finishing.'

'Good, because I wanted to have a little chat.' She curled up on my bed and patted the space next to her invitingly. 'As you know, Bud and dear Miles are flying into Heathrow tomorrow afternoon—'

'Miles? His son, you mean?'

'Yes. I'm pretty sure it's Miles, not Mike. Or maybe it's Milo . . .' said my mother vaguely. 'I haven't met him before but he's bound to be awfully sweet. And he's *practically* your own age.'

'Practically?'

'Oh yes. Well, almost. Fourteen, I believe.' Great. I have yet to meet a fourteen-year-old boy who could be described as awfully sweet. Awful sounded more likely. I'd always assumed Bud's son was still at the knee-high stage from the goopy expression Bud wore whenever he had mentioned 'my boy back home'. Which wasn't very often, come to think of it.

'And what does Mike/Miles/Milo feel about it all?'

'What do you mean?'

'Well, let's face it, it's his mother who's been ditched for a younger blonde.'

'Darling! I thought I explained the situation. And for goodness' sake, Lola and I are only a year or two apart . . . it's hardly my fault if she's been tanning herself to leather for the last fifteen years . . . Where was I? Oh yes. Heathrow. Well, I was talking the situation over with Euphoria and she feels that Bud's arrival at the airport is the *ideal* photo opportunity. The press are *bound* to be hanging around, especially if we let slip that Lady Jane and her daughter are going out there to welcome Bud and his son into their hearts the *very moment* they step off that plane.'

I stared at her, aghast.

'Now, sweetheart, there's absolutely no need to look like that. It's going to be a very *natural*, a very *spontaneous* occasion. And anyway,' she added, suddenly all practical and brisk, 'it's either got to be at the airport or here on our own front steps, and the neighbours are hardly likely to thank us if we have to go through all that again. I don't know about you, but I think we've had enough of people camping on our doorstep.'

'True,' I managed to croak. Weakly.

'Poor baby. I know how you hate this sort of thing, I really do. And, to be honest, I'm not much looking forward to it myself. But this way we get things *over* with. We take a stand. We show the world. We give the press what they want. And then we're left alone.'

'So you hope.'

My mother sighed. 'I do feel bad putting all this pressure on you so suddenly. Everything's so . . . so *new* still.' Now she looked down at her hands a little shyly. 'I haven't wanted to say this before but sometimes, since your father and I . . . well, sometimes I've been rather – lonely. Maybe I didn't realize quite *how* lonely. Bud's changed that, you see.'

Saturday afternoon and my mother and I were speeding off to Heathrow in a chauffeur-driven car. Lady Jane was surprisingly nervous, repeatedly smoothing her hair and fiddling with her watch. She had on a new outfit for the occasion – casual trousers, a sugar-pink bouclé jacket and pearls – that was a marked departure from the Scarlet Woman suit. I was in my usual jeans and a jumper and had expected a scene, but after a pursed-lipped inspection my mother had conceded, 'Yes, maybe you're right. The wholesome, homely look. So much more *approachable*.'

When we got to the arrivals lounge I felt prickly with nerves and even Lady Jane looked a bit pale. However, Frisbee and Euphoria were already there to coordinate things, as well as some security people from the airport. To be honest, I don't think this was strictly necessary as there were only a few reporters hanging around slurping coffee, but this was still more than enough to attract a gaggle of curious onlookers. I hung back and slouched down to make myself look as small as possible. Then my mother gripped my arm so hard it hurt. 'Come on, they're *here*,' she hissed. 'Smile, darling! Big smile!' And with that we were rushing, arms out-stretched, towards a large fair man and his smaller, darker shadow.

'Princess!'

'Hero!'

Bud swung my mother, laughing, around and off her feet. Mike/Miles/Milo and I looked at each other for a split second of appalled irresolution. Then we sort of collided together – less of a warm hug than a particularly clumsy bump. There was the flash and whirr of cameras around us and then Bud and Mum, hand in hand, turned to face the (small) crowd.

'It feels so great to be in this glorious nation of England again,' proclaimed Bud, clearing his throat, 'and now that I and my son have been welcomed by two people very dear to our hearts, I have no doubt in my mind that we can put the, uh, turmoil of the last few days behind us. And that's all I have to say on this occasion. Thank you very much.' Then, oh blessed relief, Frisbee and Euphoria and the security people closed ranks and we somehow shuffled off.

The rest of the journey home passed in a blur. Bud and Mum and even the driver were talking nineteen to the dozen while Mike/Miles/Milo and I sat side by side in mutual, and ever increasing, gloom. I hadn't had time at the airport to actually take in what he looked like but I'd seen enough to know that he was dressed head to toe in funeral black. Somehow I didn't think this could be a good sign.

There wasn't anyone prowling around with a camera when we got back, which was just as well given the fuss it took to get all Bud and Bud Junior's bags from the car into the house. (Mum looked rather disappointed though.) Once the chauffeur had driven off and the suitcases and we were collected in the hall there was a slightly embarrassed pause.

'Now then,' said Lady Jane brightly, 'Octavia, why don't you show dear Mi— er . . . show your guest to his room? And after you've had time to refresh yourselves, we'll all sit down to a good old-fashioned English tea.'

'Oh boy,' exclaimed Bud. 'Doesn't that sound great, Milton?'

Milton (for it was he) heaved a deep and sorrowful sigh. 'Just great, Dad.' It was the kind of voice that might have floated out of a crypt. Slowly and silently we turned and began to climb the stairs; slowly and silently we each dragged a truly mammoth suitcase step over step; slowly and silently we hauled our loads along the landing.

When we got to the guest bedroom, a tasteful confection of powder-blue drapes and lace-trimmed scatter cushions, we set down the suitcases and stood facing each other, wheezing slightly. Bud is big and blond and square-jawed and always seems about to burst out of his sober executive shirts and go wrestle a crocodile or something. His son was thin and sallow with pale-blue eyes. He was dressed all in black, mousy roots showing within a mop of jet-black hair. There was a small green skull printed on the front of his T-shirt.

'Hey.'

'Hey.'

'I'm, ah, Octavia.'

'That figures.' Pause. 'I'm Milton.'

'Right . . . as in Keynes?'

He heaved another colossal sigh. '*Paradise Lost.*'

I stared. I knew that Americans could get sentimental about ye olde motherland, but surely not even its most loyal citizens would describe Milton Keynes as a heavenly city.

'As in *John* Milton. The seventeenth-century poet,' explained Milton, with unutterable contempt.

'Right.' Another pause. 'So, er, welcome to London.' Glassy smile. 'Is this your first visit to Europe?'

'Europe,' announced Milton, 'is dead. It is the decaying carcass of the old world order, crumbling under the stinking mass of its own apathy, corruption and decadence.'

'Oh. I'm sorry to hear that.'

'I think I'm going to like it here,' said Milton, in funereal tones.

'. . . and then,' I said to Viv on the phone late that night, 'we went downstairs and had this excruciating tea – cucumber sandwiches and sponge cake galore – and Bud kept bursting into tears all the time and telling us how much he loved us.'

'Is he on some kind of medication?'

'I'm beginning to think we all should be. No, I'm exaggerating a bit . . . he wasn't bawling into the Earl Grey, exactly . . . just getting a lump in his throat and dashing away a manly tear and clenching his jaw in a heroic sort of way. And saying stuff like, "Words cannot express how much this time of loving union means to me," or, "The bond between Helena and I is more precious than diamonds and deeper than oceans." Or something.'

'Bloody hell.'

'And do you know what the weirdest thing is? He actually *means* it.'

'I thought he was some hotshot executive. You know, tough.'

'I'm sure he could still be pretty scary in a board meeting . . . I think he's been watching too many of his own TV shows lately, that's all. I always knew he went a bit moist-eyed around Mum, but this business with Lola and the tabloids has tipped him over the edge. It's like Santa Claus on Prozac.'

'No wonder Milton is a manic-depressive.'

'Yeah. I'm just worried that we're going to wake up one morning and find he's slit all our throats.'

Viv laughed. 'Merry Christmas, Octavia.'

It was now the last Monday of term and although, thanks to my mother's brush with the tabloids, I'd thought I couldn't escape the school corridors fast enough, I was now dreading the onset of the holidays. Bud and Milton's stay looked as if it were going to be extended at least until after Christmas and I didn't think I could face any more family bonding over the cucumber sandwiches. The only bright spot, as far as I could see, was Freddie Lions pulling down his trousers at a pop concert; this, and a group of asylum seekers' daring raid on a burger van in Brighton, had ensured that our touching scene at the airport hadn't made a single front page. The *Comet* hadn't even reported it at all. Lady Jane was outraged.

'I do see her point,' I confided to Viv during morning break. 'The press only really care about the bad stuff. When it's something positive, people aren't all that interested.'

'I know. It's *just* like me and Jack.' This was Katie.

'It is?'

'Totally. People weren't paying me *any* attention when we were together but now he – I mean *we* decided to move on, well, suddenly I'm hot gossip.' She tossed her head. 'Not that I'm going to oblige them. What Jack and I had was something . . . special . . . private . . . and no one can take that away from us.'

'So special,' sighed Hannah.

'Special? After one week?' Viv muttered in my ear.

'But then I'm lucky, I suppose,' mused Katie. 'I can still keep my personal life more or less to myself. I guess it must be extra hard for you, Octavia. Dating, that is. Do you think it scares guys off, the fact that they might end up all over the papers?'

'Hardly,' I said, amused. 'Who'd want to know about me? Nobody gives a stuff.'

'Aww. Poor little rich girl, does nobody care?' Ben had just come up behind us and draped an arm around my shoulder.

'Shut up, Ben,' said Viv.

'No offence meant.'

'Too bad, it was taken.' I glared at him. He shrugged and moved on. 'God, what *is* his problem?'

'Inferiority issues relating to dominant females,' said Viv wisely. 'Possible castration complex.' She winked at me.

'Uurgh!' said Katie, tossing her head again. 'Well, I don't know about castration but he's certainly *complex*. And quite sexy, don't you think?'

'So lovely and tall!' sighed Hannah.

'That's a point,' said Viv, giving me a significant look. I glared back at her – it really annoys me when people assume that any male who is as tall as I am is, hey presto, a sure-fire romantic match. Not that Ben is my height anyway. I'd say he was nearly a whole inch shorter than me, in fact.

'Ben's not in Jack's league, of course,' continued Katie, 'but I do like those moody, mysterious types . . . like that Heathcliff bloke from *Wuthering Heights*, you know? I'm sure Ben's got lots of hidden depth.'

'Ooh yes,' said Hannah, 'and those lovely green eyes!'

'He's not mysterious,' I objected. 'He's just a scruffy, self-important creep with a massive chip on his shoulder. And his eyes aren't green. They're khaki-coloured. Like pond scum.'

During the last week of school I threw myself into extra-curricular activities with mindless enthusiasm. I managed to find something to do every evening, whether it was turning pages at the piano in rehearsal for Friday's end-of-term concert or attending the Young Vegan Society's festive debate ('Christmas: A Carnival of Cruelty?') or carol singing in aid of the library fund. After these pleasant occupations came to an end I went round to Viv's or Dad's and one night even helped Katie to track down and destroy every poster for Jack's band she'd ever put up. (Jack was now 'shamelessly flaunting' his new-found relationship with Emma 'Double D' Jones, apparently.) The result of all this public-spirited activity was that the only time I was at home was spent sleeping or eating a solitary breakfast.

Bud, who usually got back from his early-morning three-mile run just as I was leaving the house, was most admiring. 'Wow! Your mom must be so proud – you're a real team player!' My mother, however, was less impressed and managed to corner me in the hall as I let myself in just before midnight on Thursday.

'Either you're embarking on a secret life of sex and drugs or you're deliberately avoiding us, Octavia.'

I affected to look hurt. 'Just because I've decided to give something back to the school community doesn't mean I have criminal tendencies.'

My mother pursed her lips. 'It's time to show a little Christmas spirit, darling. And I'm not talking about the Young Vegans.'

'How about a Young Pagan, then?' She looked confused. 'Milton. Our very own little ray of sunshine. I don't see him about to deck the halls with boughs of holly . . . unless, of course, it's in preparation for a Black Mass.'

'Shh.' She lowered her voice and looked around nervously. 'Milton is a very *gifted* boy. Gifted, but troubled. Bud says his IQ is right off the chart, you know, and this causes all sorts of *pressures* . . . the kind of pressures you and I couldn't *possibly* understand. He's taking time off school to recover from some sort of, well, *breakdown*, you see, and Bud hopes the change of scene and, er, personality, will help the Healing Process.'

'Personality? Lola, I presume.'

'Poor Lola's just *given up*, Bud says. Apparently Milton makes her *gloomy*.'

I had some sympathy with Lola on this but kept quiet. 'So you see, darling, it's very important that we all *rally round*. Show our support. If you're already feeling vulnerable, Christmas can be a very stressful time of the year, you know.'

No kidding.

*

It was the Friday afternoon before the school carol concert and 11B were supposedly occupied in taking down the decorations in our classroom and clearing up after our lunchtime 'party'. This had involved polite small talk with a few hapless teachers over mince pies and sausage rolls but had been considerably improved by the rum that somebody smuggled in with the (flat) Coke. The 'Ultimate Xmas Sound Selection' was now blasting away on the stereo while people draped in tinsel were running round chucking balloons and mince pies at each other with tipsy glee.

Those of us who weren't participating in Mince Pie Volleyball were leafing through magazines in a corner while working through a jumbo tin of chocolates. I thought all this was a huge improvement on Christmas revels at Darlinham House, which used to celebrate the holiday by drafting in extra Domestic Therapy Counsellors to help its pupils through the festive season.

'It says here that Freddie Lions is going to break all records for sales of the Christmas number one,' said someone.

'The only thing he'll break is my heart,' sighed Katie. 'That man is sex on legs.'

'Ladies, please, are you talking about me again?' asked Jack, wagging his head so that the mistletoe attached to his reindeer headdress jiggled invitingly. 'Whoa, are those hot babes or *what*?' He was looking over Viv's shoulder at her magazine. 'Check out the legs on that one in the tiara!'

Viv smiled in a superior sort of way. 'Too good even for the likes of you, Jacky boy. These are future debs and they're at a very exclusive party. With Prince Richard, no less.'

'Deborah who?' demanded Jack. You could already see the drool forming.

'Not Deborah – debutantes. Society belles. Posh girls.'

'Like Octavia,' someone explained helpfully.

'Speaking of which,' said Viv, examining the page narrowly, 'isn't that Alex in the middle? Next to the girl in the sequinned halter neck?'

With a sinking feeling, I took a look at the photo. ''Fraid so.'

'What's Alex up to now, have you heard?'

I shrugged. Actually, I *had* heard. According to Euphoria, who likes to keep herself informed about this sort of thing, he was writing a novel on the Dark Side of the Champagne Lifestyle. She told Lady Jane that his mother had bought a villa in St Moritz for him, as a sort of writer's retreat.

'Who's Alex?' asked several people.

'My, er, ex-boyfriend,' I muttered, with a reproachful look at Viv.

'This one? The tall dark one holding a cigarette?'

'Wow. He's *seriously* cute.'

'Hang on. It says here that he's the son of Sir Rich Withers. Isn't he that wrinkly rocker guy?'

'My mum still fancies him!'

'Bet Alex must have been *loaded*.'

'So did you go to parties like that?'

'Did you ever get to meet Prince Richard?'

'Why did you break up then?'

I found I was pink with embarrassment. All around

me were curious, eager, watchful faces. And Ben. Ben, who was arching his brows in a superior, knowing sort of way.

I took a deep breath. 'Yes, I went to parties like that. I broke up with Alex because I didn't enjoy them.'

'Why?'

'Because I didn't fit in. I never felt really comfortable with Alex or Alex's friends or with that sort of lifestyle.'

'Really?' asked Ben smoothly. 'Poor Octavia. You just didn't feel at home with all those posh rich kids so you decided to slum it with us instead. I hope you haven't found adjusting to our standard of living too difficult. Must have been quite a shock to your delicate system.' There was an uncomfortable silence.

'Leave her alone,' said Viv.

'Yeah,' said Jack. 'Chill. What's made you so uptight all of a sudden?'

'Three cheers for Comrade Ben, the social revolutionary,' I said, standing up. 'Very inspiring. But do you know who you really remind me of? Alex. Because you're both shallow, arrogant tossers who think they're better than everyone else. Except that Alex,' I added, 'at least had charm.' And on that devastating note, I turned on my heel and swept grandly out of the room.

Viv caught up with me in the girls' toilets, Hannah in hot pursuit. 'God, Octavia, are you OK? Ben was right out of line.'

'And at Christmas time too!' chorused Hannah, our one-woman backing group.

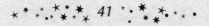

41

'I'm not upset. Just pissed off. Make that *hugely* pissed off.'

'I don't get it,' said Viv, shaking her head, 'Ben's always been a bit stroppy but I don't understand why he has it in for you so badly.'

'Maybe he fancies her.' We turned and stared. Hannah had gone red with the shock, or maybe the stress, of coming out with an original opinion of her own. 'Or maybe not,' she said, twitching. 'What do you think?'

'Not,' I said firmly.

'Yeah, you're so right,' said Hannah, relieved. But Viv looked thoughtful.

'So maybe Ben has castration anxiety after all.'

'Viv, I really don't think—'

'Not *actual* castration. It's just a metaphor to explain why men show hostility to what they desire. Female sexuality is a very powerful force, you know. And since men are afraid of surrendering to their desire in case they're "un-manned" by it, they get all aggressive. It's *defensive*.'

I snorted. 'Have you tried sharing this theory with Simon?' Simon is Viv's boyfriend. He goes to a different school to us, which is probably just as well, given that they have blazing rows every other week or so about stuff like the Dayton Peace Accords or obscure footnotes to UN Security Council Resolutions. They both enjoy these very much and Viv tends to get restless if the kiss-'n'-make-up process goes on for too long. 'No, Viv, sometimes people are just born idiots and you don't need any fancy theories or analysis to explain it.'

*

In spite of all this drama, I enjoyed my first school carol concert. Particularly as no members of my family could attend because tickets were reserved for the families of people in the choir or those in the final year. I think the lunch-party rum may have had a unfavourable effect when it came to Year Eleven's turn to sing a verse of 'Good King Wenceslas', but other than this and all the lights going off in the middle of the Head's Christmas Speech, the event was judged to be a success.

Ben caught up with me when I was at the bus stop.

'Octavia.'

I raised my brows. 'You want something?'

'Yes. To apologize. I shouldn't have said those things this afternoon. I was out of order and I'm sorry.'

'Viv thinks you have castration anxiety.'

'What? Oh.' He laughed. 'No, I don't have a problem with strong women.'

'Just posh ones, right?'

He tugged at his hair. It's a tawny colour, like tortoiseshell almost, and is always falling over his eyes; I had a sudden, irrational desire to put my hands to his face and push it back for him. 'I wasn't being fair, I know that. I didn't mean for you to take it seriously.'

'How else am I supposed to take it? Look, I can't help who my parents are or how they lead their lives and I can't help the fact that you can read all about it in the papers. But I'm not going to apologize for it. I'm not going to apologize for the parties I've been to or the people I've been with, either. I don't owe it to you or *anyone*.'

'Yeah, you're right. I understand.'

'Good.' My tone softened. 'I'm really not like those

people in the magazine, you know. Anyone can see that. So why can't you?'

He gave me one of his mocking, lopsided smiles. 'Maybe because,' he said, 'you'd be too good to be true.'

I got home just after four, in an extremely good mood, and found my mother supervising the installation of our Christmas decorations while dressed in a hooped skirt and a black wig.

'No, no, no, Archimboldo – the white doves and the gilded cherries are for the *drawing*-room mantelpiece. I want the frosted pomegranate and poinsettia garland for the dining room! Oh dear – oh, hello, darling. What do you think?' She flapped her hand distractedly at the tangle of ribbons and garlands and trinkets strewn all over the hallway. A small sulky man with a purple quiff and a nose-ring was standing in the middle.

'Lovely.'

She took me to one side. 'The man's a genius, you know, but rather *temperamental*. I suppose it was the same in the Renaissance,' she added vaguely.

'What was the same?'

'Artists, of course.'

'Right. Mum . . . why are you wearing a wig?'

'Don't you like it? I've never really thought of myself as a brunette, but it's extraordinary how the concept of having dark hair *infuses* one. Method acting, you see.'

All became clear. My mother's preparation for her role as Ellen O'Hara in the *Gone With the Wind* miniseries had already required intensive sessions with an accent coach, a Civil War historian and a black rights

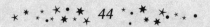

activist. A nineteenth-century-style wig and a hooped skirt were the obvious accessories.

'Welcome to my world of raven-haired loveliness. Maybe people will believe we're related now . . . does Bud approve?'

'Oh, he's been in meetings all day. I don't expect him until late. How was your last day at school?'

'Good. Surprisingly good, actually.'

'I must say, I'll be glad to have you home full-time, as it were. It will be so nice for Milton too. I've been worried it's all been a bit, well, *lonely* . . . especially with Bud having to work right up to Christmas and me with my lines to learn and all this research on the legacy of slavery to do . . .'

I did feel a bit sorry for the boy. 'So what's he been doing all day?'

'Well, as far as I can tell, he's spent most of his time on a video-link with his psychotherapist.'

'Fun.'

'I feel we haven't quite *bonded* yet, you see.' She looked worried. 'And it means so much to Bud that we get along . . . I know, darling, why don't you go up and say hello? Tell him about your day at school, what your friends are doing, that sort of thing. Maybe he'd like to help Archimboldo with the decorations.'

'I think not, lady,' said Archimboldo with a sniff. 'You don' get Mr Man who cleeps hedge to help your brain-surgeon-sir. Not unless,' he added darkly, 'you wan' mek bloody, bloody hell, OK?'

If Archimboldo had wanted to 'mek bloody hell' as part of his design brief, Milton's powder-blue-and-lace boudoir would have been a good place to start. Munch's painting of *The Scream* was taped to the wall above the bed and he'd pinned a thick black drape across the window so that the only light came from a solitary flickering candle. Which, I noticed, was dripping purple wax all over Lady Jane's white-painted Edwardian dressing table with the gilt trim.

'Hi,' I said, voice booming with this awful false heartiness. 'Just thought I'd, ah, pop in and see how you're doing.' Milton barely raised his eyes from the book he was reading. I went in anyway and sat down on the bed – which seemed to have acquired a black drape too. 'What are you reading?'

'*Being and Nothingness*.'

'Any good?'

'That would depend on whether existentialism is your thing.'

'I see.'

'Somehow I doubt it.'

Silence, broken only by the slow turning of the pages. I counted up to ten and tried again. 'Look, I'm sorry if things have been a bit hectic round here lately. I know, um, I know my mother can be a bit . . . full on . . . but she means well.' I paused. 'If you give her a chance.'

'Your mother's all right.'

'She is?' I asked, slightly disconcerted.

'You should meet mine.'

'Oh.'

Milton let out one of his graveyard sighs and put his book to one side. 'Have you ever seen a game show called *Twist of Fate*?'

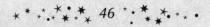

'Might have done,' I said cautiously.

'Then you may have seen a boy in a gold turban who pranced on at the end.'

'Yes . . . so?'

He gave me a haunted look.

'Oh dear God. That was you . . .'

'Do you know what they called me at school after that?'

'No.'

'"The Turkish Delight."' Hollow laugh. 'There are some things,' he said, voice fading to a doomed whisper, fingers plucking nervously at his shirt, 'that mark a person for life.'

I survived the weekend, though barely. Archimboldo reduced my mother to tears on two occasions ('Lady, with things of the arteest you are fisted ham, yes? Go away and leave me to my create'), the Turkish Delight spent all day drawing skulls in his bedroom, and Bud kept trying to get me alone for a 'heart to heart'. He succeeded late afternoon on Sunday, after Archimboldo had finally whirled off and my mother had retired to bed with herbal tea and a headache.

'Your mom is such a dear and gracious lady –' he had to pause a moment to compose himself '– that I live in daily wonder at our joy together. And that joy, Octavia, is in no small way owing to your own positivity of spirit. I realize that Milton and I came into your life in unusually, uh, pressured circumstances, and I apologize for this with all my heart. If I had my time over, you can bet I would have handled the situation differently.'

I muttered something along the lines of, 'Think nothing of it.'

'I know there will be challenges ahead and bridges to build. Even so, I think the four of us have a very special opportunity here. In fact,' continued Bud, chin jutting forth in a noble sort of way, 'just knowing that your support will blossom with the dawning of each new day . . . well, it makes all the difference in the world to me.' I nodded meekly. 'It makes all the difference to your mom too. Like I said before, you're a real team player, Octavia. I appreciate that. So does Milton.'

'He does?'

'I have this wonderful feeling,' announced Bud, eyes misting over again, 'that your example is going to let the sunshine into Milton's life.'

On Monday evening I met up with a group from my English class for an out-of-term excursion to see one of our set texts, *Macbeth*, performed in the West End. (Mum suggested that I take Milton along, but I didn't think that a couple of hours of on-stage murder and mayhem would really get the Sunshine Project off to a good start.) There were about six of us who turned up and we sat at the very back of the theatre, but even though it wasn't a particularly good production – in fact, one of our party, Tom, fell noisily asleep halfway through the second act – I still enjoyed it. In the interval I found myself queuing at the bar with Ben.

'I suppose you must know a lot about the theatre,' he said, 'because of your dad being a director and everything. He's more of a stage than a screen man, isn't he?'

I looked to see if he was being snide but he seemed

genuinely interested. I explained that, although Dad got quite a few offers to direct films after his last one, *Gatherings*, did so well, theatre is still his first love. 'I probably do get to go to the theatre more than most people and I've spent a lot of time hanging around back-stage. But Dad's tactful – he never pressures me to see things I'm not interested in. And he's more likely to tell funny stories about annoying actors or things that go wrong onstage than discuss Postmodern Performance Theory or whatever.'

'He must be pretty good company then.'

'Yes, he is.'

Then we talked about the play and the production for a bit. Normally I'd have been nervous about having this kind of discussion with Ben, as he's got a sharp tongue and gets impatient if people can't keep up in a conversation, but we found that we agreed about lots of the same things. In fact, we got so absorbed in arguing whether or not Lady Macbeth is morally redeemed by the end of the play that we talked through the end-of-interval bell and only got back to our seats just as the curtain was rising. Even in the dark I could sense Viv's raised eyebrows.

After the play finished we collected in a street at the side of the theatre. It had been raining while we were inside and the Christmas lights shone in wet rainbow wriggles down the road, where the crowds spilling out from the theatres and bars were dodging puddles and traffic with equal good humour. Our own group was slightly dazed from two hours of Revenge Tragedy so we took a long time to decide whether we should try a fast food place or go back to somebody's house and order pizza. As we were dithering, a long silver car slid past us and stopped a little way down the street near the entrance of a famous restaurant. Two burly men all dressed in black stumped out and stood to either side of the passenger door, then the chauffeur came round ready to open it while the maître d' of the restaurant hovered respectfully in the middle of the pavement. Everyone paused to look, as you do.

Tanned, elegant legs swung out of the car door, tiny feet in glittering sandals placed themselves delicately on the pavement. There was just enough time to glimpse a shimmer of violet sequins and a flick of gleaming blonde hair before the security guards and the restaurant's welcoming-committee closed in. We turned back to our burgers versus pizza discussion.

'DAVY! DARLING!'

I froze. There was the clippity-clop of stiletto heels teetering along the pavement. A blast of exotic perfume strong enough to make your eyes water. A dazzling flash of bright eyes and even brighter teeth, now bared in a radiant and ruthless smile.

Kiss, kiss.

India Withers was back in my life.

'Hello,' I croaked. 'Um . . . fancy meeting you here.'

'Isn't it *super*?' India was holding both my hands in hers, stepping back so she could look me up and down in one sweep of her lustrous lashes. 'It must be *fated*, us meeting like this.'

The rest of my group were standing back in a huddle, open-mouthed, along with quite a few passers-by. India's henchmen had followed her and positioned themselves around us in an intimidating sort of way. I freed my hands. With difficulty.

'Erm. Congratulations on your film career. Nice to see you again.' I took a step back. 'Well, I'd better be off . . . good luck with your new, er, projects and all that . . .'

'But it's been *years*, Dave! We really *must* catch up – I'm sure we've both got *so* much to talk about! All *sorts* of news!'

'Not years. Just months. I haven't seen you since you left school for the Vince Valiant film.' And since I dumped your brother, Alexis, I added silently. 'As a matter of fact, I don't really have any news. And I can read about yours in the papers. So—'

'Dave, darling, when I said it was fate, us meeting like this, I *really meant it*, you know. I've been thinking about you a *lot* these days.' Was I being paranoid, or was there something slightly threatening about the way she said this?

'You have?'

'Totally.' She didn't elaborate. 'So we'll do lunch, OK? Hook up at the Rah Bar, have a girly gossip, take a trip down memory lane and all that . . . it'll be *such* fun.'

'Such fun,' I echoed faintly.

'*Fabulous*.' We exchanged air-kisses, although I had a feeling that India would be checking in the mirror for smudges anyway. '*Must* run.' And a moment later she was gone. It was like the end of *Twist of Fate*, when Lola disappears in a puff of glitter.

'Did you *see* them? Did you see how they all looked at me? Like I was an *alien*.'

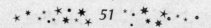

After India's grand entrance the rest of the evening was bound to be a bit of a let-down. Our theatre party had broken up without making any further plans for the night and now Viv and I were going home on the tube.

'They were just surprised, that's all. Surprised and impressed. India's very . . . um . . . impressive. In a slightly scary kind of way.'

'Ben wasn't impressed. Or scared. He looked like he was going to choke on his own contempt.'

'Since when do you care what Ben thinks, anyway?' asked Viv sharply. 'Didn't you say that he was an arrogant loser with a castration complex?'

'The castration complex was *your* theory, as I remember . . . Look, I agree that he is arrogant. And scruffy. *And* a snob. But that doesn't mean that he doesn't have certain . . . qualities . . .'

'Oh ho,' said Viv triumphantly. 'I knew it. You're falling for him.'

'Don't be ridiculous,' I snapped. 'Just because I've decided that maybe, *maybe*, he's not a villain of the darkest dye doesn't mean I'm getting weak at the knees over his smart-alec comments and green eyes.'

'Green, are they? That's funny . . . because I've heard some people describe them as pond scum.'

Suddenly it was almost Christmas, and after Christmas was my chemistry module followed by the mock exams. I managed to assure my mother that this was a legitimate reason for spending the whole of the next few days studying in the library and so had little opportunity to share my positivity of spirit with the folks back home. Milton, on the other hand, had begun to leave the sanctuary of his bedroom in favour of long and mysterious walks, preferably in the rain. My mother informed me that he had visited the Tower of London several times. Apparently he liked the ravens.

Revision aside, I was trying hard not to get too worked up about my encounter with India. Her bestest-of-friends performance on Monday was, I decided, just another example of her unnerving ability to cause me maximum embarrassment whenever I was least able to deal with it. The idea that she would soon be knocking at my door in the hope of a girly tête-à-tête over vodka Martinis was about as likely as Milton breaking into the 'Spoonful of Sugar' song from *Mary Poppins* next time he skipped down the stairs.

Given the choice between Mary Poppins or Santa Claus paying a real live visit to the Clairbrook-Cleeve-Carnaby household for Christmas, I would opt for Mary, I decided, no questions asked. I reckoned she'd be better qualified in crisis management. Dad and Michael had been invited over for Christmas lunch, which was something of an emotional milestone in itself since, as far as I knew, my mother and Michael hadn't even had so much as a cup of tea together before without Mum putting on a look of martyrdom. Times had changed but I was still nervous as to how my mother, her married lover and his depressive son, her ex-husband and her ex-husband's boyfriend would manage to share a little festive cheer beneath the mistletoe.

I was also very curious as to what Milton thought about it all. Presumably Bud had treated his son to a version of the 'Your support will blossom with the dawning of each new day' speech, which was doubtless a practice run for the 'I have asked this most dear and gracious lady to be my wife' speech. I wasn't quite sure how I felt about the situation myself; sometimes I felt resigned, sometimes resentful and sometimes impatient for them just to *get on with it*. Once Bud's verbal ecstasies had calmed down, it wouldn't be so bad, I supposed. In any case, Milton's irrepressible misery was a sort of counterbalance to his father's irrepressible good-cheer . . . perhaps with time they'd manage to even each other out. But at least I understood Bud – Milton was still a mystery. Was he just as dismal back home among all that apple-pie optimism or did England bring out the Goth in him? Either way, he didn't seem to especially resent either his father or my mother. He'd actually said that Mum was 'all right' which, coming from him, was practically a ringing endorsement. So maybe he was happiest being depressed. Maybe we should only start to worry if he ditched the black T-shirts and began putting up posters of kittens and rainbows all over the place.

According to Lady Jane's Christmas Day Itinerary, which had been drawn up with all the solemnity of a military campaign, the celebrations were scheduled to begin with a champagne and strawberry breakfast in the drawing room. But when I made my way there for the appointed time, I opened the door to find her and Bud locked in passionate embrace by the mantelpiece. My mother's hair and quite a lot of her negligee were entangled with Archimboldo's frosted pomegranate and poinsettia arrangement, but that didn't seem to hold back proceedings. If anything, it seemed to encourage them. The next moment they drew apart and looked deeply into each other's eyes.

'Oh, Princess!'

'Oh, Hero!'

I backed away and closed the door immediately, treading on Milton in the process. He gave a most un-Milton-like yelp. 'Shut *up*!' I hissed, shooing him back into the hallway.

'And a happy Christmas to you too.' He was still wearing black, but this time his T-shirt was printed with a crucifix dipped in blood. I motioned him to be silent and put my ear to the door.

'I want to find out if he's just proposed to her.'

'You'll find out soon enough if he has. Why hasten the misery?' He slumped to the floor and closed his eyes. 'We should prolong the bliss of ignorance while we still can.'

'I thought misery *was* your bliss.'

At this point the door was flung open by a beaming Princess and Hero, looking somewhat flushed and dishevelled, if the truth be told.

'Merry Christmas, my darlings!'

We were all swept up in a group embrace, although not before I took a quick look at Mum's left hand and saw that her ring finger was still bare. Rather to my surprise, I felt a twinge of disappointment as well as relief. Milton had obviously checked out the bare finger too and raised his brows at me from under Bud's armpit (he was attempting to wriggle free from one of his father's death-grip hugs, but had got stuck halfway). Eventually we managed to disentangle ourselves and settled down to our champagne breakfast. This bit was nice; we picnicked on the floor and opened presents and it was all quite relaxed. Bud didn't make any speeches, just silly jokes, and held Mum's hand and kept the champagne flutes filled. They both looked very happy.

Mum gave me two pairs of trousers, one smart and one more casual. She'd got them tailor-made so they were the exact fit – normally it takes me ages to find trousers because I'm so tall. She'd also found me a new pair of party shoes; they had sexy pointed toes embroidered all over with jet beads and were, most importantly, flat. I was touched, especially as I knew that what she really wanted to see me parading around in was itsy-bitsy kitten heels and teeny-weeny skirts. I gave her a voucher for a beauty treatment at her favourite spa and a set of note-cards illustrated with famous fashion icons.

Milton had bought me a black candle scented with 'Essence of Midnight: belladonna, cypress flower and yew'. I gave him a book that told you where all sorts of hideous crimes had been committed in London through the ages so you could follow in the exact footsteps of Jack the Ripper, etc. I think he liked it; at any rate, he said it was time he started on some light reading. Bud – who was still labouring under the delusion that I was the cheerleading type – presented me with a charm bracelet that had little silver pompoms, a cupid, muffin and tiara hanging from it. He got some silk handkerchiefs printed with the Union Jack on one side and the Stars and Stripes on the other from me, and a beautiful tweed jacket from my mother (she's always had a soft spot for the Designer Squire look). She also gave him a silver hip flask engraved with his name and what she claimed was the long-lost Carnaby coat of arms, tracked down on some 'family heritage' website. But the most successful gift of all was undoubtedly Bud's present to Lady Jane: an original framed poster for the 1939 movie of *Gone With the Wind*, signed by Vivien Leigh and Clark Gable. The raptures of gratitude he received probably outdid the film itself in heaving bosoms and breathless melodrama.

After the fuss with the presents was over we went our separate ways to get started on cosmetic/domestic preparations for the day. Michael had offered to come round early to do some or all of the cooking since food preparation isn't really Lady Jane's thing, but she had hit upon an arrangement that guaranteed a kitchen-free morning while preserving her status as hostess. She'd hired a chef. Ahmed was now busy sweating over the stuffing while Lady Jane tweaked the flower displays and arranged the canapés into ever more elaborate patterns.

Bud's a natural icebreaker, I'll say that for him. As soon as Dad and Michael arrived he strode over to them and clasped both of their hands in turn, beaming fit to burst. 'Glad to know you, boys! Glad to know you!' They both looked a bit taken aback, but that might have been due to Archimboldo's efforts with the Christmas tree, a glittering construction roped in pearls and gilded cockle-shells and crowned with a plaster replica of the goddess of love in Botticelli's *Birth of Venus*. (As a matter of fact, I was ready to bet that Botticelli would have charged a lot less than Archimboldo. Since she's become the face of Avilon cosmetics, Lady Jane's tastes have got positively queenly.)

Lunch itself went quite well. Ahmed had done himself proud on the smoked turkey breast with cranberry confit, and the caramelized plum and amaretto pudding went down a storm, even if we weren't quite so convinced by the cream of Brussels sprouts and pancetta brûlée. However, before everyone got the chance to tuck in, Bud cleared his throat in a significant, man-about-to-embark-on-a-mission-statement kind of way.

'I just want to let you know how proud I am to be here with you all today. I realize that some folks might think we make a somewhat, uh, unconventional family gathering, but that's OK. In fact, when I look around this table, I realize how much we have to cherish, both in ourselves and in one another.' His voiced choked up for a moment, then he recovered enough to raise his glass. 'So I would like to propose two toasts, the first to an exquisite hostess and a very dear lady, and the second . . . well, my second toast is to the bonds of love and esteem between us on this most wonderful occasion.'

We all solemnly raised our glasses, me trying desperately not to catch Dad's eye. But to my surprise, conversation flowed along nicely after this. Bud and Dad got into a really good discussion on the problems facing the British film industry and it turned out that Michael's legal firm had done some work for Tempest in a libel action so he and Bud had several acquaintances in common. My mother unbent enough to pull a cracker with Michael and actually laughed when he read out his joke. Milton didn't say anything at all, which helped.

I think Michael felt a bit sorry for him; at any rate, when we moved into the drawing room for coffee he went over to talk to him specially. I don't know how he began the conversation, but it was obvious that he wasn't getting very far.

'Um. Milton's an unusual name. After John, I suppose?'

'You suppose right.' Milton was busy shredding a poinsettia.

'Milton's mom majored in English,' explained Bud. 'She's always been a lover of this great literary heritage of yours.'

The poinsettia-shredding became yet more agitated. 'She used to whisper Milton's poetry over my cradle while I slept.'

'How lovely,' said my father politely.

'Actually, that would depend.' Milton closed his eyes and began to recite, his voice echoing eerily:

'. . . *No light, but rather darkness visible*
Serv'd only to discover sights of woe,
Regions of sorrow, doleful shades, where peace
And rest can never dwell, hope never comes
That comes to all; but torture without end . . .'

Nobody could really think of anything to say after that, but Lady Jane, who'd been conferring with Ahmed during the beginning of the conversation, now rejoined us, smiling brightly.

'Milton, why don't you give your mother a call? I'm sure she's longing to hear from you.'

Milton looked at her blankly, ground-up flecks of petal scattered bloodily around his feet. 'My mother doesn't believe in Christmas.'

'What, she reckons there's no such thing?' I

couldn't help asking. 'That's quite a big conspiracy theory.'

'Ahem. Yes, perhaps I should explain,' said Bud, hearty smile now looking a little fixed. 'Lola usually spends Christmas on a retreat with her holistic counsellor, Guru Abdiel-Jones. They like to spend the time in fasting and meditation. It's apparently very, uh, cleansing.'

'I can imagine,' said Michael, rallying. 'Just the sort of thing one needs after the excess of the festive season.'

'Excess?' enquired my mother, eyes narrowed.

'Well, er, you know. One does tend to overindulge at this time of the year . . .' said Michael nervously.

'I see. Next time I make my preparations for Christmas I'll be sure to bear that in mind,' said my mother coldly. 'I wouldn't want you to think that I was *overdoing* things.'

The conversation failed to really get going again and Michael and my father said their goodbyes soon after. Just before he left, Dad took me by my arm and spoke in an anxious undertone. 'You know, Octavia, if you ever find you're getting inexplicably . . . gloomy –' here he gave a meaningful look in Milton's direction '– you will *tell* me, won't you?'

Mum and Bud left the house themselves about ten minutes later to 'get some fresh air'. It was nearly dark now, but never mind. After I cleared the coffee cups from the drawing room and helped Ahmed pack his stuff into his van I went to track down Milton. He was alone in the dining room, making little holes in the Christmas cake with a cocktail stick.

'"Regions of sorrow"? "Torture without end"? Was that really necessary?'

'Sometimes I can sense a lot of pent-up aggression in you, Octavia.' He offered me a cocktail stick. 'I like it.'

'You should try a bit of penting yourself some time. It might make you feel better. And it would be a lot less painful for the rest of us . . . couldn't you a least *pretend* to feel cheerful occasionally?'

He gave me a disgusted sort of look. 'So Dad was right about you. Three cheers for Little Miss Congeniality.'

'Yeah, well, every time you come out with your world sorrow crap I have this uncontrollable urge to paint my nails pink and bake muffins.'

'Pity,' he mused, digging away at the icing. 'I had hopes of discovering your darker side. It might have been interesting.' He sighed. 'Now I see that you're just as shallow as you seem.'

At this point Bud and Lady Jane burst into the room.

'There you both are!' they exclaimed, obviously thrilled to bits to see their offspring communing over the Christmas cake.

'Oh, darlings! We have such marvellous news for you!' My mother was bubbling over with excitement. 'Now, this might come as a shock—'

'And I know it seems very sudden—'

'I can hardly believe it myself—'

'But we think you'll understand—'

Milton and I looked at each other. The time had come. Bud came and sat beside Milton and my mother sat down beside me. Each of them took each of us by the hand, then glanced at each other encouragingly. I steeled myself for the grandaddy of all speeches.

But when the Bud's big moment came, words, for once, failed him. All he said, in a slightly stammering rush, was 'Um, because we love each other very much we're going to um get married and we um hope you don't mind.' Then my mother burst out crying.

After this, of course, everyone jumped up and exclaimed and hugged one another and made the right sort of excited noises. Luckily Milton and I didn't have to say very much because after the announcement was made Bud and my mother were tumbling over themselves in their eagerness to explain it all – how Bud had proposed that morning on impulse (hence no ring), how they'd planned to announce it at lunch but then decided to break the news to the two of us first, how nervous they were about telling us but how sure they were that it was the right thing to do and how fantastic everything was going to be . . . I found myself agreeing, in a daze, to go wedding-dress shopping with Mum in the next couple of weeks. 'We'll have the ceremony just as soon as the divorce papers come through!' Then Bud and she whirled off to get yet more champagne. And, presumably, have a celebratory snog under the mistle-toe.

Silence descended on the dining room. I sat down again across the table from Milton and pushed my cock-tail stick through the icing a couple of times. Hard. Actually, it *was* kind of therapeutic.

Milton left the day after Boxing Day to spend the New Year with his mother (presumably Lola could bring herself to 'believe' in January the first, if not December the twenty-fifth). I found that I had to work extra hard at being sunny and obliging now that Milton wasn't around to provide the dramatic contrast, so it was probably just as well that Bud and Mum were pre-occupied with arrangements for their New Year's Eve do. I think Mum was disappointed I wasn't going to be on hand at the party when they announced the engage-ment, but I'd used the fact that I'd been bullied into spending New Year's Day with my loathsome grand-father as justification for missing out on the fun.

I was seeing in the New Year at a party at Jack's house instead, along with most of Year Eleven at Jethro Park. Katie and I met up at Viv's house beforehand to discuss hair strategy and compare notes on Yuletide family meltdowns.

Viv's mother, Mrs Duckworth, is Lady Jane's num-ber one fan. Viv is named after Vivien Leigh, who played Scarlett O'Hara in *Gone With the Wind One* (as my mother and the television company were now calling it), so the prospect of Mrs Duckworth's best-ever film being remade with her best-ever actress was almost too much for her to take in. Although it did take a while for her to grasp that Helena Clairbrook-Cleeve wouldn't actually be playing the heroine, but her mother.

'*Ellen* O'Hara? Oh. I suppose that does make sense, age wise. But . . . surely . . . doesn't she die early on?'

'Yeah, but because it's a TV miniseries, not a film, they're spending more time on the early part of the book. And we get to see a lot more of Ellen's relationship with the slaves on the plantation. The producers want to make it a bit more politically, um, sensitive.'

Viv raised her brows. 'You can't make *the* great Southern epic of the Civil War politically correct. What are they going to do? Have Martin Luther King intoning "I have a dream" over the end credits?'

I shrugged. 'Mum'll be happy just as long as she gets to swish around in big silk petticoats looking sad and saintly. She's been practising her deathbed scene for weeks now and they don't even start shooting until June.'

I thought I heard a snort from Mr Duckworth's corner. Rumour has it that he bore a passing resemblance to Clark Gable in his youth, but it's hard to see now. He is quiet and balding and tends to keep out of everyone's way, especially when his wife gets started on the Golden Age of Hollywood or his daughter holds forth on phallogocentrism in the post-feminist age.

'You're so lucky, Octavia,' said Katie. 'I bet you'll get to meet all the stars. I read how they're getting that fit Irish actor to play Rhett Butler. Whatshisface. The one who was the baddie in the last Vince Valiant film.'

'Ah, but there'll only ever be one Clark Gable,' said Mrs Duckworth, shaking her head. 'And I haven't even *heard* of the girl who gets to play Scarlett. Isn't she from a terrible American teen soap or something?'

'You mean *Casey's Brook*,' said Katie. 'And it's a *drama*, not a soap. It's all about the importance of showing loyalty to your friends and being true to your innermost dreams. They all have such beautiful emotions . . . and such beautiful clothes.' She sighed. 'I wish I could have gone to an American high school.'

We could probably have talked about Hollywood Sirens and Southern Belles all night, but Viv suddenly remembered that she should have met up with Simon, her boyfriend, fifteen minutes before and we left in a rush. Even so, I thought we'd arrive too early for the party to have really started. I was used to the Darlinham social scene, where turning up to anything before ten was seen as just a bit too keen. However, when we got to Jack's house it was clear that the celebrations were already in full swing, with people spilling out the front door and packed all up the stairs. Jack met us in the hallway.

'Hello, my lovelies. Do I get a New Year's kiss from my favourite girls?'

Katie, who'd perked up no end now that Emma 'Double D' Jones was no longer decorating Jack's arm, wasn't about to miss an opportunity like this. Viv and I took advantage of the distraction to slip past, but I didn't want to tag along after her and Simon all night (especially as they seemed about to launch into a blazing 'debate' on the merits/injustices of the North American Free Trade Agreement). Much as they enjoyed this sort of thing, it was something of a relief to part ways in between the lounge and the kitchen. That was another nice thing about not being a Darling any more; you could go to parties and didn't need to share a drug habit with someone before you could strike up a conversation. Then Vicky and Meera sidled over.

'Hi, Octavia. *Gorgeous* shoes.'

These were my Christmas ones. 'Thanks.'

'Oooh, they look really expensive. I bet they're designer,' said Meera. I just smiled and pretended I hadn't heard her – not difficult, considering the blast of Freddie Lions that had just started up in the lounge.

Gimme gold, he warbled, *and I'll lose it, gimme fame, I'll abuse it, but gimme lurrrve and I won't ask for nothin' m-o-o-o-re* . . .

'I heard about your friend,' said Vicky loudly. 'The one who's a movie star? We went to see her in the Vince Valiant film only a couple of weeks ago. Tom says she's even more stunning in real life.'

'She's not really a friend. Just . . . someone I used to know.'

They exchanged meaningful looks.

'Someone you used to know . . . like the boy in that magazine, for instance?'

I didn't like the eager, almost greedy way they were watching me so I turned away and began scanning the room for somebody else to talk to.

'And how's your mum?' asked Meera, holding on to my sleeve. 'Is it true she's going to be in a, like, *really steamy* love scene in her new drama series?'

'She's fine. And no, it's not true,' I said, moving away abruptly. 'The only occasion when she needs to get steamy is when she's dying of fever.'

However, I managed to keep out of their way for the rest of night and spent an enjoyable couple of hours chatting to people I hadn't seen since the end of term and eating vast quantities of tortilla chips. Towards mid-night it got very hot and rowdy in the main room and I decided to get some fresh air. I wandered out on my own and sat on the little wall between Jack's front garden and the street while I drank some water and cooled my cheeks. Then I heard someone else come out and stand behind me.

'Oh. Octavia. Hi.' It was Ben and he sounded rather disconcerted to see me.

In fact, he was shifting his feet about in a way that suggested he didn't know how to go back inside without it being obviously rude. I remembered the way he'd looked at me after India's little performance – it was a bit how Milton looked when he said I was too shallow to be interesting. But to my surprise Ben sat down on the wall beside me. There was a short pause.

'Good party.' Oh, well done, Octavia. Most impressive. 'Um. Good Christmas?'

Ben looked at me sidelong. 'It was all right,' he said at last, clearly bowled over by my sparkling conversational skills. 'Yours?'

'Fine.' This was ridiculous. If we could manage an intense discussion of megalomania in *Macbeth*, surely a little party chit-chat couldn't be beyond us. I tried again. 'Actually, no – it was weird. A month ago it was just me and my mother getting ready to hang balls on the tree. Then her long-distance, part-time boyfriend suddenly became local and long-term and brought his son along for the fun. And now it turns out they're for life, not just for Christmas.' I tried to sound flip but didn't quite pull it off. At any rate, Ben turned to look at me.

'That's rough,' he said seriously.

I shrugged. 'I'll get used to it.'

Ben was quiet for a while. '"Getting used to it" is only the half of it . . . You know, my dad got divorced from my stepmother a couple of years ago. She'd been around since I was quite a little kid and suddenly she wasn't part of our lives any more. And when I wanted to go and spend some of the Easter holidays with her last year both Dad and Mum just didn't get it. They kept on saying, "But it's not like she's *family*."'

I tried to imagine what it would be like if Dad and Michael split up and shivered.

'Sorry,' he said. 'That wasn't very helpful. I guess I should have said something a bit more . . . constructive. Upbeat. And you know, things probably will sort themselves out—'

'It's OK, Ben. You don't have to cheer me up or anything.'

'Right.' He smiled, a little ruefully. 'I just don't want you thinking I'm Mr Bitter-and-Twisted, skulking in a corner and shaking my fist at the world. I can be cheery too, you know.' He glanced at me. 'In fact, I'm even capable of mindless optimism.'

'Oh yes? What are you so mindlessly optimistic about then?'

'Things I don't deserve to be.' He moved a little closer. 'Octavia,' he said softly, and it was like a question. His eyes were bright through the tawny fall of his hair and I had that desire again to put my hands to his face and push it back for him. I think I may even have moved my hand up to do it but then someone stumbled out of the door behind us and called out.

'Oi, are you lot coming in or what?' It was Jack, Katie following after him. 'It's nearly time for the countdown to midnight! Auld langs whatsit and all that. Wheee!' He put his arms out and did a half-spin that only just missed whacking Katie in the head. 'Ooops.'

Katie giggled. 'Maybe they prefer being outside. I hope you're keeping Octavia nice and cosy, Ben.'

Ben got down from the wall and dusted off his

jeans. 'Just practising the art of conversation, Katie. You should try it some time.'

So back we went into the noise and crush of the party. You could hardly hear, let alone see the television broadcast of Big Ben ringing in the New Year, but it didn't really matter as everyone put their arms around one another and bawled out the final countdown together. I stood a little back from the main crush, next to Ben, and though he didn't put his arm around me or even say a word, we stood very close, so that our hands were just touching. Where his skin brushed mine, it felt hot and my mouth went dry. And when the bell pealed out midnight and everybody shouted and cheered and pressed together even more tightly, Ben turned to me and smiled. It was a serious, private sort of smile, nothing mocking about it at all, and I was suddenly overwhelmed with shyness. But then Viv and Simon and some others swept me up into a confusion of New Year's hugs and exclamations and the next time I looked, Ben was already at the door and making his goodbyes.

Our eyes met briefly and he raised his hand. That was it: nothing had happened between us, nothing at all, and yet I felt the exhilaration go fizzing through me, like sherbet or champagne. If Milton had been there I think the sheer force of my optimism would have sent him to an early grave.

I tried to hold on to this feeling the next morning when I was packed off to have pre-luncheon drinks with my grandfather, Lord Clairbrook-Cleeve. He disowned my father fifteen years ago when Dad left Mum for another man, and for a while it looked like he had washed his hands of me as well after my mother and he had a spectacular bust-up last year. This suited me fine since Grandpa Cleeve has spent a long and spiteful life in perfecting the art of humiliation and likes nothing better than practising it on his nearest and dearest. Unfortunately, he had reconsidered his position on the grounds that I am, after all, the Last in Line and so my visits had recently started up again under an uneasy truce.

When I was shown into his murky drawing room I found the other guests were already assembled. All of them were familiar to me from previous gatherings: the very ancient Earl of Morthaven (referred to, mysteriously, as Binkie), the frog-faced Mrs Blenkinswick-Sudsbury, her even froggier-faced daughter, Miranda, and a fourth cousin of mine called Rory. He's an investment banker in his fifties and on both the last two occasions we'd met had made a blatant pass at my mother. Rory was quite obviously nursing the hangover from hell and stood in a corner with mottled cheeks and bloodshot eyes, swaying slightly.

'Why, if it isn't Little Octavia!' cooed my grandfather, his cold, clever face as malevolent as ever. I bent down to brush his cheek with my lips.

'Happy New Year,' I said with as much enthusiasm as I could manage. 'You look very well.'

'Indeed? I have only lately returned from France, you see. So refreshing. I am accustomed to spend Christmas there,' he explained to the others, 'on the estate of my dear old friend the Comte d' Malfeux. I find England has become increasingly *vulgarized* at this time of year.'

Cue much shaking of heads and sighs of agreement. The decline and fall of western civilization has been a favourite topic of Lord C-C's ever since he got involved in the League for the Promotion of Christian Decency, a well-heeled pressure group set up to make life as unpleasant as possible for homosexuals, immigrants, single parents and other undesirable types. The type of people who're disqualified from the 'love thy neighbour' bit of the commandments, presumably.

Somewhat to my relief, however, the conversation moved on to the charms of France, which would, as everyone knows, be perfectly delightful if it were not for the French (with a few well-bred exceptions, of course). This topic was inevitably followed by long discussions on the boorishness of the Germans, the dishonesty of the Italians and the general dreadfulness of Americans.

'Didn't I hear that your mother is, ahem, involved with one? An American, that is?' enquired Mrs B-S. I nodded, not daring to look at my grandfather who must, I knew, have been following the whole business with much grinding of the teeth.

'And how does that make you feel?' asked her daughter with a froggy smile.

'Oh, you know these colonials . . . a bit rough and ready, but they mean well,' I said blandly. Mrs and Miss B-S nodded in an understanding sort of way.

'Octavia, you must understand, is very liberal-minded these days,' put in my grandfather. 'She has chosen to attend her local so-called comprehensive. Though, to my mind, there is nothing more socially and intellectually restrictive than an education dictated by the state.'

'Absolutely.' This was Rory. 'And nobody *does*.'

'Does what?' I asked, confused.

'Well . . . go to these schools,' said Rory. Then, with breathtaking lack of logic, 'I hear they're terribly over-crowded.'

We sipped our sherry in silence for a while. Finally, the ancient earl quavered into life.

'Your mother . . . hrm . . . your mother was that . . . hrm . . . woman. That woman in the papers.'

'The actress,' said Mrs Blenkinswick-Sudsbury, in the kind of way one might say 'the strippergram' or 'the kleptomaniac'.

The Earl drew himself up and fixed me with a watery eye. 'The only occasions on which a lady should be mentioned in the papers is when she is born, when she marries and when she dies.'

I didn't think there was much point explaining that sometimes you don't have the choice.

Milton returned the Tuesday night before the start of term; I was rather surprised to see him back so soon but apparently ten days was the maximum Lola could take of his company or he of hers. He was as melancholy as ever but the next morning he actually walked me to the bus stop and stood outside the shelter while I waited, his face upturned to the dark sky and drizzling rain. 'It's good to be back,' he said.

I could have said the same as I went through the school gates. Now that term had started I could finally put the whole Clairbrook-Cleeve-Carnaby soap opera behind me – it would almost be a relief to settle down to a timetable and a nice orderly deadline or two. Even the exams had their advantages: the perfect get-out clause for embroiling myself in wedding plans. I was also looking forward to seeing Viv and Katie and the rest again. And Ben, of course . . . I felt a flutter of anticipation as I began walking towards the entrance the Upper School block, especially as I spied somebody who looked like Ben loitering by the door. It seemed as if he were waiting for someone – was it, *could* it be me? Yes: our eyes had met across the crowded playground. It was as if no time had passed since we'd exchanged smiles at the New Year countdown; I was filled with a sense of glorious certainty. Fate. If this had been a film, it was the moment when everything around me faded away as the two of us began to draw together in graceful slow motion, accompanied by throbbing violins and yearning looks. I quickened my pace.

'Darling!'

It took a moment for me to grasp that it wasn't Ben who was speaking. In fact, Ben hadn't even opened his mouth. It was then that I realized a figure was standing next to me – a small, blonde, horribly familiar figure. Something had gone very, very wrong.

'It's me! India!' Pause. 'Surprise!'

I now understand what people who've stared death in the face mean when they say that their life flashed before their eyes. My own zipped past in a series of grotesque tableaux – of India's glittering stilettos teetering down the pavement towards me, of the sneer on Alex's face the last time I saw him, of all the Darlings raising their disdainful eyebrows and sniggering in unison . . . After the first shock had passed I became aware that life was, incredibly, still going on; that Ben was standing back and frowning, first in puzzlement, then in dawning recognition; that all over the playground people were beginning to turn and stare; that the bell for registration was shrilling on and on just like all the alarms going off inside my head . . .

'I *told* you we were going to meet up again! That night in the West End, remember? Poor Dave – you're looking unwell.' India's voice was syrupy with concern. 'Hadn't you better sit down?'

'No . . . no . . . I'm . . . fine.'

'Your face is really *very* green. But maybe it's just your uniform that's making you look so sallow.' She put her head to one side and inspected me with furrowed brow. 'Yes, if I were you, I should try and avoid that shade of maroon.'

India, of course, glowed with sun-kissed good health. She was wearing a long dark tapestry coat with gorgeous chocolate fur at the hem and collar and nothing but a slinky sort of slip underneath in rose-coloured silk. Plus knee-high suede boots with a dangerously spiky heel and toe. Although it was the sort of January morning where the sun needn't have bothered getting out of bed, a pair of dark glasses was perched on top of her golden curls. From the look of things, I wasn't the only one wondering what someone who clearly belonged on a red carpet in Beverly Hills was doing on the cracked tarmac of Jethro Park Comp. A gaggle of onlookers had already gathered by the Upper School entrance and their numbers were growing. 'I take it you're not here to discuss fashion,' I finally managed to say, hustling her away to a more secluded spot behind a rubbish skip.

'Don't be silly!' Charming laugh. 'No, I'm here for my education – just like you!' Please God, no. This could not be happening. Not to me, not now. I gripped the side of the skip so hard my knuckles turned white. 'Well, it's more for research, as a matter of fact. My latest role, you know.' She paused in an expectant sort of way but I just looked at her blankly. 'Yes, well, this next film is going to be a totally new departure for me. You know what a fan I am of classic French literature—'

'So you've got a part in the new Asterix movie? Congratulations.'

India gave me a pitying look. 'Classic *nineteenth-century* French literature, Dave. The original book was written by one of the three musketeers, you know.' She thought for a moment. 'Or by the man who wrote *The Three Musketeers*. I can't remember. Anyway, it's about a girl first corrupted, then crushed by society so it's *ideal* for an update. Our version's going to be very contemporary, very gritty and political: *La Dame aux Camélias* on a council estate. I'm taking the part of Cam, you see – a young girl forced by desperate circumstances into prostitution but redeemed by the love of a good man. Her school guidance counsellor, in fact. But then the powers that be intervene and, well, it all gets very sad . . . It's a bit like *Pretty Woman* really. Except she dies in the end.'

'Tragic.'

'Oh, I know. And yet, despite all the abuse in her life, at heart she's still so beautiful and idealistic and pure. I can relate to a lot of this, naturally.'

'*Naturally*,' I repeated through gritted teeth. Irony was never one of India's strong points.

'We're talking about a *major* artistic breakthrough here. Of course, I've always been very socially aware, but it still requires *intense* preparation to get into a role like this. We've been working on character-motivation for several weeks, but Jed – my director, adorable man – thinks we need a different approach. The poor thing's had to take a little break (some sort of nervous disorder, apparently) but now he's suggested that I try *total immersion*. The slum of a council estate where my character lives, her run-down inner-city comprehensive . . . I have to go where my art takes me.'

It was all becoming horribly clear.

'Wait, India. Jethro Park isn't – look, just because it's a state school doesn't mean it's the sort of place you're after. I mean, *doctors* send their kids here! And accountants!' I was getting desperate. 'In last year's league tables we—' But India swept on regardless.

'At first I didn't know where to start. And then I remembered how when you had your breakdown and had to drop out of—'

'I DID NOT HAVE A BREAKDOWN.' Too late, I remembered that we were in the middle of the pre-registration rush. Great. So now the whole school would know me as the posh lunatic in 11B.

'Whatever.' India patted my arm soothingly. 'I admire you, actually – it must have taken a lot of guts to admit you couldn't cope with the more high-profile lifestyle. I can see that you're *so* much more comfortable down at this level . . . and I suppose if you only have low expectations of life, you'll never be disappointed, will you? Anyway, it was all *very* simple to organize – Dad got on the phone to the school governors and a couple of letters later, here I am!'

'I'm sure our governors are thrilled that their school's been chosen as the model for an educational sin bin. Not forgetting all the schoolgirl prostitutes who throng the corridors.'

'Yes, but it's such a *moral* story,' she said. 'So cautionary. We explained to the board that Jed's interpretation of it will very inspirational, very motivating . . . not that we needed to go into great *detail* about it all. And after Dad helps out with the new music suite I'm sure *nobody* will call this place bog-standard any more.'

So in other words, India had bribed and bullied her way into getting what she wanted, just like she always did. I felt some reluctant sympathy for Jed, the nervously disordered director – perhaps he'd packed his starlet off for a spot of 'total immersion' in the hopes that she'd get knifed behind a bog-standard bike-shed. A tempting prospect, I thought, eyeing up a rusty spike that was poking out of the skip by my elbow.

'Now you *know* I'd love to spend all morning chatting to you, Dave. But I *must* get on – I'm due at the Head's office now and I've got a zillion and one things to organize before I start tomorrow . . . We'll catch up later and you can introduce me to everyone, OK?' India squeezed my arm with such eager affection that her nails dug into my flesh. 'I can't *tell* you how thrilled I am that we're going to be school chums again!'

The second bell for registration had been and gone long before I got to 11B's form room, pale of face and wild of eye. Even so, I was still ahead of Mr Pemberton, who arrived too late for a proper roll-call and immediately shooed us off to assembly in a most absent-minded manner. In normal circumstances I would have been thankful to escape the usual jibe at young ladies who think poor punctuality is a fashion statement. This time, unfortunately, Mr Pemberton's distracted air could only mean one thing: he had doubtless just been informed that his class would be playing host to an aspiring movie star.

I immediately squeezed ahead of the rest of the class in the vain hope of getting to assembly and then to lessons without having to say anything to anybody. Blind panic was gradually giving way to white-hot fury. The *bitch*. She'd done this on purpose – tracked me down in all the schools of all of London just so she could brush up on her sadism skills. After all, what was a little ritual persecution between old friends? For a girl like Indy, there wasn't much fun in being very rich and semi-famous unless you had somebody's life to ruin. Poisonous, conniving bimbo-from-hell . . .

However, in spite of the touching reunion scene between India and me in the playground, most of 11B seemed too absorbed in post-holiday greetings and gossip to pay me more attention than a cheerful, 'Hello, Octavia – where's the fire?' as I elbowed my way ahead. Perhaps I'd imagined all the staring and whispering in the playground. Perhaps the stress of the mocks had got to me more than I realized and the whole encounter with India had been some kind of manic delusion. But on the other hand, there were the marks of India's nails in my arm, and there were Meera and Vicky bearing down on me, eyes bright and ears pricked, noses twitching at the scent of second-hand celebrity . . . I broke into a trot, only to find myself face to face with Ben, who for some reason was ambling along in the opposite direction to the school hall. He raised his brows and started to say my name, but I clenched my jaw and shouldered past regardless. The whole Ben issue was something I just wasn't ready to think about at the moment.

'Oi – what's with the sudden enthusiasm for assembly?' Viv was pushing her way through a swarm of Year Sevens. 'You know we'll only get that Chinese parable about the giant chopsticks in heaven again . . .' She took another look at me. 'God, whatever happened to you? You look like the hounds of hell are after you.'

'Hello, hello,' said Jack, panting up behind her. 'What's the word on that hot babe I saw you chatting with outside? Rumour has it she's that fit Swedish tennis player—'

'Wait, Octavia,' chorused Meera and Vicky. 'We know who—'

But I had already slipped in to take my place in assembly. God knows what it was all about – as far as I was concerned the Head could have been rambling on about anything from metaphysical chopsticks to Saving the Great Crested Newt. From my air of rapt attention, however, you would have thought I was soaking up moral enlightenment with every word.

Alas, all good things must come to an end – even fundraising appeals for great crested newts followed by the full five verses of 'Lord of the Dance'. By the time lessons started I had to face the fact that word of India had now spread through the school like wildfire and that I was the first point of enquiry. It didn't seem to matter that hardly anyone knew what, exactly, India was famous *for*. Presumably the people who'd been present that fateful night in the West End had made the connection, but there were far too many conflicting rumours for anyone to be certain of anything.

Most of Year Eleven were careful not to appear overly thrilled; after all, you don't have to be a Darling to think that fainting with excitement over a flash of semi-famous flesh is not very cool. However, there were still plenty of people who kept sidling up to me and muttering about my 'friend the tennis player/pop singer/lingerie model/TV presenter', and was it true that she'd come to Jethro Park to 'sponsor the tennis team/promote her single/shoot a centrefold/talent-spot for her show'? I managed to ignore most of these questions, but if there was absolutely no way I could get out of giving an answer I would say that yes, she was a girl from my old school, yes, she'd been in the papers quite a bit and, as far as I knew, she was coming to the Upper School to give a little talk on The Dark Side of the Champagne Lifestyle. Yes, it was a new government initiative, I believed; all sorts of media personalities were involved – India was touring schools to warn us of the dangers of binge drinking and sexually transmitted diseases. Genital warts were her speciality. Well, I had to get my kicks somehow . . .

I wasn't in any of the same classes as Viv that morning, but she met up with me at lunch, when I was skulking in the computer room. (The system crashes on such a regular basis that most people have given up even attempting to log on. As a result, the room makes quite a nice hideaway.)

'Is it true?' she demanded.

'Is what true?' I asked grumpily. I'd had more than enough interrogations for one morning.

'Ooh, let's see. That we're having a Swedish pop star host a chat show in the gym?'

'Not as far as I know.'

'OK, how about the lingerie model who's going to hand out leopard-print thongs in the school hall?'

'Sounds like Jack's been daydreaming aloud again.'

'Amazing how these rumours spread . . .' Viv grinned sardonically. 'So come on – tell me the one about the Darlinham socialite turned wannabe movie star.'

I groaned. 'Make that the Darlinham socialite turned wannabe movie star turned West London schoolgirl.'

'You don't mean – what, she's coming *here*? *India*? No way.'

'Welcome to my hell.'

'My God – no wonder you were so freaked this morning.' Even though Viv's never actually met India she's a bit of an expert on the subject, having spent a lot of time getting me through my Post-Traumatic Pygmy Blonde Disorder. 'And I thought India turning up was just a social call . . . Wow. Has Rich Withers gone bankrupt? Or has India's sordid past caught up with her at last and they've sent her here for community service?'

'India thinks she's doing the whole world a service just by breathing the same air as the rest of us.' I slumped back in my chair, realizing that I'd have to explain everything from the beginning. 'In fact, she's got such a right-on social conscience that she's playing a schoolgirl prostitute in her next film. It's a modern take on this French costume thingy . . . something about carnations. No – camellias. And being corrupted by society.'

'I thought being corrupted by society was every It-Girl's dream.'

'Not that kind of society. I think her director's one of those arty earnest types – wants to expose the dark underbelly of the welfare state, that sort of thing.' Dad knew a number of people like this and in my experience they were either deeply scary or deeply dull. 'But since India probably only got the part by taking her clothes off or her wallet out he's packed her off to get some "experience" of how the other half lives . . . you know, give her some sort of credibility. She reckons Jethro Park is where she's going to impersonate her way into a life of squalor and suffering.'

'Because only slum kids and mental retards go to comprehensive schools, of course.'

'Of course.'

'So why hasn't she started here already then?'

'Who knows. I think – I hope – this is going to be a part-time sort of arrangement. Back in the good old days, India's attendance at school was always rather erratic, with the result that she was a year older than the rest of us in her class. But whether at Jethro Park or Darlinham House, India's still got an industry to seduce and a world to conquer.'

'Poor old Mr Pemberton – he'll hate having a diva in the class almost as much as you will. Oh, Octavia . . .

think of Vicky and Meera! Think of Jack!' Viv's eyes gleamed. 'You know, I have to admit I am quite curious to meet the girl . . . Everything's got so dull and exam-fixated lately – a bit of controversy could be just what's needed to get things going again.'

I nearly fell off my chair. '*Viv*. You can't mean it! This is *India* we're talking about! *India*. Who spent the whole time I was at Darlinham House doing everything she could to humiliate and manipulate and spoil—'

'Exactly,' said Viv calmly. 'I've heard so much about her – I've even got within spitting distance of the girl – and now I've finally got the chance to see what she's like first hand.'

'And what about *my* chance for a nice normal quiet life? Don't you see that this research farce is only a cover, an excuse for hunting me down and ruining everything? You know she's never forgiven me for going out with and then dumping her precious brother. Plus she still blames me for the time she made a total prat of herself in front of Drake.'

'Hmm. I'd forgotten about that.' This referred to the occasion when India had bullied me into getting her an introduction to Drake 'Mega Star' Montague, who was acting in one of Dad's films. Unfortunately for India, Drake proved to be more than just a pretty set of pecs, and her seduction scam had seriously backfired. Just remembering this used to bring a smile to my face, but now I was feeling slightly sick.

'India hasn't forgotten it. This is *vengeance*, Viv.'

Viv rolled her eyes. 'It all seems a bit far-fetched to me. But if what you say is right and India's taken all this time and trouble just to get one up on an old school enemy, don't you see how desperately pathetic she must be?'

'Pathetic, maybe. Poisonous, definitely.'

'And you've moved on from all that. Look, you've not got Alex to complicate things any more – you're a free agent. India can be as charming or as psychotic as she likes because as far as you're concerned she's yesterday's news. Right?'

'Right. Yesterday's news.' I sighed and picked up my bag to leave. 'Viv . . . do you think maroon makes me look sallow?'

Mr Pemberton looked strangely jolly for someone whose class was about to be invaded by an egomaniacal It-Girl halfway through an exam year. I had confidently expected that with Mr Pemberton, at least, India would have her work cut out – after all, not only had she been dumped on him at extremely short notice, but she also personified all the things he most disliked about popular culture/twenty-first-century society/the modern female. But when he marched into our classroom after lunch he no longer had the irritable, harassed look of the morning. His bald spot gleamed with confidence and his teeth were bared in a nicotine-stained smile as he informed the class that he had some very special news for us.

A buzz of speculation immediately started up, in which 'Swedish lingerie model' and 'genital warts' could be clearly heard. Mr Pemberton put up his hand for silence.

'I see that the rumour mills have already started. I don't know who is to blame for spreading all this non-

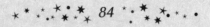

84

sense,' said Mr Pemberton, with a glare in my direction, 'but I will say that it was a very irresponsible, some might say *inflammatory*, thing to do. Now, Jethro Park has a long and proud tradition of promoting the arts. Our annual Shakespeare production is always a highlight of the summer term and, er, I'm sure you're all enjoying the Year Seven still-life drawings on display in the cafeteria . . .' The class stirred restlessly. What had a few badly drawn fruit bowls got to do with pop stars playing tennis in their underwear? 'But now a great privilege and, dare I say it, opportunity for us all has arrived.' Significant pause. 'A very promising, indeed pioneering, young film-maker has taken an interest in our school.' He raised his voice as the class broke into a babble of excitement. 'Silence, please, ladies and gentlemen. Unless, of course, you do not want to hear about your role in all this? No? Right . . . To continue. Ahem. I understand that Mr Mosley will be drawing on a literary and romantic classic – Alexandre Dumas's *The Lady of the Camellias* – as the inspiration for his film. What's more, he wishes to adapt this wonderful text in such a way as to promote a fresh, dynamic and above all *authentic* view of life in Britain today. And to this end, he is sending a youthful cast member here to join in our routine and learn about day-to-day life in our little community.' The babble was now a roar and Mr Pemberton had to rap on his desk several times before a semblance of order was restored. 'Some of you may recognize her from her appearance in a certain popular movie franchise. However, I am assured that Miss Withers is a serious and committed young actress. Her father is, after all, a very well-known musician and patron of the arts.'

Right. Sir Rich Withers: one time drug-fuelled, sex-crazed rock star, now a national hero of high culture.

'You will all get the chance to meet India tomorrow. Sadly, her various commitments will prevent her from taking part in school life on a full-time basis, but this has only made her more determined to settle down to life in Jethro Park in as natural and unobtrusive a way as possible. Which brings me to an important point.' He looked at us sternly. 'As you are well aware, this is a critical year for you all. Much depends on your academic performance over the coming weeks and months. Most of you, in fact, will be starting your mock exams on Monday. In light of this, I have to say that I had serious misgivings about the, ah, distraction that Miss Withers might pose. And if I find that her presence here is disrupting the academic routine *in any way* I will have no choice but to end the arrangement.' We all stared back at him solemnly. After an impressive pause, Mr Pemberton continued in his most stately manner. 'Since India is an exceptionally mature young lady, I can only hope that you will rise to the occasion and respond in a similarly adult manner. I think you'll find that she is a very down-to-earth, very *sincere* girl who is here to learn, just like the rest of you.'

And that was that.

The rest of the afternoon passed in a miserable daze. All around me was the happy chatter of people convinced that India Withers was going to transform life at Jethro Park into a glitter-strewn celebrity gala. Nobody seemed to believe Mr Pemberton's protestations that she was going to be Just Another Regular Schoolgirl. I reckoned they'd be even less likely to believe that India was only coming here so she could take notes on being desperate and downtrodden. Even Viv, who knew exactly what India was up to, seemed cheerfully unconcerned, almost as if she was looking forward to having a fame-crazed superbitch in our midst. Oh well, I thought grimly, they'd soon find out what India was really like and then they'd be sorry . . . Or would they? What if – even worse – India went on a charm offensive so that everyone spent the next few months saying what a sweetie-pie she was?

I set off for home feeling that if I met one more person who wanted to know about India's favourite designer label or celebrity pal I'd do a pretty good impression of unbridled evil myself. So when I heard someone calling after me as I headed for the bus stop I did my best to ignore it. Then I realized it was Ben and that he was looking fairly pissed off.

'Have I done something to offend you?'

'No. Of course not.'

'Then why have you been ignoring me all day?'

'I haven't been ignoring you.'

'Yes you have.' He gave me one of his glowers. 'Every time I've come up to you or even caught your eye you've completely blanked me. So now I want to know what the problem is.'

God he was sexy when his voice went all low and growly . . . It was very distracting. I tried to concentrate on the matter in hand. 'There isn't a problem, it's just that—' But Ben cut in before I could finish.

'I thought we sorted everything out before

Christmas. I'd been behaving like an idiot and I apologized for it. Fine. And after Jack's party –' there was the tiniest pause '– I thought things were cool between us. But now—'

'If you'll just let me get a word in edgeways I'll try to explain.' We glared at each other. He had his arms folded across his chest, waiting. It was then I realized I wasn't exactly sure what I was going to say. 'Um, you know that girl I was talking to before morning registration?'

'India Withers is quite hard to miss.'

'Yeah . . . I guess you'd have to be deaf, dumb and blind not to notice the uproar she's caused, especially after Mr Pemberton's news this afternoon. And as you probably knew from that night we went to the theatre, India and I, er, used to go to school together.'

'So?'

'So it was a big shock to see her again. And then with all those crazy rumours and everyone coming up to me hoping for an exclusive I suppose I may have been a bit . . . distracted. I'm sorry if I was rude. Really. I promise you I didn't mean to be.'

Ben wasn't glowering any more but he didn't look particularly convinced either. I didn't blame him. The problem was how to explain the fear and loathing India inspired in me without going into the whole sordid history of our relationship and without sounding . . . well, bitter and neurotic and slightly crazed. Then if Ben was taken in by India's sweetness-and-light routine I'd be left looking like the villain of the piece. I tried again. 'The thing is, there's a bit of history between India and me.'

'You dumped her brother, didn't you – the bloke in

that magazine? Are you saying that she's still pissed off about it?'

Hell's bells. Oh well, he'd have worked it out sooner or later. 'India and I haven't ever got on for a number of reasons. My, er, thing with Alex was only one aspect of it . . . and anyway, that really *is* ancient history,' I added firmly, hoping I didn't look as flustered as I felt. 'But you can appreciate that I was a bit spooked to find out that she's coming here.'

'Yeah, I guess.' He ran his hands through his hair in that half-shy, half-exasperated way of his. 'I suppose I was feeling a bit paranoid but . . . after New Year, you see, I kind of hoped that things between us were . . .'

'Yes?' There was a tight, breathless feeling in my chest. Like asthma, but nicer.

'Good.' He was staring at his feet. 'I want things to be good between us.'

'Right.' *Good?* What the hell was that supposed to mean?

'OK.' Pause. 'I've got football practice now.' Pause. 'So I'll, er, say goodbye then.'

'Right.'

'Bye.'

'Bye.'

'See you tomorrow.'

'See you tomorrow.'

He had already turned to go back to school. I watched him lope off to the end of the street. Then he looked back at me. 'By the way,' he called out, grinning, 'for an international superstar, that India's a bit of a midget, isn't she?'

It may have been a delusion of my fevered brain,

but at that moment a ray of sun seemed to pierce the evening sky.

Back home, all was sweetness, light and domestic harmony. Bud, my mother and even the Turkish Delight were assembled in the kitchen, where Bud was teaching Mum how to make burritos. Cookery has never been high on Lady Jane's list of desirable accomplishments, so it was something of a shock to see her up to her elbows in flour and with a smudge of tomato purée on her nose. She was wearing her brunette wig and hooped skirt again, which made negotiating the space between the sink and the central workstation a little difficult. Milton, meanwhile, was leafing through a mail-order catalogue and cutting out the eyes of the sportswear models. New Orleans jazz was blasting out from the stereo.

'Look, sweetheart – I'm learning how to make burritos! We're making the most *frightful* mess!' Mum held out her gunky hands for inspection and beamed at me delightedly.

'You're doing great, Princess,' said Bud, every inch the red-blooded male even when wearing a polka-dot apron and with flour in his hair. (There wasn't much that hadn't been covered in flour actually. Even Milton wore a light dusting.) 'I hope you're hungry, Octavia. By the time we're done there's going to be a whole heap of these things to get through.'

'After the day I've had, I've kind of lost my appetite,' I said in my most long-suffering tone. No reaction. I slumped into a chair and tried again. 'Not to mention the will to live.' Milton looked up briefly but when he saw that I hadn't, as yet, slit my wrists with the vegetable knife he went back to his magazine in a disappointed sort of way. I noticed that he was now filling in the sportswear models' smiles with black ink. 'In fact,' I said, raising my voice above the tootling jazz trumpeters, 'I might as well be dead.'

'Something bothering you, darling?' My mother was trying to free her petticoats from the pedal bin. 'Goodness, things must have been a lot less *crowded* in the olden days . . . I thought those horrid exams of yours didn't start until Monday.'

'It's not the mocks.' I got up and switched off the stereo. 'It's more serious than that. It's India. She's back.'

There was a confused silence.

'India? Really?' said my mother at last. 'Rich and Tigerlily's youngest, you know,' she said to Bud in explanation. 'Octavia and she are old school friends.'

'Mum! How can you say that? Don't you remember last year at all? We *hated* each other.'

Bud shifted his feet uncomfortably. I had a feeling that he was about to turn those honest grey eyes on me and tell me that Hate Is A Very Strong Word. Milton, however, looked almost perky. 'You mean she's your nemesis?'

'If that means she's made it her mission in life to make mine miserable, then yes.'

He leaned towards me intently. 'Cold-blooded and black-hearted, is she? And utterly ruthless?'

'Sounds about right. Only each time she sticks in the knife she does it with this fluffy-bunny, candy-coated charm . . . She's made public humiliation into an art-form, though blackmail is her weapon of choice. Pure acid runs in her veins.'

'Aaaah.' Milton closed his eyes in ecstasy. My mother pursed her lips.

'Yes, but what has she done this time, Octavia?'

I summed up the situation with a few well-chosen and forceful words. Bud and Mum made various sympathetic noises but, as usual, Lady Jane managed to pick up on the least significant aspect of it all.

'But how *riveting* that India's a disciple of the Stanislavsky school!'

'What? No, Mum, it's Jethro Park she's—'

'School of *thought*, darling. Stanislavsky is the Father of Method Acting, you know. When you use your own emotional memories to develop the characterization of a part by thinking and feeling as your character does, living the way they live . . .' She smoothed out her skirts self-consciously. 'I can't tell you what it's done for my understanding of life as a plantation owner's wife.'

I started to point out all the ways in which a plantation owner's wife's petticoats, inner-city deprivation and India Withers had nothing to do with each other. But what was the use? It was all hopeless. Milton was right. There was no reason, no purpose to existence. We were all crumbling under the stinking mass of our own apathy, corruption and decadence. I may have said as much as I left the kitchen, but the jazz record had started up again and I don't think they heard me.

Mum came up to me just as I was leaving for school the next morning. She looked a bit shamefaced.

'Octavia, darling, I'm worried that I wasn't properly supportive last night. I really don't want you getting all upset about India again, not when you're doing so well at this new school and everything. I'm *sure* you and Indy will be able to sort things out. And anyway, you've got so many nice friends now . . . have you ever thought that India might just be, well, *lonely*?'

Yes, that would explain it – poor little Indy was only looking for someone to be her friend. Put this together with Viv's pathetic-and-desperate theory and it was clear that each of India's acts of persecution was actually a Cry For Help. And here I was, wallowing in self-pity, when India was the one in need of sympathy and support!

Viv was waiting for me at the main entrance, Katie and Hannah in tow. Somewhat to my surprise, there were no groupies gathering to slobber on to the tarmac and it appeared that everything was business as usual. Either India had already made her entrance or people were taking her plea for anonymity more seriously than I'd expected. I hoped it was the latter for the simple reason that nothing was more certain to piss her off. Her moment of Vince Valiant glory notwithstanding, the fact remained that outside the Darlings' cosy little circle, India was a still long way from breaking into the major league.

Viv solemnly presented me with a four-leaf clover hairclip as we went in. 'To keep the evil spirits at bay,' she explained. 'I usually save it for exams.'

'Who's evil?' asked Katie.

'No one,' I said quickly. 'I'm just very superstitious. My, er, horoscope said that Thursday is an unlucky day.' Since everyone, including Mr Pemberton, seemed hell-bent on falling for the infamous Withers charm, I felt that insincerity was my safest option. I had decided that I would be polite both to and about India, at least until the others had had a chance to see what she was really like.

'Octavia's a little nervous about seeing India again,' said Viv before I could stop her.

'That'll be because of Alex,' said Katie wisely. 'Seeing his sister after all this time must bring up all sorts of painful memories. Like with me and Jack.'

'Jack doesn't have a sister,' said Viv. 'And you see him all the time without breaking down in tears.'

'She's right, you know,' said Hannah.

'Ah, but it's the little things which bring it all back . . . Even now, there are certain songs I can't listen to without getting all choked up and I know it's the same for him.'

'Exactly the same,' agreed Hannah.

'I suppose Alex took the break-up badly?' asked Katie, reluctantly tearing her thoughts away from Jack and their five-day Romance of the Century.

'Oh no, he was fine.' I noticed that Ben had come up and joined us and felt myself blushing. 'Alex is – was – fine. I'm fine. India's fine. Everything is absolutely fine.' Dear God, I was already babbling like an idiot and I hadn't even seen India yet. Deep breaths, I told myself as we walked into our classroom. Deep breaths and happy thoughts. Roses and rainbows and chocolate ice cream. Ignore all fantasies involving that iron spike in the skip outside. Sunshine and puppies and cherry lip balm . . .

'*There* you are, Dave! Isn't this fun?' India was perched on a desk surrounded by an adoring cluster of, among others, Meera, Vicky and Jack. When she saw me she got down for the ritual air kiss. Cheekbone to cheekbone. Mwah, mwah. 'I already feel *so* at home.'

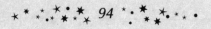

'I see you've dressed for the part.' She was, indeed, wearing a sort of haute couture version of our school uniform. Her charcoal wool skirt was tighter and shorter than even the most daring Jethro Park slapper could construct out of safety pins and grey polyester. Sleek black stilettos set off her tanned legs to their best possible advantage and she wore a beautifully tailored shirt in crisp, snowy cotton, open just one button too many to be strictly decent. Slung carelessly over the back of a chair was a burgundy-coloured sweater that I didn't have to touch to know was made from the softest cashmere and a million miles away from the scratchy maroon material of the regulation variety. Her nails were painted the same dark red as the sweater, her hair was swept back in a gleaming chignon and a silk tie was loosely knotted around her neck. She looked like a cross between a boardroom vamp and a dirty magazine's fantasy schoolgirl. But the really irritating thing about this was that she didn't look cheap. India Withers could wear the shortest skirt, the flimsiest frock, the skimpiest top and still look expensive.

'You know, I'm beginning to see why you were always so desperate to fade into the background. It's such a relief to get away from the spotlight for a while, pretend I'm just one of the crowd . . .' Another dazzling smile. 'By the way, Tallulah and Twinkle send *lots* of love. And Asia, of course. They're all *longing* to see you again.'

'I'll bet.' Fiends reunited. However, we didn't have time for further chit-chat because at that moment Mr Pemberton strode in. He was wearing a new tie for the occasion (purple, zigzagged) and his face was shiny with self-importance.

'Settle down, please, ladies and gentlemen! I see you've already had a chance to meet your new classmate. Welcome, India. Welcome.' He stood there rubbing his hands and grinning like a maniac. 'Splendid. Ahem . . . I, ah, trust you've already had a little tour of the sights, as it were, and had a chance to familiarize yourself with the timetable?'

'Yes thank you, Mr Pemberton. Everyone has been *so* helpful.'

'Splendid. Now, as it's your first day, I think it would be a good idea if someone were on hand to show you the ropes. Take you along to the cafeteria, sit next to you in lessons, that sort of thing. If we could have a volunt—'

A dozen hands shot up. India smiled dazzlingly. 'That's so kind. Perhaps if Dave – Octavia, I mean, wouldn't mind? After all, we go back a long way and it's nice to see a familiar face. Everything's still a little . . . overwhelming.' She dipped her head and looked bashful. 'But I really wouldn't want to be any trouble.'

'Well, that's settled then. Splendid. You've been assigned to most of the same classes as her anyway. Octavia, can I trust you to look after India and see that she settles in?'

'It will be just like old times!' said India, clasping her hands to her chest in gratitude. I could sense the awe and envy of the rest of the class settle around me like a fog.

'Splendid,' I said sourly.

It took until morning break before someone asked India the inevitable question: 'Why do you call her Dave?'

Nearly all of 11B and as many of 11A and C as could

squeeze into our form room had gathered to admire Jethro Park's newest and shiniest acquisition. A crowd made up from the other years was collecting in the corridor outside, still hopeful of admittance into the Inner Sanctum. This time India was lounging on Mr Pemberton's desk, swinging her legs girlishly and sipping from a bottle of designer mineral water. The straw in the bottle was the exact same colour as her nail varnish. Another button on her shirt had come undone. Jack's tongue was practically dragging on the floor.

'Dave? Oh, it was always everyone's pet name for Octavia, back at our old school. She's so big and tall and, with that cute, boyish crop, you know. Octavia, 'Tavia, 'Tavy, Davy . . . silly, really. But there were other names as well—'

'So what do people call you, then?' asked Ben. He'd been reading a newspaper in the corner furthest from Mr Pemberton's desk and had, up until now, apparently been oblivious to events at the other end of the class-room.

'Darling, mainly.' Tinkling laugh. 'I've never been a great one for nicknames.'

'Really?' asked Viv, all innocence. 'If I were you, I'd always want to know what people called me behind my back.'

It was probably just as well that Meera, or it might have been Vicky, piped up at this point. 'Are you allowed to tell us anything about your new film, India? Or is it a secret?'

'If it's a love story, does that mean you're going to have to do a sex scene? Will it be with someone famous?'

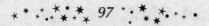

97

'Are you actually going to be filming here, at Jethro Park?'

'Does that mean we get to be extras?'

'Yeah, come on, India,' I said, folding my arms across my chest, 'why don't you tell everyone about what you're researching here at Jethro Park?'

'But, Dave, you *know* that I've signed a confidentiality agreement. My professional integrity means a great deal to me and I hoped that you would respect that.' India sounded hurt and Vicky and Meera looked at me reproachfully. 'All I can say is that a lot of the film is set in a school like this one and it's the very touching story of a girl who has a lot of problems, and yet still manages to be redeemed by the power of love.' India's bosom heaved and her voice trembled with emotion. 'She's had a lot of heartache, a lot of *exploitation* in her life; in fact, some might say she's been emotionally damaged by her experiences.' Now her head was bowed, and her voice had faded to a whisper. 'Sometimes I . . . well, I – I can understand how that feels.'

There was a respectful silence as India bit her lip and smiled at us bravely. Behind all the glamour and the glitz, everyone could see that here was just an ordinary, tender-hearted girl struggling to come to terms with some mysterious inner sorrow. Never mind that the most tragic thing that had ever happened to India Withers was the time her gold card was rejected at Harvey Nichols (a technical blip, but just recalling that moment used to bring tears to her eyes).

During lessons India sat quietly at the back of the class, apparently drinking in every word, but her sex-kitten-turned-trauma-victim act proved so irresistible that she spent every free moment besieged by yet more people clamouring to be her new best friend/guidance counsellor. This meant she had little chance to share her oh-so-hilarious anecdotes from Darlinham House and, for the time being, I was able to watch the action from a safe distance. At least I had Katie to keep me company – she confided to me that it was a bit of a disappointment to see India in the flesh because, 'without any airbrushing I really don't see what all the fuss is about. And that is *so* obviously a padded bra.' Alas for Katie, Jack was not so discriminating and was following India around like a lost puppy. He seemed incapable of saying or doing anything other than croak 'wow', weakly, at irregular intervals.

Viv, on the other hand, was much more eloquent. She announced with relish that India represented 'the über-feminine ideal as determined and conditioned by the male gaze' and as such was a perfect example of 'how blurred the line between genuine femininity and womanliness as a masquerade has become.' Her eyes gleamed as she informed me that girls like India are 'paradoxically both victims of the Beauty Myth and willing proponents of the phallogocentric social codes it perpetuates.' Then she said that India was an A-grade pain in the backside and with a bit of luck the novelty of having a micro-celeb in the class would soon wear off and everything would get back to normal. But neither of us looked entirely convinced.

After the final bell had gone I planned to slip away without entangling myself with the über-feminine ideal and her newly appointed entourage. She ran me to ground, of course, outside the girls' locker room.

'I couldn't let you head off without saying thank you for making my first day here so much fun. And we've hardly even had a chance to talk properly! I want to hear about *everything*. Your poor, poor mother, for instance – I was at Boo Swartzburger's the other day and she and Herbie were saying that Bud *drinks*. That's why Lola kicked him out, apparently. He's not turned violent yet, has he? It's all *such* a shame . . . Such a terrible waste. But now I've simply got to run – an interview with *Hollywood Scoop* in the Rah Bar, you know. *So* tedious.' Mwah, mwah. 'See you tomorrow!'

At last she was gone, presumably to sink her pert little bottom into the leather seats of a waiting limo. There was a brief surge of people after her, the babble of comment and bustle among those who remained, and then, finally, the last stragglers collected their things and shuffled off home. Even Viv and her post-feminist theories had left, already late for her date with Simon. I sat down on the grubby linoleum, leaned back against a locker and closed my eyes. Peace at last.

'So now I know why you're so secretive about your past.' Ben was lolling against the door. I immediately straightened my shoulders and tried to look a little less like the kind of social reject who spends her spare time huddled on the floor of deserted locker rooms.

'Oh yes? Would that be my star-studded adventures among the rich and shameless or my double life as a top MI5 agent?' I really hoped Ben hadn't come looking for me just to get the low-down on India's career at Darlinham House.

'Both sound interesting. But I guess your tales of global espionage are censored by the Official Secrets Act.'

'And my adventures among the stars are covered by the libel laws. Sorry.'

'All this mystery!' he said teasingly. 'You know, some might say you've got something to hide.'

'Or I could just be trying to make myself look interesting.'

'As feminine mystique goes, it's very effective.' He grinned. 'And talking of effective females . . . I seem to have spent the whole day reminding Jack to put his tongue back in his mouth. You know what he's calling India? A Pocket Venus.'

'Otherwise known as the Poison Dwarf,' I muttered before I could stop myself. Wasn't my mother forever telling me how Real Men Don't Like Bitchy Women? The Pygmy Blonde's string of conquests may have cast this theory into doubt but even so . . . 'Of course, she *is* stunning,' I added in what I hoped was non-neurotic, breezy, girl-power sort of way.

Ben laughed. 'Oh yeah. In the original knock-out-blow-to-the-head meaning of the word. I think we're all feeling slightly . . . concussed. Seeing stars, you might say.' Then he reached out his hand and helped pull me to my feet. 'Come on, time for home.'

We started to make our way out of the school. It was bucketing down with rain, so much so that Ben didn't attempt to be self-sufficient and macho and ducked his head under my umbrella as we trudged along. I found myself wondering if this situation would have more romantic potential if I was wearing a fantasy-schoolgirl outfit in luxury fabrics. I remembered enthusing to Mum about how wonderful it was to have a proper school uniform at last – no more stressing about what to wear every morning, no more fashion fascists gathering in the locker room to bitch about how your trainers were *sooo* Last Season. After today, however, I realized that while all uniforms are equal, some uniforms are more equal than others. Did Ben now see me as just another drop in a muddy maroon ocean? As we waited in the leaky bus stop and I saw the raindrops spatter my uniform with darker shades of sludge, I thought how nice it would be to slip into some super-stylish outfit, ready to be whisked off to some posh bar in a gleaming limo. At this very moment India was probably being plied with Cosmopolitans while a journalist asked searching questions like, 'Do you ever get tired of being so fabulous?' and begged her to share her beauty tips.

'Do you really not miss it at all? Life as a . . . Darling? Is that what you call them?' It was almost as if he'd been reading my thoughts.

'I wasn't a Darling, not a proper one. As I keep telling you.'

'Look – I'm not having a go. Now that I've seen how India operates I get why you've been a bit, er, tense recently. But I'm still curious . . . seeing her must bring it all back and not just the bad stuff. All those Beautiful People, those glamorous parties – most of the girls I know would kill to live that sort of life. Surely you must miss it *sometimes* . . .'

I felt a spurt of annoyance. Why did my conversations with Ben always have to lead back to Darlinham House and my so-called celebrity lifestyle? But although he was frowning, it wasn't a proper glower. It was an uncertain, working-it-out sort of frown, so I tried to keep the irritation out of my voice.

'Of course some of it was fun. But it's hard work, keeping up with people like India, trying to be part of the pack. It's weird – they pride themselves on being so individual and original while actually everyone's desperate to fit in with everyone else . . . I'm not saying I was this amazing free spirit or anything. I just wasn't any good at all that, you know, social networking.'

'I'm not so sure.' He looked at me sidelong. 'It looked to me like you've got that air-kissing thing down to a fine art.'

I couldn't tell if he was teasing or testing me but decided to take the risk.

'I suspect my technique's got a little rusty.'

'That would be a shame,' he said solemnly. 'A girl shouldn't neglect her kissing technique.'

At this point my bus came wheezing up to the stop. Through its steamed-up windows I could see that it was packed with damp, grumpy people. I had the beginnings of a headache, my bag was dragging at my shoulder and even with the umbrella I'd got very wet. In spite of these things, or maybe because of them, I suddenly felt light-hearted. Reckless.

'Well, you know what they say. Practice makes per-fect,' I said, and kissed him lightly on both cheeks. Then I jumped on to the bus and we wheezed off into the rain.

I went to bed nearly as soon as I got home, suddenly too tired to face company, too tired to think about the science module on Monday, too tired to eat. Instead, I lay on my bed, not really thinking about anything, just staring at the ceiling in a sort of daze. At around eight o'clock the phone rang and I heard my mother's voice float up from the hallway. 'No, Hector, she can't talk to you. No, I don't know how she got on with India. She's gone to bed. Yes – went straight upstairs and now she's out cold. Oh, Hector, you don't think it could be this horrible glandular fever thing, do you? Academic stress is very damaging to the health, you know, especially for vulnerable young girls . . . anorexia . . . depression . . . drugs . . . should I call the doctor, do you think?' Poor old Dad, I thought, then I rolled over and fell fast asleep.

I think I may have spent a bit too long in bed; after nearly eleven hours of sleep I woke up the next day feeling groggy and disorientated. Nobody else was around at breakfast, though there were the dregs of Bud's wheatgrass 'n' vegetable juice smoothie in the blender. Bud swears by it – 'No better way to kick-start your morning!' – but now I couldn't help remembering India's hushed voice as she told me, 'Bud *drinks*.' I took a cautious sip, feeling a louse. It tasted like poison but was alcohol-free.

Unfortunately, I needed more than a dribble of vegetable juice to get me going that morning, and even though I legged it all the way from our house to the bus stop I still managed to miss the bus I usually get. In theory, there's only supposed to be five to eight minutes between them, but this morning it was more like twenty and so I didn't get to school until after assembly. This meant that Viv and I went off to our different classes before I could fill her in on my encounter with Ben. Spontaneity was all well and good but now it was time for what Viv calls FAB tactics – Foresight And Back-up. (Exhaustive analysis of the meaning, motivation and significance of everything said and done. Speculation on likely developments. Suggestions for further action, with extra points for cross-relationship referencing. Et cetera.)

And talking of back-up . . . 'Where have you *been*? I need to talk to you,' India said with a voice of silk and eyes of steel as I walked into French. 'It's *important*.' She was waiting for me at the front of the class, hands on hips, oblivious to Meera and Jack and Co. hovering at either side, and immediately grabbed my arm to pull me down to the seat she'd been saving next to her. Now was the time to summon a muscle-bound henchman or three to wrestle her to the ground and drag her out of Jethro Park and my life forever. But before I could shake her off or she could say anything further, Mademoiselle Bertaut marched into the room and everyone immediately sat down and shut up. It has to be said that the members of staff who have this effect on us are few and far between, but then Mademoiselle Bertaut is A-grade henchwoman material: muscly, military and mean as hell. I was quite looking forward to seeing what she'd make of India.

I was ready to bet that India had a personal tutor holed up at home ready to do her homework for her and maybe even prepare for the odd lesson, but if the general squalor of comprehensive-school life didn't put her off, I was still hopeful that she would crack under the pressure of a real live learning environment. Of course, one of the reasons India was so dangerous was because she was smart, but I liked to think this was more animal cunning than intellectual brilliance. It certainly didn't owe much to her education. Although the standard of teaching at Darlinham House was, on the whole, fairly good – after all, our parents had to have something to show for all the money they threw at the place – even the staff thought it was a bit uncool to pay *too* much attention to passé subjects like physics or history or whatever. So it was surely only a matter of time before India was exposed in class as an educationally subnormal bimbo with about as much depth as a coat of nail varnish.

Unfortunately, I'd forgotten that not only was India a devoted follower of Paris Fashion Week, she'd also nearly had a French stepfather, the heir to a famous cosmetics company who had entertained mother and daughter at his chateaux on the Loire over the course of several summers. After a heartfelt speech on the wonders of French literature in general and Alexandre Dumas in particular, Indy proceeded to lisp and smirk her way very prettily through a role-play exercise set in a Parisian hotel. Not that it took much linguistic skill to look good next to India's role-play partner, Dan – one brisk flutter of her eyelashes and he was incapable of forming a coherent sentence in English, let alone French.

The result of this was that for the rest of the lesson most of Mademoiselle B's time and energy was taken up with persecuting Dan. Even India had the good sense to sit tight and shut up so I was able to let my eyes glaze over with the rest of my class while devoting the next half-hour to going over every conversation I'd ever had with Ben. We were flirting last night. Definitely. And I was pretty sure he'd come looking for me. He'd been waiting for me that first day back at school, after all. Then he'd been angry, upset even, when he thought I was deliberately ignoring him. Put this together with our encounter at New Year and all the signs were good. Very good. And yet . . . sometimes I felt that Ben was still making his mind up about me. After all, it wasn't so long ago that he was convinced I was some kind of spoilt rich kid playing at being an ordinary just because I was bored/rebellious/attention-seeking/whatever. But he *had* apologized, he *had* admitted he'd got it wrong . . . and now that he'd met India he could appreciate what I was escaping from. At least I hoped he could. I hoped that India being here would make it easier, not more difficult, to prove to Ben that I wasn't that sort of girl, that I never had been. I hoped the more he saw of India the more ridiculous and less alluring he would think she was. And, most importantly, I hoped I'd get another chance to demonstrate my kissing technique. Only this time there wouldn't be any buses or rain or unflattering maroon blazers to spoil the moment.

It was almost a relief to find that Ben wasn't in school that morning, since I knew I wouldn't get the chance to have a proper talk with Viv until lunchtime. I know I sound like one of those gormless girlies who can't choose a flavoured lip balm without consulting their bestest chum, but I felt the need for an outside opinion. Viv can be forthright to the point of ruthlessness, but I knew she wouldn't ever tell me some rose-tinted rubbish just to make me feel better. It would be too awful if I'd got the signs wrong, particularly as it's not as if I have a long and glorious history of success with the opposite sex (how had India or Asia or Twinkle once put it? Oh yes, Dave the romance-retard). This time I wanted to be 110 per cent sure I wasn't just seeing what I wanted to see.

I found Viv in the cafeteria, where she was sitting with Katie and Tom and a few others. I was hoping that one whiff of the starch-and-lard selection on the cafeteria hotplates would be too much for India's delicate stomach but, as always, I had underestimated the girl. Just as I was settling down to my plate of chips I felt a manicured nail tap my shoulder. 'Dave. I said I needed to talk to you. Didn't you hear me calling after you in the corridor?'

'She was *waiting* for you,' said Meera.

'She said it was *important*,' said Vicky.

'Is there anything I can do to help?' asked Jack, Dan and Tom at the same time. Then they turned and glared at one another.

India waved them all back with an impatient hand. 'I need to talk to Davy in private. It's about a *personal* matter.' That didn't sound good. Already the people on the other tables were beginning to turn and stare as the Withers Effect began to kick in. It didn't help that Dan's girlfriend, Carrie, had just fled the room in tears.

'All right, all right,' I said, lowering my voice and sliding my tray to the other end of the table from the rest. 'You've got five minutes. Then you can go and play with your friends and I can play with mine. OK?'

'Fabulous.' She broke into an angelic smile. We sat

opposite each other, me tucking into my chips in a defiant sort of way as India nibbled delicately at a single lettuce leaf.

'So I've been thinking, Dave—'

I put a ketchup-'n'-mayo-dunked chip back on my plate. 'Whoa. Stop right there. I think it's time we got something straight.' I leaned in and spoke very slowly and clearly. 'My name is Oc-tave-ee-ah. It's a bit of a mouthful, I know, and it's maybe not the most sensible-sounding name in the world. But it's what I'm called. Not Dave or Tavy or the Obelisk or Goliath or the Incredible Hulk or any other of those sweet little pet names you've thought up in the past. I'm Octavia. So if we're going to have this conversation – in fact, if we're going to have any conversation *at all* – you're going to have to start remembering that. Got it?'

India sighed. 'There's no need to be so *aggressive* . . . have you ever thought you might have a testosterone imbalance, Dave? Octavia, I mean? It would explain a lot more than just the whole height issue—' She saw I was pushing my tray back down the table and changed tack hastily. 'No – wait. That's fine. Oc-tave-ee-ah. I've remembered, see? Anyway, as I was *saying*, we need to talk. This is only my second day here, I know, but I have to say that so far the whole experience has been something of a let-down.'

'So you're leaving us then?' I struggled to keep the unbridled joy out of my voice.

'Don't be ridiculous. Why would I want to do that? No, I can see this place has potential. I just need you to make my time here more relevant. More *authentic*.'

'More authentically what?'

'Deprived. Rough. Desperate. Working-class, obviously.'

'Look, India, this really isn't my problem. *You* decided Jethro Park was the place for you, *you* fixed it up with the governors, *you* were all set on coming here even though I tried to tell you it wasn't the educational slum you were looking for. I'm sorry if we've turned out to be a bit more well-heeled than you were expecting—'

'I wouldn't go *that* far,' said India, looking around us with distaste. 'But I was certainly hoping for a bit more obvious disadvantage. Surely *some* of these kids must have criminal relatives. What about physical abuse? Drugs? Broken homes?'

I had to laugh at this point. 'If it's drug problems and broken homes you're after you should have stuck to Darlinham House.'

'As a child of a one-parent family I don't really see the funny side of marital breakdown,' she said primly. 'In fact, I think it makes me uniquely qualified to empathize with the *alienated* and *dispossessed* of our society. As I explained to Jed, at my first casting.'

I saw that Ben had turned up from wherever he'd been all morning and was now sitting next to Viv. They were both looking over at me with commiserating expressions and I took courage from it.

'Oh, for God's sake, India! You're the only daughter of a multimillionaire knight of the realm, not some crack-addict's kid from a high-rise tower block. So why don't you stick to what you know best and go back to playing beauty queens and cheerleaders. Then maybe the rest of us social dropouts will get some peace.'

India's eyes flashed but she spoke in the same sweet, sorrowful voice as before. Only louder.

'Poor Dave, Octavia I mean. I should never have brought up the whole broken-home issue. I should have realized that you're a little oversensitive when it comes to family matters . . . Just between ourselves, don't you think it's about time you talked over your abandonment issues with your psychiatrist?' People were starting to turn round and lean in again. She smiled and raised her voice even louder. 'It's only natural for you to feel that way. I mean, first your dad deserted you and your mother when you were only a baby, running off with another man – well, it was a series of men, wasn't it? – and now your mother's been publicly exposed as the mistress of a Z-list alcoholic. No wonder it's taken you so long to come to terms with Alex breaking up with you . . .'

It seemed as if the whole cafeteria had paused to listen.

'But I thought you said that *you* dumped *him*, Octavia,' said Vicky, or it could have been Meera, both of whom had left their own table and were now hovering behind India again.

'That's because I did,' I said through clenched teeth.

'Still in denial,' said India, shaking her head sadly. 'My brother,' she confided, 'has a bit of reputation. He's a sweet boy at heart but rather *wild*. Girls are always going crazy over him . . .'

At this point Ben got up from the table and walked out of the room. His face was set and he wouldn't catch my eye. I had a sudden, desperate urge to go after him, to explain, but that would look like running away . . .

and would probably draw even more attention to myself. In that moment of indecision, India took further control of the situation. 'Octavia was in *floods* of tears for days after,' she explained to her new audience, dinner ladies and all, 'coming round to the house at all hours of the day and night, begging me to change Alexis's mind. I felt very sorry for the poor girl, but what could I do? Lex and I thought that after she dropped out of school and came here she'd be able to make a clean break, put it all behind her . . . but now I can see that she's still not over him.'

'That is absolute crap and you know it,' Viv said clearly.

'Yeah,' put in good old Katie. 'Octavia's not the kind of girl to go loopy over a bloke.'

India gave them both a long, measuring look. 'You didn't ever meet Alexis, did you? Hmm? I think your loyalty's very touching, of course, but you should bear in mind that you only ever heard one side of the story.'

I felt a red mist descend over my eyes. 'Stop right there. *You're* the one who's obsessed. You're the one in denial. You just can't accept the fact that your precious brother wasn't good enough for me and I decided that I could do better. A lot better.' Then I got up and began to go after Ben. India would have to be dealt with sooner or later but right now, I decided, I had other priorities.

'You believe that if you want to, Octavia,' India called after me, voice dripping with sympathy. 'But remember – the sooner you face up to reality the sooner the healing process can begin!'

*

In hindsight, the sensible thing to have done would have been to stay in the cafeteria and have it out with India right there and then. If necessary, I could have given a blow-by-blow, warts-and-all account of everything that went wrong between Alex and me, with Viv to back me up. I could have described the scandals and sensations of India's own love life in lurid detail. I could have said that she'd given her director a nervous breakdown before filming had even begun, that she thought roughing it at Jethro Park for a week or two was Suffering for the Cause of Art and that this, in India's eyes, was the kind of sacrifice worthy of Nobel Prizes and Academy Awards. Finally, I could have broken the news to the Withers Adoration Society that India only tolerated them because she wanted to know what it was like to spend your life surrounded by illiterate yobbos.

I told myself that I wasn't ready for this sort of direct action just yet. A no-holds-barred public slanging match with India was bound to be messy, unpleasant and prolonged, and I knew all too well that even if I did end up with the upper hand, India could inflict quite a bit of damage along the way. A decisive victory would require energy and resourcefulness, neither of which was in huge supply at the moment. If only I could get her on her own and find some way of forcing her to back down quietly . . . but what were the chances of that? No, the only way to deal with India right now was open confrontation and I knew it. The real reason I left when I did was Ben.

I'd been thinking of Ben for most of the morning – wondering, hoping, debating about Ben – and seeing him walk past me with that cold, almost contemptuous look on his face had suddenly thrown all these thoughts and feelings into sharp relief. I could cope with Vicky or Dan or whoever thinking I was a lovesick fantasist with abandonment issues, but not Ben. Not Ben.

It was with a feeling of déjà vu that I finally caught up with him in the covered passage at the back of the science block. During the weeks before and after Christmas we'd both done a fair bit of chasing after each other with challenges and excuses and apologies. Maybe this was the time to put an end to it once and for all. I felt a sudden lurch in my stomach at the thought that this could be the last time I would be able to feel the sense of possibility, the lovely uncertainty, which hovered around all my thoughts of him. Almost without realizing it, we'd caught one another's eye or brushed past on the stairs or even sulked and snapped at each other, and the moment had been lit by a sparkle of anticipation. *Shared* anticipation. Or *was* all this the delusion of a lovesick fantasist?

Ben didn't look overly pleased to see I'd come after him. In fact, he acted surprised to see me at all.

'I didn't expect to see you back so soon.'

'Back from where?'

'Your little trip down memory lane. India and you obviously have a lot of catching up to do.'

'And you obviously haven't ever heard of false memory syndrome . . . come on, Ben, don't tell me you believed all that crap India was spouting back there.'

'I don't know what to believe. Like I said before, you're a woman of mystery.' He said this carelessly, like he was already bored with the conversation, and made to move on down the passage, but I blocked his path.

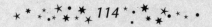

'More fool you then. You've known India all of five minutes whereas we've been in the same class for over a term now. Can't you see what she's doing?' In spite of my forceful tone, I was only just resisting the impulse to hang on to his shirtsleeve and beg. 'That whole performance in the cafeteria was stage-managed to create maximum fun for her and embarrassment for me.'

He shrugged. 'Look, I don't know the rights and wrongs of whatever's gone on between the two of you. Maybe you did dump her brother, maybe she is exaggerating things. But it's fairly clear that Alex or Alexis or whoever he is has got an overactive charisma drive and it's even more clear that you've still got issues about him.'

The red mist descended over my eyes again. I couldn't believe I'd raced after him to explain myself when all he did was patronize me. 'Issues? What do you mean, "issues"? So you think I'm such a poor shrinking violet I still haven't recovered from my fling-of-a-lifetime with India's big brother, do you? As amateur psychology goes, that's not only crass, it's *insulting.*'

Ben glowered. 'I'm not blind. I've seen how you go flushed and twitchy-looking whenever anyone mentions Alex's name – you do, you know – and it's not just when India's around.'

All the anger suddenly went out of me. Behind the glower, Ben's face looked uncertain, lost. He looked how I felt, in fact. Only now I realized that I wasn't feeling uncertain any more – that *I* was the one in control here and I didn't need any debate or tactic-plotting to know what I had to do. I may have lost my nerve with India but this was different. This time there was no way on earth I was going to back down.

'And what if I do?' I moved towards him and looked him in the eye. 'What's it to you if I broke up with some guy you've never even met or if he broke up with me? Why does it matter so much?'

'You know why,' he said in that low growl of his.

'Then tell me.'

'I – you – because – oh, for God's sake—' and then he kissed me.

We both drew away and looked at each other in surprise, and then relief. The tension of the last hour had caught up with me and I started to giggle, but he kissed me again, half-laughing himself, and that sparkling, lucky, light-headed feeling flooded over and into me.

'This isn't going to be a one-off, is it,' Ben said at last, and it wasn't a question.

'No. I hope not.' We stood there grinning at each other like a pair of idiots. I don't think we would even have realized the bell had gone if Mademoiselle Bertaut hadn't passed by in a high-speed stomp and shaken her wristwatch at us in a threatening sort of way.

'I suppose we'd better go,' I said reluctantly. 'I don't want to be late again . . . where'd you get to this morning, by the way?'

'Dentist's. Impeccable timing, really – it's not every day I get to lock lips with the class princess. I can't afford pink diamonds so the least I can manage is pearly whites.'

I laughed but mention of the class princess had brought me back to reality with a nasty jolt. 'Ben, I hope

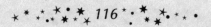

you don't mind, but I'd rather we, um, kept this to ourselves. Just for a bit.'

'I wasn't planning on a *national* broadcast, you know. I thought we could start off small – a little announcement in assembly, then local radio, maybe a billboard or two . . .'

'Look, I know it sounds ridiculous. But – well – life will be a lot easier if people continue to think we're just friends and no more.'

Ben stopped in his tracks and looked at me narrowly. 'And why's that?'

'India,' I said simply. 'Once she works out there's something going on there'll be no peace for either of us. She'll try and ruin everything, she always does. Honestly, it won't be for long – I just need a bit more time to decide how to deal with her. And who knows, she might be gone by next week.'

'You're going to have to sort things out with her sooner or later.'

'I know. I will. But in the meantime – please?'

'OK, OK. If it's really not going to be for long . . . then secret rendezvous in the broom cupboard it is.' He gave me a mischievous look. 'Could be fun.'

'And, er, maybe if you acted a bit off with me? Like you were before? It's just so that she doesn't suspect anything . . .'

Ben rolled his eyes but didn't look seriously annoyed. 'All right, Agent Double-O Cleeve – I suppose if we have to do it at all we might as well do it properly. In which case, you'd better go into the classroom first and I'll come in five minutes behind you.'

*

All afternoon, I had to work hard at avoiding Ben's eye and not staring into the distance with a big syrupy smile all over my face. I should, of course, have been miserable. Viv was clearly exasperated with me for not standing my ground in the cafeteria, India oozed smugness from every pore, and Vicky 'n' Meera and Co. kept giving me the sort of sorrowful, pitying looks you reserve for the terminally insane. Now that India's second full day at Jethro Park was drawing to a close it was all too clear that my worst fears had been realized. Already, all manner of intrigues and rivalries were beginning to simmer under the surface of school life.

Our entire year was now split into factions, by far the largest of which was the Withers Adoration Society. Its members were completely in thrall to the promise of glamour and stardom that India represented along with, of course, her Commitment To Her Art, her hints at a secret sorrow and her touching concern for the mental health of her old school chum, Dave. First among India's inner circle were Jack, Dan and Tom, at one time the most determinedly macho of the Jethro Park Romeos, but now reduced to stuttering, slobbering shadows of their former selves. When they weren't squabbling over who got to carry India's nail file they united to close ranks against any other male who tried to muscle in on the Withers turf. In the meantime, Carrie, Dan's girlfriend, kept breaking down in tears and was tended to by Katie and a couple of other girls to whom the novelty of India's oh-so-fabulous life and invincible sex-appeal was beginning to wear thin. Their rebellion was limited to muttering in corners and tossing their hair in a defiant sort of way.

Like I said, I should have been miserable. Instead, I was glowing. Through cunning use of text messaging, Ben and I arranged to meet up on Saturday morning, so I had to concentrate my thoughts on the chemistry module on Monday and the next stage of India's smear campaign in an effort to look a little less delighted with life. I must have been successful, because when the final bell went Viv took my arm and asked me how I was bearing up. She'd obviously decided to let me off the hook for my failure of nerve in the cafeteria. 'I know you wanted to talk to me earlier – how about we go for chocolate fudge cake in that cafe down the road? It's nice and grotty so we'll be safe from you-know-who.'

'I'd love to but I can't, I'm afraid. I'm going straight to Dad and Michael's tonight – I haven't been round for ages. Oh, Viv!' I started giggling in spite of myself. 'I've got so much to tell you – *good* things, for a change.' I saw Katie and Hannah coming up and lowered my voice. 'But it'll have to wait. I'll call you this weekend, OK?'

The four of us walked out together to the main entrance. Katie and Hannah were obviously dying to ask me about my run-in with India, but I didn't give them any encouragement and Katie's attention soon wandered from the conversation. 'Octavia, don't turn and stare, but a *really* cute guy has just driven up in a Mercedes,' she said in awestruck tones. 'I think he's, like, *signalling* at you.'

I turned and stared, then laughed. 'Oh, that's Michael. He must have got off work early.'

'Who's Michael?' asked Hannah.

'Dad's boyfriend.' Katie and Hannah looked dismayed – so India had been telling the truth about my dysfunctional family after all. But I couldn't be bothered to explain, just winked at Viv, waved, and made my way over to Michael's car with a sigh of relief.

'Happy Friday,' said Michael, opening the passenger door for me. 'Glad it's the weekend?'

'Like you wouldn't believe.'

He pulled a sympathetic face but didn't ask any searching questions. He and Dad had been out on the Wednesday night of India's arrival at Jethro Park and so, apart from leaving an anguished and incoherent message on their answering machine, I hadn't yet had the chance to bring them up to speed on the whole Withers fiasco. And now, I found, I didn't have the energy for a proper rant. But although Michael's a lawyer and is actually pretty hot at cross-examination and the rest of it, he's also one of those people you can just sit and be silent with in a peaceful sort of way.

Over a supper of grilled scallops followed by lemon cheesecake I perked up, however, and launched into a long and indignant catalogue of India's crimes. Dad let me run on for a bit, then scratched his head and looked thoughtful.

'But you do realize who the financial backer for this film of Jed's will probably be, don't you? Tempest UK. Of course, it's not been confirmed yet—'

'*What?* But that's who Bud works for – he would have *said* something, surely – I can't believe—'

'I'm sure there was something about it in the last issue of *Cinema Scope*. Wait a sec and I'll dig it out.' After a brief rummage in the pile of books and papers stacked in the hall, he came back with one of his trade journals. 'Here you go: "Tempest Films UK have begun talks with

Jed Mosley's Stakeout Productions after Stakeout's partnership with the Campion media group unexpectedly fell through before Christmas. Shooting on Mosley's new film, a radical reinterpretation of *La Dame aux Camélias* set among London teenagers, has been postponed until financial backing—"'

I practically snatched the magazine out of his hands. Most of the article was a lot of boring bumf from Tempest's Creative Director about how committed his company was to 'fostering talent' and 'investing in quality' and 'supporting the UK's most distinctive film-making voices'. But the last paragraph was what really made me choke on my cheesecake: 'Mosley's debut feature, *Rat Dancer*, acquired something of a cult following but failed to make much of a commercial impact due to distribution problems. If Tempest do decide to back Mosley, what began as a low-budget art-house flick may well make the crossover into box office success.'

No wonder India was so keen to be old school buddies again – she must have known about Bud's connections with Tempest right from the start, I fumed.

'This is so bloody typical: India clawing her way to the top and once again trampling all over my life to get there . . . and do you know what *really* gets to me? Bud. He must have known all about it but he listened to me going on and on about India and this film and didn't say a word.'

'He probably couldn't,' said Michael. 'It wouldn't be professional – or ethical, come to that.'

'Bud's in charge of marketing, right?' said Dad. 'Then I'm sure he'll be kept informed of the latest developments, but it's not as if he's responsible for deciding whether they're going to back the film or not. And don't forget, Tempest will have at least five or six other projects in the pipeline.'

OK. So maybe Bud was off the hook. Maybe India wouldn't be able turn the Carnaby–Tempest connection to evil advantage after all. Maybe. None of this changed the fact, however, that any kind of link between India's life and mine was Seriously Bad News. With a sigh, I began to read the biog note on 'The Talented Mr Mosley' that *Cinema Scope* had helpfully provided. It told me that Jed had begun his career as a political journalist and documentary film-maker and that his first film, *Rat Dancer*, was about a young boy with a poetry-writing drug dealer for a mother.

'I remember the reviews,' said Michael. 'Snappy dialogue, stylish camera work and a soundtrack to make your eardrums bleed.'

'Yes, I think Jed's ambitious as well as talented,' said Dad. 'It was a big risk casting someone like India but I'm sure it helped get the project off the ground. I don't really see what's in it for Ms Withers though.'

'Come on, Dad, you know what India's like! She's convinced she's destined for Great Art, not playing rent-a-bimbo in slasher flicks or whatever. And look what being in one of your films has done for Drake Montague's image,' I pointed out. 'People used to think he was just another dumb hunk. Now they want to know his opinion on everything from American foreign policy to sexism in Shakespeare.'

My father looked thoughtful. 'Well, it'll be interesting to see how much pressure Jed will be under to make his work more populist . . . he's always been a bit of an eccentric and that makes financing his projects difficult.'

'It's not just money he's got problems with,' I said. 'Poor old Jed's already had to take time out because India's made him ill.'

'And yet I don't get the impression that all this righteous indignation with India is out of concern for "poor old Jed",' Dad said drily.

He was right, of course. The bottom line was, I couldn't care less whether or not India ground the Great Hope of the British film industry into dust beneath her heel. The only hopes or plans I gave a stuff about right now were mine.

I stayed the night at Dad's place and for a few groggy moments on Saturday morning had to struggle to remember why I'd woken up with butterflies in my stomach. Ben-smitten butterflies. I rolled over on to my back and stretched luxuriously with a happy sigh. It struck me that it wasn't just the romance of the situation I was looking forward to; I was also excited about being proper *friends* with Ben at last. Up until now, our attempts at friendship had always been frustrated by all those thoughts and feelings left unsaid or misunderstood. We still had a lot of finding out about each other to do. Thinking about all the conversations we could have, the stories and jokes and opinions we could share, made the grey morning outside my window seem bright with opportunity. Little Miss Sunshine rides again.

Dad was clearly relieved to see me looking so cheerful when I came down for breakfast. 'Sleep well?'

'Yup. Not a single paparazzo, suicidal stepbrother or

vengeful prom queen to spoil my dreams.' I meant it as a joke but he looked at me with a concerned expression.

'Hmm . . . you really have been in the wars lately, haven't you?'

'Oh, well. Never a dull moment and all that . . . has Michael had breakfast? Because if he's not here soon I'm going to finish off that last bit of bacon.' I didn't want my good mood spoilt by yet another in-depth discussion of my woes. But Dad wasn't ready to change the subject.

'I've been thinking about our conversation last night and I must admit I'm a little surprised and, ah, worried by how much this Withers girl has got under your skin. I think of you as being so much more happy and confident these days and yet you seem to feel that all that old Darlinham House nonsense has some sort of . . . well, *power* over you still.' I shrugged but felt a bit uncomfortable. It *was* disconcerting to find myself so panicked by India after all this time. I thought I was doing so well with my nicely organized new life, but India's arrival had made me question this hard-won sense of security – surely a truly self-assured person wouldn't be reduced to a neurotic wreck after just a couple of days in the company of an old school fiend?

'Don't worry about it, Dad, honestly. I think I probably went a bit OTT with the dramatics last night. And I feel loads better after having had a good whinge.'

'Well . . . if you're sure.' He brightened. 'At least you've got proper back-up this time. If I were ever in a tight spot, I'd want to have a girl like Viv fighting my corner.'

I smiled but didn't say anything. I had a suspicion

that Viv was actually quite enjoying having India in the class – hadn't she said that school life could do with a bit of livening up? Viv has always liked a bit of commotion and confrontation and I knew that my failure to go after India with all guns blazing was something of a disappointment to her. Which was fair enough, but then it wasn't *her* past that India was muckraking over so merrily and it wasn't *her* future that India could put at risk in one blink of a baby-blue eye.

I stopped off at home to change clothes before going to meet Ben. There were no signs of life when I let myself in; the happy couple were presumably off choosing matching monogrammed napkin rings or whatever while Milton's black window drapes were still drawn and his door firmly closed. This suited me fine since the last thing I wanted was to get the maternal third degree on why I was looking so nice and where was I going and was I, perhaps, meeting a Special Friend? In some ways I would have liked to have shared the glad tidings with Dad, but if I told him and Michael I'd have to tell the other half of the family and I didn't think I could cope with Mum and Bud's combined raptures.

As for the whole what-to-wear minefield . . . I've always been a jeans-and-T-shirt kinda gal, although since I left Darlinham House, ironically enough, Mum's had more success in getting me to branch out into the occasional girly skirt and sparkly top. A short skirt and sparkles were clearly not appropriate here but I was nevertheless determined to banish all Ben's memories of sludgy polyester, at least until Monday. Something flattering and sophisticated then. But not *too* sophisticated of course. Nothing obviously pricey and princess-like . . . I had come to accept that everyone – male or female, celebrity or civilian, fashion conscious or fashion clueless – makes assumptions about you from what you wear. Most people make these assumptions without being really aware of it. Darlings, however, have made label-labelling into something between an academic discipline and a spectator sport.

When I finally left the house I was in a corduroy skirt, boots and a wrap-over cardigan. A lovely soft raspberry colour – not a speck of maroon in sight. I thought about Bud's charm bracelet but decided that silver cupcakes were a step too far. Even though the clothes issue was resolved, however, I still felt a little nervous; it was going to be odd to see Ben outside Jethro Park and away from all the familiar props and rituals of our school routine. There had been the theatre trip and Jack's party, of course, but this was different. Just the two of us . . . Nothing to distract us but nothing to fall back on either.

As the only child of divorced parents, Ben, like me, often spent his Saturday mornings with his dad. However, while my mother and father were at least reconciled to sharing the same postal district, Ben's parents had fled to opposite ends of London. This had slightly complicated our rendezvous arrangements, but in the end I settled on going to meet him halfway on his return trip. I got the impression that Ben wasn't one hundred per cent convinced I knew how to find my way round the tube but I informed him, slightly sharply, that I'd been using public transport for the last six years without ever needing a stretch limo on standby.

Once I came up from the underground at Tower Hill, I started looking around for Ben and had a flash of panic that maybe I had after all got the tube station wrong or the time wrong or something, but he was there, of course, looking out for me on the other side of the road. When I walked over to where he was waiting we didn't kiss or anything, just stood there smiling at each other and suddenly feeling rather shy.

'Hey.'

'Hey.'

Pause.

'So—' we both started to say at once, then stopped confusedly.

'You first,' I said.

'I was only going to ask if you'd had lunch yet, cos there's a nice cafe round the corner – everything from fish and chips to sun-dried whatsits. Or we could get sandwiches and sit out somewhere if you want.'

'I never say no to a sun-dried whatsit and chips.'

'Your wish is my command,' he said, sweeping an extravagant bow. Then he gave me a mischievous look, and my last trace of nervousness was gone.

The cafe was a small, bustling place where the waiters bawled instructions to each other in cockney-accented Italian and an ancient cappuccino machine hissed and steamed behind the counter. There was a bit of a wait to find a table since we'd arrived right in the lunchtime rush: a cheery mix of workmen taking a break from digging up the pavement and of tourists en route to the Tower. We finally squashed ourselves into a table right at the back and settled down to the tricky business of eating toasted panini without dripping melted mozzarella down our fronts. There was some general chat but after a while I got the feeling that Ben had something on his mind.

'I'm really glad we're doing this,' he said abruptly. 'Just the two of us at last, sitting down, talking, no hassle.'

'Me too,' I said, surprised.

'It's a shame we didn't do it before. Right from the beginning, I mean – maybe then I wouldn't have been such a pain in the backside.' He half-smiled, then went back to fiddling with the sugar packets. 'I think I owe you more of an explanation for why I've been so stroppy. It's just . . . sounds stupid, I guess . . . but when I saw the photo of Alex in that magazine . . . all those glossy people and buckets of champagne . . . I've always thought that sort of world rather ridiculous. Laughable. Like a bad soap opera, you know, trashy and quite fun but not *real*?' I nodded to show I understood. 'Seeing the picture of Alex and imagining you there with him made it real, you see, but it wasn't so funny any more . . . I felt as if I knew exactly what Alex was like. Rich and good-looking and oozing charm. I don't blame you for falling for someone like that. And, well, you *do* go all flustered whenever he's mentioned.'

'Part of that was just the general embarrassment of being put on the spot. Especially as you always seemed to be there and, er . . .'

'Sneering?'

'Well, you certainly looked very *knowing*. The thing is, I'm pretty much a beginner at the whole relationship thing.' I found that I was flushing slightly. 'And you're right – my time with Alex *was* a bit like a bad soap opera.

Even if he could be funny and charming when he wanted to be and occasionally, well, quite sweet.' Ben was frowning again. 'I'm only telling you this so you understand why I did get mixed up with him. Otherwise I'd either have been criminally shallow or criminally stupid, neither of which are desirable qualities in a girl, right?'

'Right.'

'So what about you?'

'What about me?'

'Well, I think it's high time you took a turn in the spotlight. Any abandonment issues you'd care to share? Or is there a high-profile ex with a psychotic sister I should know about?'

'Nothing so exciting, I'm afraid.' He shrugged. 'I've been out with a couple of nice people, but nothing special, no dramas. Maybe that was the problem. The spark's never been there . . . so I guess I'm a beginner too.'

I felt my heart lift. We Had A Spark. A *special* spark! I concentrated on stirring the foam on my coffee to hide my glee. Maybe Katie was wrong about me after all – maybe Octavia Clairbrook-Cleeve *was* the kind of girl to go loopy over a bloke.

I think we were both relieved that we'd had this conversation and could now move on to more cheerful things. At any rate we shamelessly lingered over our coffees, nattering away and doing our best to ignore the hovering waiter. After we'd finally paid the bill and come out of the cafe I was afraid there was going to be one of those 'what now' moments, but Ben had obviously got other ideas.

'Come on, there's something I want to show you.'

'Oh yes?'

'Yup. How are your legs?'

'Excuse me?'

'You've got a bit of a climb ahead.' Oh God. He'd booked us into some 'fun' activity session, like rock-climbing up plastic cliffs at a sports centre. And I'd have to pretend it was a lovely romantic gesture . . . Ben saw my face and laughed. 'Don't look so tragic. You'll like it, I promise.'

We walked for a bit, though Ben had to stop occasionally to get his bearings. We were right in the heart of the City by now, not a part of London I know well, where all the big finance companies count their millions behind smoked-glass windows. During the week it must have been bustling with people in suits charging around from conference call to coffee shop, but on a Saturday afternoon it had an oddly deserted feel. Finally we turned into a street that led to a tube station and Ben came to a halt. 'There you go.'

'There we go where?'

'*There*. Up. We're going up.'

I looked up and immediately felt a fool because we were standing right at the foot of a stone tower.

'It's the Monument. To the Great Fire of London, you know. This is where it started. You see, I've always wanted to put you on a pedestal . . .'

It looked even higher than Nelson's Column and had a kind of gold plume right at the top; the base had an ornate marble frieze showing seventeenth-century London in flames. But in spite of all this stateliness it looked odd and rather forlorn in the midst of all those offices and newsagents and trendy sandwich shops, almost as if it had been put down there by accident and then forgotten about. At any rate, the little old man in the ticket office was clearly thrilled to see some customers and bombarded us with an array of Monument-centric facts before he would let us up the narrow spiral stairs. I concentrated on not tripping over my own feet and suppressing my wheezes rather than working out how many of the three hundred and eleven steps I had left to go.

'Welcome to my penthouse apartment,' said Ben when we finally stepped out on to the viewing platform. Below us, the streets were almost eerily quiet: a few relics of seventeenth-century grandeur still sticking out among the jumble of office blocks, the grey Thames sliding through. It was one of those dull, wintry days and all the buildings were in the same muted tones – greyish, brownish, glints of blue and silver from the flashier ones – so that the only real colour came from the occasional red or yellow crane. Some trick of perspective made them tower over the dome of St Paul's.

'It's lovely up here,' I said, and I meant it. It wasn't a dramatic sort of view, like the one from St Paul's or the London Eye perhaps, but I could feel the surge of the city around us, sleek crammed against shabby, ancient jostling with new.

'I thought you'd like it.' Ben was looking towards Tower Bridge. 'I guess you must have travelled a fair bit – New York, Paris, those kinds of places – but London's always full of surprises. It's a kaleidoscope city.'

'How poetic.'

London wasn't the only thing full of surprises. Now

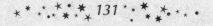

that I'd overcome my initial dislike of self-important creeps with chips on their shoulders, I was beginning to appreciate this particular creep's Poetical Charm, Emotional Maturity and – let's face it – raw sex appeal. Close up, the green spark in his eyes and the ever-so-slightly crooked slant of his smile were even more adorable . . .

'Well, you know, my mum says I've always been a very sensitive boy,' he said modestly.

'As well as "mindlessly optimistic"?'

'Of course. Not to mention hopelessly romantic—'

My first kiss at one hundred and thirty-three feet.

I got home at teatime, full of the joys of life, and raring to get started on a spot of chemistry revision. First of all, however, I bounced into the drawing room to spread a little happiness among my nearest and dearest – only to find that I'd walked straight into a Council of War. Bud, jaw clenched and eyes stern, stood clasping my mother's hand as she sat enthroned on the pink brocade armchair. She was looking her most pale and angelic: Saint Helena at the stake. Malcolm was sitting on a chair beside her, taking notes in a leather-bound notepad, while Euphoria paced up and down, chewing her nails and swearing under her breath.

'Whatever's happened?'

Lady Jane was too overcome to speak, but gestured weakly towards the television. Which, I now realized, was playing Suzi Sanmartini's chat show, *Tell It Like It Is*. From the date at the bottom of the screen, I realized it must be a recording of yesterday's show, express posted from the States. A woman with a lot of foxy red hair and smoky eye make-up was looking mournfully into the camera. Uh-oh.

'. . . Of course, my career means a great deal to me,' she was saying, 'but at the end of the day, all I've ever wanted to be was a good wife and a loving mom.' Her bronzed bosom heaved with emotion and there was a murmur of sympathy from the studio audience. 'When I lost Bud, I didn't just lose a husband and a mentor – I lost my best friend. And now my little boy's been taken halfway across the world . . . I've always been a deeply spiritual woman, but I tell you, Suzi, sometimes I don't know where I find the strength to carry on.'

The camera cut back to Ms Sanmartini, all a-quiver with insincerity. 'I think every woman watching this today can feel the pain of what you're going through,' she cooed. 'Tell me, Lola – Helena Clairbrook-Cleeve has been called America's favourite English Rose, but I imagine your feelings about her are rather different, is that right?'

Lola raked a long scarlet-painted talon through her hair, then sighed. 'Helena's a very complex person. I don't mean to judge, but she comes from a very different world to me, with very different values. I'm just a hard-working girl from Brooklyn, you know? I had a real tough time growing up but, even if there weren't a whole lot of social graces to go round, we were all instilled with certain principles. Loyalty. Integrity. Commitment. I can't blame Helena for her background, but those old English families . . . you do hear strange things. I mean, look at their Royal Family, right? *Completely* wacko. Maybe it's the inbreeding. Or those creepy boarding schools they all go to . . .'

'For God's sake – *surely* that must be libellous?' interjected Euphoria, robes billowing, bracelets clashing, eyes ablaze. 'I mean, she's practically accused Helena's family of *incest*! And insanity!'

Malcolm coughed discreetly. 'Ahem. It is far from clear whether the latter allegations relate to Helena or the monarchy and, frankly, in respect of our beloved Royal Family, few people would regard Ms Salanova's claims as excessively controversial . . . no, I'm sorry, but this is the fifth time we've played the tape and I still can't see anything that would stand up in court. It's all too generalized.'

My mother pressed a button on the remote and the Lola 'n' Suzi show was abruptly cut short.

'Words cannot express—' began Bud, and then stopped. Obviously on this occasion they couldn't. Euphoria was still chewing her nails frantically.

'OK, people, OK. Let's keep calm. Let's keep it together here. Let's focus.' She paced up and down some more. 'This is only one crappy lunchtime show. Lola's not got the clout to break into the prime-time stuff – and Suzi's slipped down the ratings lately too. She's schedule-padding, not headline-grabbing these days. We have to keep this in perspective.'

'I still can't believe Suzi would do this to me,' said my mother in martyred tones. Mum is something of a *Tell It Like It Is* regular, and has often been invited to sit on Suzi's couch and relate amusing anecdotes about the time the Marquis of Bath guest-starred on *Lady Jane* or chair a discussion on Why Manners Make The Man.

'If Helena's reputation is damaged because of this I will never forgive myself,' said Bud, eyes gleaming with anguish. 'This is all my fault. Now that we're through with the divorce courts, Lola knows that the surest way to punish me is to hurt The Woman I Love.'

'I wouldn't take it too personally,' said Euphoria firmly. She was regaining her composure – even her bracelets had stopped jangling. 'This is as much about timing as anything else. Lola's contract is up for renewal at the end of the month and my guess is she's hoping that a public spat with Helena is just the thing to give her profile a boost.'

'God damn it, if only the people in that audience knew what I'd been through with that woman—' I had never seen Bud so worked up before.

'Yes, but the last thing we want to do is start mud-slinging. That would be playing into Lola's hands.'

'I agree,' said Malcolm. 'Damage limitation by all means, but no direct retaliation.'

'Of course, as soon as the publicity machine for *Gone With the Wind* gets into gear we can put this behind us once and for all,' continued Euphoria. 'But for the time being, sincerity should be our watchword. We need to show Helena's side of the story. We need to focus on Helena as the loyal wife-to-be, the loving mother. A few well-placed comments from a trusted friend or two . . . then maybe just one in-depth interview . . . something family-based and domestic . . . nothing too obviously gloating, of course . . . perhaps if I had a word with my friend at *Stellar!* magazine . . .'

'What do you think, Octavia?' asked my mother suddenly. Throughout all this I'd been leaning against the wall and listening to them in silence. 'What do you think I should do?'

There was a moment's pause. Euphoria nodded her head slowly. 'Octavia,' she said in a speculative sort of way, 'could be something of an asset.'

I looked round the room at them all. I'd come back from my afternoon with Ben feeling so happy, the upset of India put behind me, everything straightforward and pleasant and relaxed, like life was supposed to be. And now this. And once this had been sorted out it would be something else. I'd got my wish to be ordinary all right, but what was the use of that when everyone around me was putting all their energy into being exceptional? No matter what I did or where I went there would always be some new showbizzy sensation ready and waiting to turn life upside down.

'It doesn't matter what I think,' I said, 'because this hasn't got anything to do with me. It's between you and Bud and Lola. So I really don't care what you do and, as a matter of fact, I would appreciate it if you left me out of it.' Then I went up to my room, shut the door with a bang and opened my chemistry file.

They left me in peace for the rest of the evening, although Mum did come up to deliver a supper tray. She hovered in my doorway for a bit but I remained steadfastly engrossed in the Periodic Table so she eventually took the hint and went away again. To my utter surprise, my next visitor was Milton.

He came in without knocking and wandered round my room for a while, shuddered at my cuddly toys, sneered at my Burne-Jones poster, then flopped down on a chair with one of his floating-up-from-a-crypt sighs. I was forced to remind myself that if I was finding the prospect of a PR war between Lola and Lady Jane difficult to deal with it must be a hell of a lot worse for Milton. Had he seen the tape, heard the discussions? I waited for him to say something, but after nearly ten minutes of total silence my nerve broke.

'This situation must be very awkward for you—'

'Please. Spare me your amateur Care Bear crap.'

'But your mother—'

'My mother,' said Milton, 'is nuts.' He thought for a bit. 'So is yours, of course. But whereas Helena is acutely annoying, mommy dearest is borderline psychotic.'

'I'm sure she's, er, not that bad.'

Milton gave me a look. 'You're talking to the fruit of her womb here, remember. Do I seem well-balanced to you?'

I wasn't quite sure how to respond to this. 'So what's your point?'

'Nothing in life has any point – *that's* the point. Humankind is condemned to live a life of uncertainty and absurdity in a meaningless universe.' He got up and began to trail towards the door, where he stopped and fixed me with one of his unblinking stares. 'The thing is, Octavia, existence means the freedom to choose who you are. But more importantly –' significant pause '– what you commit to. *Or to whom.*' He gave me another death-stare, then turned and sloped away.

I returned to my books feeling completely confused, and not only by the evils of kinetic molecular theory. Had Milton just given me a pep talk on the importance of interpersonal commitment? Could it even have been a declaration of solidarity?

*

Even after my heart-to-heart with Milton I was in no mood to cooperate with whatever Lola-bashing scheme Mum and Euphoria had cooked up between them. When I went into the drawing room the next morning for a little light breakfast television I found the TV had been replaced by a huge whiteboard on which Phase One and Phase Two of the battle plan had been drawn up with lots of bullet points, diagrams and red ink.

From what I could make out, Phase One was 'Press Management'. There was a list of various media contacts, both American and British, who could be called upon for a little discreet spin-doctoring, a breakdown of *Stellar!*'s distribution figures and then some draft interview questions, colour-coded in order of importance. Someone, Euphoria I assumed, had written out in capital letters the watchwords of the day – EMPATHY, DIGNITY, DISCRETION. Phase Two was 'Public Exposure' and a timetable of possible photo opportunities.

First up on the list was the Harlequin Trust. This was a charity recently set up by Dame Tilda Sweeney to teach stage skills to Third World street kids; I already knew she was throwing a cocktail party for the main patrons because Dad had been talking about it only last week. (He'd turned down an invitation on the grounds that, 'The slums of Calcutta are grim enough without inflicting Dame Tilda on the poor sods.') Tempest Films UK, however, were less discriminating and had pledged a hefty donation. I'd assumed Bud and Mum would be going as a matter of course, but now, with a sinking heart, I saw my name and Milton's written up with a big red question mark. This time the key phrase was UNITED FRONT.

Like I said, I had more than enough on my plate without getting dragged into a tabloid-courting cat fight. But that was before I opened up the arts supplement of one of the Sunday newspapers only to find India's face smirking up at me. The strapline read 'Rise of a Reluctant Princess'.

I'd seen India featured in magazines before; first in the society pages of the *Prattler*, of course, and then the promotional stuff for the Vince Valiant film – photo shoots involving lots of tousled curls, ripped denim and a wisp or two of chiffon for modesty's sake. This was different. This was the 'culture' section of a broadsheet newspaper, not a glossy mag or tabloid. The photograph was an artsy black-and-white portrait of India leaning back against an old brick wall, her hair blowing free, her expression dreamy. She was wearing a plain white shirt and little visible make-up. This wasn't the kind of styling I'd ever associated with India the rock-chick party poppet. This was . . . pale and interesting.

India Withers, I was told, has got it all: looks, brains, attitude and a career in the ascendancy. Only just turned seventeen, she got her big break in the latest Vince Valiant film, Cut and Thrust, *where she stole the show in her role as feisty Bliss Kendall, the diplomat's daughter who escapes her Afghan kidnappers and helps save the world from nuclear meltdown. At the time, some critics sniped that if it wasn't for certain friends-in-high-places, India might never have made her red-carpet debut. After all, the daughter of rock royalty Sir Rich Withers and society beauty Tigerlily Clements must have an address book to die for. And in a cut-throat industry chock-full of bright young things on the make, who could blame her for making the most of her* connections? Yet India, with a determination that belies her tender years, has resolutely turned her back on the super-starry world in which she grew up, preferring to strike it out on her own and pursue the kind of projects that 'stir my heart and grip my soul'.

It is a brave, some might say reckless, decision, but one that India takes very seriously: she is currently attending a West London state school where, instead of rubbing shoulders with It-Girls and Playboys, her friends are 'ordinary, down-to-earth people – the children of nurses and electricians, not fashion designers or pop idols'. She readily agrees that the Vince Valiant experience was 'a wonderful, wonderful opportunity', but has a word of caution for all those aspiring starlets out there: 'It's all too easy to let that showbiz stuff go to your head, to lose your sense of perspective, of who you really are.' She says she has never felt comfortable with the A-list lifestyle and, after years of struggling with low self-esteem, has finally found a new sense of purpose and balance in her life.

Years of struggling with low self-esteem? The nearest thing India got to an identity crisis was deciding whether she preferred men with blue eyes or brown. I was tempted to bin the article before I read any further, but had turned the page before I knew it.

However, India might not be able to avoid the limelight for much longer. Although she has broken free from the celebrity circuit, her determination to be taken seriously as an actress is even more impressive than her famous family or screen-siren looks. And now, as she prepares for her role in a new film by Jed Mosley, one of Britain's hottest young directors, it looks as if her determination has paid off. Loosely inspired by Alexandre Dumas's classic tale of a tragic young *courtesan, La Dame aux Camélias, Mosley's latest feature is a coming-of-age drama set in inner-city London. The action takes place not in elegant Parisian salons, but in litter-strewn school playgrounds and the stairwells of tower blocks, Dumas's cast of aristocratic roués replaced by teenage dropouts and small-time crooks. The exact nature of the script is still under wraps, but if it is anything like Mosley's debut, the critically acclaimed* Rat Dancer, *this latest film will be stylish, edgy and uncompromising, the kind of film that gets you noticed for good or ill. Will India be up to the challenge? Jed Mosley certainly thinks so. 'India,' he enthuses, 'is a force of nature. She's so strong, so dynamic – she just blew me away.'*

India is equally admiring of Jed. 'This man is a hero to me. His integrity, his commitment to his vision . . . for Jed, inspiration is a way of life.' Does she feel any apprehension about taking on such a demanding project at such an early stage in her career? 'I need to find a creative outlet for all the energy, all the passion, that's firing me up inside. That's why I've turned my back on the whole showbiz thing. If you're not challenging yourself and taking risks, then what's the point of being an artist?'

At last I folded up the paper and pushed it to one side with a groan. At the same time I heard a heavy sigh from the other end of the kitchen table. My mother was sitting there in her dressing gown, a decomposing bowl of cereal by her elbow, a spread of news clippings in front of her, gloom on her face. It didn't look like she'd had much sleep last night. Her magazine was open on a double-page spread and even from the opposite end of the table I could see the headline: LOLA SALANOVA:

HOW HEARTBREAK MADE ME STRONGER. Mum sighed again and rubbed her eyes.

It was then that I understood. I mean *really* understood. Lola was her . . . how had Milton put it? Nemesis. Lola was Mum's nemesis, just like India was mine. And right there and then I decided that if Mum still needed me, I'd do what I could to help.

Viv came round at teatime, all flashing-eyed and flushed after her latest set-to with Simon. This one had been about the evils of neo-imperialism masquerading as humanitarian intervention, apparently.

Mum gets nervous when Viv launches into this sort of stuff but Bud was full of admiration. 'You English girls are just the greatest – such passion! Such energy! Such get-up-and-go!'

'He's sweet,' remarked Viv after the lovebirds had left us.

'He has his moments.'

'So where's Satan's Little Helper?' It was at that moment Milton himself wandered into the kitchen, gave Viv and me a long stare, went across to collect a carving knife from the drawer, then stalked off again. 'Er, should we be worried?'

'I don't think so. I think he just uses it to carve stuff into his furniture.'

'Like "God is Dead"?'

'Exactly.'

'You know,' said Viv, tilting her head to one side, 'there is a sort of family resemblance between the two of you.'

I put my cup of tea down so hard it slopped on the

table. 'Excuse me? Between me and Milton? You have *got* to be kidding.'

'Well, let's face it, neither of you much resemble Mr and Mrs Sunny Delight. You're both of the, what-d'ye-call-it, "pale and interesting" variety.'

I started arguing the point but realized I was unlikely to get very far. Viv doesn't back down easily. And talk of pale and interesting types had put me in mind of the India article, which I now got out and displayed on the table. To my annoyance, Viv was rather admiring.

'You have to hand it to her, the girl's got nerve,' she said when she got to the end of the piece. 'But I'm kind of surprised she's still being so loathsome to you. After all, her film's on hold cos they've run out of money, and your stepdad-to-be works for the company that might come to the rescue, right? I'd have thought India would be acting like your dearly beloved long-lost sister right now.'

I pulled a face. 'Why waste the energy? India knows I wouldn't ever fall for her Sugar Plum Fairy act. I don't even think Bud has much say in whether her stupid film gets backed by Tempest or not.' All the same, I *was* starting to wonder. It was hard to believe that India wouldn't find some fiendish way of turning the situation to her advantage.

I was suddenly fed up with the whole business and began to tell Viv all about the momentous events of Friday lunchtime and Saturday afternoon instead. Recent events might have put a dampener on my whole blissed-out-by-Ben feeling, but as I started describing our adventures at one hundred and thirty-three feet I could feel that inner glow spread through me again. Viv's reaction could not to be faulted: exclamations, gasps, coos and, finally, a whoop of congratulation.

'This is so cool! I *knew* the two of you were secretly pining for each other – first they bicker, then they kiss . . . I'm always right! Ha! . . . Just wait until Katie finds out!'

'She can't,' I said, feeling a twinge of panic. 'You mustn't tell *anyone*, Viv. You've got to promise.'

'Huh?'

'India again. If she finds out she'll try and find a way of wrecking everything. I know she will. Ben and I had a talk about it – we're going to act as if nothing's happened until India's out of the way.'

'And when's that going to be exactly? Ben's a nice guy but he's not the most patient person on the planet.'

'It'll be fine,' I said with a certainty I was far from feeling. 'It'll make life easier for everyone concerned.'

'Yeah but—'

'Viv. Please. Just let me enjoy the moment, OK?'

'OK.' We ate some more cake. 'By the way, Mum's desperate for an update on the *Gone With the Wind* situation. Apparently she's read an interview where Lola Salanova says Helena's going to lose the part because she can't manage a Southern accent.'

'Oh, God. Don't tell Mum that, she'll go mad.'

'Has the feud started up again or something? I thought it would all be over by now.'

'So did we. But Lola's gone and launched a new offensive . . .' I briefly summed up the *Tell It Like It Is* fiasco. 'Now it looks like Mum's got a celebrity cat fight on her hands.'

'Eek. I'd stay well out of it, if I were you.'

'That,' I said wearily, 'is going to be easier said than done.'

It was hard to decide which was the more painful: the real-life chemistry exam and the mock everything-else which followed it, or the little pep talks Mr Pemberton insisted on giving in between them. He seemed a bit disappointed we weren't more stressed; in fact, I got the impression he was looking forward to the genuine exams and to finally seeing some real trauma hit the class. When I wasn't proving how much I still had to learn about hydrogen chloride/quadratic equations/the Weimar Republic, I was working hard at my kissing technique and extending my expert knowledge of a certain Ben Harper. Ben and I were actually finding the whole secret romance thing quite enjoyable and did a lot of hiding round corners and sneaky texting and stealing off behind the gym – childish, but fun.

It had come as something as a surprise to find that you could be with someone you fancied like mad and still feel relaxed in his company, but when I was with Ben I forgot to worry about how my hair looked or if I'd worn the right sort of shoes or whether I'd understood his jokes properly. (Even if I sometimes had to watch what I said – I'd made a casual remark about preferring the oyster bar in Harvey Nick's to the one in Harrods and Ben *still* took the piss about it.) Of course, life was made a lot easier by the fact that India was sitting out the exam week back home at Chateau Withers. God knows what state India's educational qualifications were in, but although she was ready for drug abuse and gang-warfare in the school corridors, she clearly wasn't prepared to come face to face with the full horror of the National Curriculum.

On Thursday evening after school Ben and I went to one of the big bookshop chains where they sell everything from musical glitter-pens to pecan pie. Sometimes, if you're really lucky, you can find a book or two. We were supposedly looking for a study guide on *Great Expectations*, but wasted most of the time reading out the especially stupid bits from the self-help section ('Adolescence can be an emotional roller coaster – and hormones don't come with safety harnesses. So remember: buckle up before the ride!'). Then we went for hot chocolate in the cafe at the end of the CD section.

'So,' said Ben, 'I was thinking maybe we should go to the cinema this Saturday. I know the film industry's a bit of a sore point at the moment, but there's this really good Italian film everyone's talking about. A comedy – just what we need to make a full recovery from that chemistry module.'

'Ah. The weekend. You see, I was going to talk to you about that . . .'

All day I'd been wondering how to bring up the subject of the Helena Clairbrook-Cleeve-Carnaby comeback – or, more particularly, my own part in it – in a light-hearted, no-big-deal sort of way. After my moment of revelation over the Sunday papers I'd recklessly committed myself to active participation in Phase One and provisional involvement in Phase Two. My mother had responded to the news with tears of joy, but I had a feeling Ben's reaction wouldn't be quite so ecstatic.

What did normal people think about this sort of thing, anyhow?

'You see, there's been some stuff in the papers this week – more about this business with Mum and Bud, and Bud's, er, ex.'

'He and your mum are getting married soon, aren't they? So you're getting stuff ready for the wedding this weekend, is that it?'

'Sort of.' I cleared my throat. 'Actually, it's more about PR . . .'

How had Euphoria put it last night? Ah yes – 'Putting family values right at the heart of the Clairbrook-Cleeve image.' It had been the closing sentence of her PowerPoint presentation, in fact, and was followed by a slightly awkward silence while the Clairbrook-Cleeve-Carnaby household wondered if we should applaud or not. (Even Milton had turned up, though he'd been slumped under the dining-room table for most of the presentation.)

'Thank you so much, Euphoria,' Lady Jane had said at last. 'You've done a marvellous job and I'm sure you've got everything under control . . . is it definite that *Stellar!* will be able to run the interview at such short notice?'

'It's all fixed for next Saturday and my contact there has promised it will make the next issue. A six-page photo-spread plus interview.'

'The US edition too?'

'Absolutely. Now, my plan is to have a proper briefing session nearer the time, with Octavia in attendance . . .'

My mother exchanged glances with Bud. I felt a

speech coming on, but this time it was Lady Jane who did the honours. 'Ahem. Bud and I realize that Octavia, and Milton in particular, have been put in a very difficult position by recent events. Divorce is such a *messy* business and the media interest has been most unfortunate. In many ways,' she said piously, 'there are no villains here. *Everybody* has been hurt. And so, as you know, Octavia was very reluctant to get involved with this campaign. I don't blame her for wanting to be left in peace. In fact, I think she was *right* to say that this wasn't something she should be involved in.' She smiled at me. 'But now she's agreed to help with this interview and I can't tell you how much that means to me. It's a wonderful, generous thing you're doing, darling, and I want to say thank you very much.'

Once again we all wondered if we should break into applause. Bud was clearly raring to go but I managed to forestall him by getting up and giving Mum a hug. Milton made a retching sound from under the table. Then Bud had hugged Milton, Euphoria hugged me and we all hugged Mum. And after that there was no backing out.

I explained all this to Ben, putting especial emphasis on my three conditions for doing the interview with my mother: 1) that I would choose what I wore for the photographs; 2) that I would appear in no more than two photographs; and 3) I would be able to vet any questions I was asked. I had decided to take one thing at a time and not mention the United Front's photo op at the Harlequin Trust party until a bit nearer the date. Then I waited anxiously for his response.

He didn't say anything for a while, just sat there

with that slightly sarcastic expression of his. (It's actually quite sexy, but I didn't feel this was the right time to tell him so.)

'Right. So you can't come out with me this weekend because you're "talking exclusively to *Stellar!* at your fabulous home"?'

'Mum's doing most of the talking. I'm just lurking in the background.'

'I see – so you can show the world what a yummy mummy she is and what a well-adjusted daughter she's raised. Is she going to talk about the hardships of juggling a celebrity career with the Joy of Parenting?'

I wasn't sure if he was teasing me or having a go. I sighed. With the Darlings you never had to bother explaining this sort of thing – it was just business as usual, like prenuptial agreements and lifestyle gurus and ex-lovers who tried to sell your secrets to the press.

'It's part of Mum's job. It's the sort of stuff you have to do when you're in the public eye, especially if you've got someone like Lola Salanova out to get you. Mum needs all the support she can get at the moment and I'm helping out, that's all.'

'So is this going to take all weekend? What about Sunday?'

'Er . . . that might be difficult too, I'm afraid.' I explained that on Sunday Bud was flying out to the States for a week on Tempest business and Mum had taken the opportunity to dedicate the rest of the weekend to us both Bonding With Milton. (I'd assumed he'd be going with his dad, but no such luck . . . though I reckoned he'd be on that plane pronto if he knew what Lady J had in store for him.)

'OK. Family promotion and family bonding it is.'
Ben gave me a lopsided smile. 'I am trying to understand this, really. It just seems so . . . strange. It's going to be weird to think of opening a magazine and seeing you there.'

'It's going to be weird for me too. This isn't something I've done before.'

Now there was a wicked spark in his green eyes. 'So can we expect a centrefold of you posing in a bikini?'

'If you're really lucky, I'll also be wearing a diamond necklace and have a French poodle tucked under my arm.'

'Stop,' said Ben, eyes closed in mock-ecstasy. 'The anticipation is all too much for me.'

The first people to arrive on Saturday morning were Frisbee and Euphoria. They were at the house by half past nine and Frisbee immediately bustled round making coffee for everyone while Euphoria went over things with Mum and me for the third time in as many days. An hour later the stylist arrived. She'd already had an in-depth consultation with my mother on Friday and now disappeared to set up a 'green room' in my bedroom. Then the photographer and his assistant came and started tramping all over the house making marks on the floor with bits of tape, taking measurements, fiddling with the blinds and setting up light-screens and tripods everywhere. One person, at least, who we didn't have to deal with was Archimboldo – Lady Jane was all set for him to come and do an 'installation', but Euphoria and I managed to persuade her that one of his palm-frond, ostrich-feather and velvet-drape arrangements wouldn't really evoke the cosy domestic look we were hoping for.

The journalist who was going to be doing the interview was the last person to arrive. She turned up at twelve o'clock, looking as if she was in the grip of an evil hangover; at any rate, when I opened the front door she was clutching her head, swigging water from a bottle and wearing those massive sunglasses that cover half your face. Mind you, the glasses could have been to shield her from the glare coming off her clothes: a pink satin skirt worn with an itsy-bitsy lime-green cardigan. She was probably in her early forties but it was hard to tell, what with the sunglasses and the bleached streaks in her hair and lime/pink combo. She introduced herself as Daisy. 'And you must be the lovely Octavia!' Then she asked me if people ever called me 'Occy'.

'No,' I said, suppressing a shudder. I have been called lots of things in my time, but Occy, thankfully, was not one of them.

'Delightful!' I wasn't sure if she was referring to my name or our hallway, which she had inspected in one sweeping glance. 'So sweet. So *compact*,' she murmured, lowering the dark glasses again. 'Well *hello* there – it's Milton, isn't it?'

Milton was, indeed, lurking on the stairs. '*Love* the T-shirt! Post-millennium neo-Goth! What fun! . . . Milton, I don't suppose you'd be a pet and see if there's any paracetamol in the house, hmm? Thank you *so* much! . . . I was at the Swartzburgers' last night,' she confided to me, 'covering their anniversary bash. To be honest it's all a bit of a blur . . . Helena! *Wonderful* to meet you at last . . .'

I left them to it and went to sit with Bud and Euphoria in the study, where we played cards and ate toasted bagels while listening to Bud's jazz records (we couldn't use the kitchen any more because it was all set up for photographs). It was quite fun: even Milton joined in after a bit and then went on to win every game, although this only seemed to make him more dismal. Throughout our poker-and-bagels session my mother was being photographed in various poses in various outfits in various rooms around the house, with Euphoria and the stylist in attendance. The plan was that everyone would meet up for a quick tea break before taking a couple of photographs of the two of us together, then Lady Jane would do the actual interview with Daisy at the end of the afternoon.

When my turn came at last I was relieved to find that there was no mention of bikinis, let alone French poodles or diamonds. Mum was good as her word and didn't even blink when I said to the stylist that no, I didn't want to try hair extensions, thanks, and that no, I didn't think I'd like to slip into something a little more formal. So I got my way and was photographed in the same clothes I'd put on that morning: my favourite jeans and a fitted red shirt. I let her fiddle with my hair though, and apply some of that extra-posh make-up that makes you look like you're not wearing any. After all, I reasoned, there wasn't much point in looking hideous for the occasion. Especially if our six-page photo-spread was going to make an appearance in every dentists' and hairdressers' reception in the land.

And let me tell you: in order to appear cosmetic-free yet camera-friendly it was apparently necessary to wear three different layers of foundation, five shades of eyeshadow, mascara and eyebrow gloss, blusher, powder, bronzer, lip pencil and lip stain – all in various shades of 'natural', 'neutral' or 'nude'. This all took about forty-five minutes at the hands of the stylist, who continued to retouch and re-tweak at three-minute intervals throughout the shoot. The end result was that I looked like the kind of girl who only dines on organic fruit and mineral water, swims with dolphins and advertises herbal face creams for a living. I was afraid to move my facial muscles in case all the layers of paint cracked.

I don't know how my mother can stand the endless smiling-for-the-cameras part of her job, though I suppose she must be used to it by now with all the interviews she's done and air-kissing media-fests she's turned up to. Even though I was only going to be in two pictures, one on my own in the drawing room and one of the two of us sitting on my mother's bed, the photographer must have taken at least fifty shots for each location. Some at a distance, some close up, some with natural light, some with artificial, some with this expression, some with that, some with this pose, some with the other . . . my mother had been doing this all morning, and with half a dozen costume changes and make-up retouching sessions in between, and yet the sparkle in her eye was undimmed, her smile as naturally radiant as ever. Whereas I kept blinking whenever the camera flashed, had to be continually reminded to relax my mouth/keep my chin down/stop hunching my shoulders/smile and didn't even know which my 'best side' was. Maybe I should have been more sympathetic when all the part-time models at Darlinham House started whining about what hard work the last cover shoot for *Venus* magazine had been. Then again, maybe not.

My contribution to the interview was less than gripping stuff, though from the way Daisy nodded and cooed at my every word you would have thought I was outlining my plans for peace in the Middle East. Anyway, I made a few vague remarks about how pleased I was for Mum and Bud and how well everybody got on and at long last I was free to go.

I had a number of phone calls that evening from people wanting to know how it had gone. First was Dad, who was full of anxious questions along the lines of, 'Are you sure you weren't pressured into doing anything you were uncomfortable with?' I reassured him that it was a mother–daughter photo op, not a Page Three audition. Then Viv called to voice her outrage at Cuthbert Shamrock, the tycoon who owns *Stellar!* and who is, according to Viv, 'a sworn enemy to freedom of the press'. Then Katie rang to find out if my photograph was going to be airbrushed and if they'd used that special spray-on foundation that has to be applied in a sort of sealed box with a pump (it's 'all the rage' in Beverly Hills, apparently). One person who didn't call, however, was Ben. Instead, I got a text that was so brief he almost needn't have bothered: 'hope it went ok c u in skool x.'

On Sunday morning, Bud flew out to the States for his business trip. There was a touching farewell scene after breakfast and Bud had to keep clearing his throat and wiping his eye while Lady J draped herself delicately all over his chest. I got the feeling that she would have liked to enact the parting in her hooped skirt, maybe fluttering a handkerchief from the upstairs window. Milton and I exchanged looks of mutual embarrassment.

The rest of the day was, as threatened, taken up by Mum's plans to welcome Milton into the Clairbrook-Cleeve family bosom. To my surprise, this was not the complete disaster I was confidently expecting. Before lunch we went to Richmond Park, where our walk was cut short by an unfortunate incident involving a deer and a speeding Land Rover. Milton spent a lot more time admiring the road kill than he did the landscape. Then in the afternoon we went on an excursion to the Royal Academy, where my mother was hoping to banish memories of squashed stag with an exhibition on 'Pomp And Circumstance: English Court Life Through The Ages'. But that turned out to have finished the week before, so we went instead to a show called 'UpRoar!™', which was very cutting-edge and had lots of flashing lights and bodily fluids and more mutilated animals all over the place. Lady Jane retreated to the tea room in a faint and let Milton and I get on with it – he said it was 'predictably banal' but 'sporadically amusing'. After that we went for an early supper at a restaurant round the corner, where Milton took the opportunity to bring my mother (and our fellow diners) up to date with all the artworks she'd missed when she'd fled the gallery. By the time he'd got to describing the swastika made out of frozen custard and disembowelled rats he was looking quite animated, and after we'd waited twenty minutes for a taxi in the rain I even thought I saw a smile on his face.

*

After the excitements of the weekend, I had a bad attack of the Sunday Night Sinking Feeling. This was partly because I was feeling guilty/annoyed about the lack of contact with Ben and partly because I'd be getting my mock maths exam returned first thing on Monday, but mostly because I knew India would be back in school this week. The previous week had been a bit weird what with the exams and the *Stellar!* business and all the sneaking around with Ben; our secret snogging had been fun but I had a suspicion that the novelty would soon wear off, especially once we were hiding from India 'for real'. However, my Sunday-night gloom seemed to have been uncalled for – Monday morning brightened up no end when I found a little box of heart-shaped chocolates in my locker, and the whole world seemed to burst into song when Mr Pemberton got to 'Withers' in the register and nobody answered.

'She's probably had enough of us already. Bet you she's sunning herself on some Caribbean island right this minute,' said Ben. We'd bunked off assembly and were scoffing chocolate in the computer room.

'I s'pose . . .' If I were India, it certainly wouldn't take long for the novelty of living in the real world to wear off. So perhaps Ben was right: she'd had her fun, gained some street cred, and was now safely back in the bosom of the glitterati.

'Great. So are we official now?'

'Official?'

'Yup. I'm looking forward to the day we can finally start skipping hand in hand down the corridors.'

'So am I. But I'd still like to give it another day or two, just to be sure. After all, we've only been undercover for a week. And it's not been too bad, has it?'

'That's not the point. I want everyone to know we're together.' He leaned close and touched my cheek gently. 'Then maybe I'll really believe it myself.'

'Just another day or two. Please, Ben. So we know we're definitely in the clear.'

He sighed in a long-suffering sort of way. 'OK, fine, I guess another day or two won't kill me. But I still think you're overreacting. I mean, what are you so afraid of, exactly? India may be out to cause trouble, but she's not got demonic powers. She can't turn me into a frog or get you kidnapped by Albanian gangsters or anything.'

Albanian gangsters? No, India's methods were far more subtle. It was possible I was being just a *little* bit overcautious, but I knew India a lot better than Ben did. And, more importantly, India knew me. She knew every little anxiety, every little blind spot and insecurity that I had tried so hard and for so long to hide. I didn't know exactly how she'd take advantage of my feelings for Ben, but I knew she'd find some way to worm her way between us. Maybe she'd set out to dazzle him with sweet-talk and flirtation. Maybe she'd try to drag Alex back on to the scene. Maybe she'd bring up all the old Darlinham House humiliations so he'd know just what sort of a loser his new girlfriend was . . . Nine times out of ten, my brain told me that this was complete rubbish of course. Nine times out of ten, however, wasn't enough.

I liked Ben, I liked him a *lot*, and I knew that he liked me. But it was still very early days in our relationship and when push came to shove, I wasn't one hundred per cent confident that we were Withers-proof.

During the rest of the day, a number of people came up to ask me when India was coming back. Vicky and Meera even asked Mr Pemberton if he knew where she was, but the grumpiness of his reply proved that he didn't have a clue where his most high-profile pupil had got to either. The Withers Adoration Society had taken all her interview sound bites at face value so were stubbornly clinging to the belief that she was now a full-time member of Jethro Park rather than just a passing visitor. But, perhaps because we'd had a whole Withers-free week, India's whereabouts/career-plans/cleavage were not such a hot topic of conversation as I'd expected, and I even began to hope that things would start getting back to normal before too long. No doubt the sensation of her arrival at Jethro Park would still be making waves for months, maybe even years, to come, but I thought I could live with that if she turned out only to be a two-day wonder. Of course, I knew very well that India had never intended to find long-term fulfilment with all us 'ordinary, down-to-earth people', but the difference between two days, two weeks or two months of her company was a lifetime of misery as far as I was concerned.

Ben and I had arranged to go to the cinema that evening and I decided there was just enough time beforehand to go home, change my clothes and grab something to eat. I was starting to feel more relaxed at last, as if things were about to turn a corner. Maybe, just maybe, my luck was changing. I let myself into the house, dumped my bag in the hall and went into the drawing room to let Mum know I was 'going out with friends'. I found India there instead, lolling on the sofa and gazing deeply into Milton's eyes.

'What the hell are *you* doing here?'

Even I was surprised by the outrage in my voice, but India merely twirled a lock of hair and smiled up at me angelically. 'Nice to see you too, Oc-tave-ee-ah.'

'Cut it out, India. Why are you here and what do you want? And, more to the point, when are you leaving?'

'Well,' she said, pouting, 'since I couldn't make it into school today I thought I'd better pop round to find out what work I've missed, maybe even have a cup of tea and a natter with an old friend . . . I expected you to be here *ages* ago, but luckily Milton was able to let me in and so we've been having a *lovely* chat while waiting for you to show up. I feel we've *really got to know* each other.'

'So I can see.' I looked at Milton, who stared back at me coldly. Next to India in her lacy red knit-top and denim micro-mini he looked even more deathlike than usual. 'Seeing how you're so eager for a heart-to-heart, how about we have that little talk you came for?' Neither India nor Milton showed any signs of movement. 'In private,' I added, with my best glare.

'You know I *always* have time for you, Oc-tave-ee-ah.' India got up from the sofa with a movement that was something between a slink and a wiggle. 'Bye-bye, Milton,' she cooed, flashing him another angelic smile. I grabbed her arm and hustled her out into the hall, then pushed her into the study and shut the door.

'Stop it. Now.'

'I don't know what you're talking about. And I would appreciate it if you let go of my arm . . . I know how rough and ready they all are at that school of yours, but there's no need for *violence*.'

'That's something we can agree on then – we don't want anyone to get hurt. So leave Milton alone.'

'Milton looked perfectly happy when we left him.' She got out a compact mirror and began to check her hair.

'Milton doesn't "do" happy. He does bitter and miserable. And strangely enough, I don't think you're going to be the one to kiss him better. For God's sake, India, he's only fourteen!'

India raised her brows. 'Really, Octavia, I would have expected more of you. I thought you militant feminist types were all for breaking down the conventions of age and sex and the rest of it. And as I remember, there was a three-year age-gap between you and Lex.'

'Yeah, well, Alex was very immature for his age.'

India was now reapplying her lipgloss. 'In all seriousness, do you *honestly* believe that I would be interested in seducing your stepbrother? No offence to your charming family set-up, but he's hardly hunk-of-the-month material, is he? Maybe I just enjoy his company. He's very intelligent, you know.'

My phone started to go off in my pocket and I turned it off impatiently. 'India, sweetie, if I thought you were only after Milton's brains we wouldn't be having this conversation. Hell, if I thought you were only after his body I could probably cope . . . but you're not really after Milton, are you? It's Carnaby Senior and his connections at Tempest you're interested in.'

'Carnaby Senior?'

'Yeah, Budwin H. Carnaby. The Z-list, alcoholic, wife-beating love rat himself. Who just so happens to be part of the outfit that maybe, just maybe, will stop your little vanity project – sorry, cinematic breakthrough – from going belly up.'

India yawned. 'What are you accusing me of, exactly? Seducing a minor so that I can, let's see, black-mail his dad, who'll then persuade his boss to bankroll my film? As far as conspiracy theories go, that's not just crazy – it's *pathetic*. Not to say libellous.'

'Shut up. The only crazy and pathetic—' But at that moment my phone went off again and I realized, with a guilty start, that it must be Ben. Who I was supposed to be meeting in five minutes. Flustered, I got it out and managed to mutter, 'Can I call you back – emergency – going to be late – yes, I'll make it – OK, bye –' before ending the call. I put it back in my pocket, my face hot, only to find that India was watching me with a knowing sort of air.

'Running late for a date, Oc-tave-ee-ah?'

'No. As I was saying—'

'Don't let me keep you. I'd hate to think I was hold-ing you back from a romantic encounter with one of the love gods of Jethro Park. Who could it be? Will, maybe? He's quite sweet in a geeky sort of way. Liam? He barely comes up to your elbow of course, but some men have a thing for oversized women . . . Ooh – I know. How about the tall scruffy one who's always so sarcastic. Ben, is it? With the green eyes?' She was leaning towards me

with this little smirk on her face and I realized that in the space of a few moments I'd completely lost the upper hand.

'All wrong,' I said defiantly. 'And it's none of your business.'

'Then,' said India, sauntering out of the room, 'whoever *I* choose to socialize with in my free time is none of yours. See you in school, Dave.' The front door slammed shut behind her.

I unclenched my fists and counted slowly and calmly to ten before I marched back into the drawing room. OK, so my confrontation with India hadn't exactly been a roaring success but I reckoned I stood a better chance with Milton. Forthright yet tactful, friendly yet firm: that was the way to go. I found Milton still sitting on the sofa and reading something called *The Myth of Sisyphus.* He didn't bother to look up when I came in so I reached down and took the book off him.

'I don't think you'll find it to your taste,' he said coolly. 'Long words and no pictures.'

'*My* personal taste isn't the issue here.' Back in the study I'd only thought of Milton as the defenceless victim of India's wiles. Now, however, when I saw him sitting there all chilly and superior I had to resist the impulse to smack him around the head with that book of his. 'Time for some sisterly words of advice.'

'Ooh, goody. Is this when you tell me that India is an evil, conniving bitch who's out to ruin your life and upset my fragile mental balance in the process?'

'Something like that, yes.' I tried to soften my voice. 'I'm serious, Milton. I know she puts on this lovey-dovey, cutie-pie routine, but I promise you it's just an act . . .'

'*Obviously* it's an act,' said Milton with withering scorn. 'What kind of idiot do you think I am?'

'I just didn't want you being taken in by—'

'India,' he said with relish, 'is quite clearly everything you said she was. A ruthless, manipulative, black-hearted Harbinger of Doom . . .' His face took on a dreamy expression. 'I think she's the most wonderful girl I've ever met.'

I stared at him in disbelief. 'You're sick.'

'Maybe,' he said, taking up his book again, 'but at least I'm not boring.'

I didn't get to the cinema in time for the film. Ben was waiting for me outside the cinema when I ran up, still in my school uniform, purple-cheeked and breathless, a frenzied gleam in my eye.

'God, I am so, so sorry. You wouldn't believe what just happened—'

'Don't tell me. Prince Richard popped round and it would have been rude not to offer him a drink?'

'Much worse – it's India – she was in my *house*. With *Milton*. Milton! She was all over him and it was so awful and I know it's because—'

'Octavia. Will you do me a favour?'

Something in his voice made me stop in mid-flow. 'What?'

'Can we *not* talk about India? Please? Just for a change, I would like to be with my girlfriend, in public, and have a nice normal conversation that does not involve India Withers.' He was looking fairly pissed off.

Oh, God – I was turning into the girlfriend from hell: unreliable, neurotic and slightly crazed. I had a feeling that Ben wouldn't fall for the 'at least I'm not boring' line.

'Sorry. You're right. Sorry. I'll shut up now. Sorry. Is there another showing of the film tonight or, er, somewhere else? Somewhere near by?'

'No there isn't and no there's not. But the evening really will have been wasted if you spend the whole time apologizing. So let's forget about the film and go do something else. Have you had anything to eat yet?'

So we ended up just going for pizza in one of the chain-outlets near the cinema. Somewhat to my surprise, it turned out to be a fun evening in spite of its unfortunate start. By unspoken agreement we avoided talking about school for most of the time, but before the end of the meal got to speculating about what life would be like when we were in Year Twelve and had to start thinking about jobs and university and the rest of it. We had quite a lot of fun predicting what our classmates would be doing in ten years' time: Jack would be working as a world-famous porn star, Katie would be a romantic novelist and Hannah a diplomat for the UN. I told Ben that Viv couldn't decide whether she wanted to be a politician or a journalist and we came to the conclusion that she could never be objective enough to be a journalist. 'Can you imagine Viv hanging around to report *other* people's opinions?' he asked. Then he wanted to know if I ever thought about going into the media industry myself. 'I know you wouldn't want to be an actress or presenter or anyone public like that, but there must be loads of really interesting, creative, behind-the-scenes jobs. And you've already got all the contacts.'

I pulled a face. 'Even if you're behind the scenes you're still dealing with all those showbizzy types on a regular basis. I kind of feel I've already had enough of that to last me a lifetime.' But I felt we were getting back on dangerous ground and so moved the conversation on to other things. Like pinpointing the exact moment when Ben realized that I was the only girl for him, and listing all the reasons why Brunettes Have More Fun.

On the face of it, the return of the Reluctant Princess to Jethro Park caused surprisingly little commotion. After a week's cooling-off period it seemed that a lot of people, in the upper school at least, had resolved to appear a little less obviously star-struck in India's presence. However, it was noticeable that all the girls suddenly spent a lot more time checking their hair in the toilets and that most of the boys fell into a special swagger whenever India appeared on the scene. (Mr Pemberton celebrated India's return by cracking five dreadful puns in the space of ten minutes at morning registration.) If anyone asked her where she'd got to over the last week India said that she'd been working on character development with Jed – 'He calls me his Muse, you know. Isn't that sweet?' When asked how much longer she'd be here and when filming started she would look grave and mysterious and refer to her 'confidentiality clause'. If anyone asked her anything further about this, Jack 'n' Dan 'n' Tom would close in, in a menacing sort of way.

On the Tuesday of India's return she announced that she was going to accompany me on my journey home. 'The public transport experience is part of my brief, you know. Do you have rats on the buses or is it just in the underground?' She swept on board leaving me to sort out her ticket, turfed a small Year Seven out of its seat ('Delicate ankles are a medical condition, OK?'), sat down on the Year Seven's coat ('For all I know, these seats are *crawling* with bacteria.') then spent the entire journey yakking away at top volume on her mobile phone ('Yah – sweetie – cackle cackle – yes but the *people* – sweetie – you've no idea – cackle cackle – yah'). Which suited me fine, except that when we got to my stop she got off too and followed me down the road towards my house. Where Milton was waiting on the steps.

'Milton's taking me to a late-night viewing of "UpRoar!™",' India informed me brightly. 'I hear Freddie Lions was spotted there last week. Don't wait up!' And with that, they were gone.

I went into the house and slammed the front door behind me with the kind of force guaranteed to get my mother squawking in the hallway.

'Darling! Gently, please! The whole house is *shaking*—'

'Never mind that. Did you know Milton was going out tonight? Or, more importantly, *who* he was going out with?' I demanded.

'Milton never tells me anything. He's even more secretive than you are,' she said plaintively, 'and of course I'm a great believer in respecting people's privacy. But now you come to mention it . . . that *was* India I saw in the street with you just now, wasn't it?'

'It was. She's the most wonderful girl Milton's ever

met, apparently. And now they're off on a jolly jaunt to see the dead rats and custard swastikas. Mum, how could you let him go?'

'Well, for a start, I didn't know anything about it. And even if I did, it's not really my place to interfere.'

'Of course it's your place! It's your house! You set the rules! He's only fourteen – he's just a kid, for God's sake! You could have grounded him or locked him in his room or insisted he stay home and make burritos with you or something . . .'

'I don't set the rules for Milton,' my mother said gently. 'If Bud were here, that would be different. But it's too early in my relationship with Milton for me to start interfering in his personal life.'

'It wouldn't be interference. It would be an act of mercy. Milton is going to be *terminally* screwed up if India gets her talons into him. She's only interested in him because she wants to start sucking up to Bud and his friends at Tempest . . .' I explained the situation with Mosley's film and the hunt for financial backing.

'More fool India, then,' said my mother tartly. 'Bud is far too professional to be influenced by personal considerations. I know that he comes across as an easygoing kind of chap, but you seem to forget that he's spent his entire working life in one of the most cutthroat industries on the planet. Don't you think he'll be able to see straight through someone like India? Because believe me, darling, they're a dime a dozen in his line of work.'

'But Milton—'

'Octavia, sweetheart, please listen. Now I agree that the situation is less than ideal and I understand why you're worried on Milton's behalf. It's very touching, actually. But let's get this into perspective – they've gone to see an exhibition of contemporary art, not eloped to Las Vegas. Bud's back at the end of the week and if this Milton–India thing is still an issue I'll have a talk with him then, I promise. And did I tell you,' she added, all perky again, 'Milton's actually agreed to come to Dame Tilda's cocktail party with us on Wednesday? Isn't that wonderful?'

Wow. Did existential nihilists go to cocktail parties? I found it hard to share my mother's enthusiasm, since if Milton (Milton!) really was going to this thing, there was absolutely no way I would be able get out of it. I found it even harder to imagine Milton schmoozing with Dame Tilda and friends – from what I'd seen at Christmas, the Prince of Darkness wasn't a natural at the whole chit-chat-'n'-canapés scene. But then I hadn't ever imagined him setting off on cultural excursions with India Withers either.

'Just between us, darling,' my mother continued, 'I think we're reaching a bit of a breakthrough with the poor boy, especially when you think of all those dreadful therapies Lola put him through. Not to mention that creepy guru of hers who's always lurking in the background . . . Anyway, I don't find Milton all that depressing, do you? Only the other day he told me he always wears black because he's in mourning for the world, which, when you think about it, is really rather sweet.'

Oh yes, adorable. Funny how Milton was perfectly able to whoop it up at art exhibitions and cocktail parties but was still too psychologically fragile to attend school or do the dishes or make polite conversation like the rest of us lesser beings. Apparently World Sorrow wasn't just a state of mind – it was a full-time leisure activity.

'. . . and speaking of sweet', my mother continued, 'I was just looking over the JPEGs from our photo shoot when you came in. *Stellar!* have emailed a selection for approval. Want to come and see?'

I did indeed. For the moment, I pushed my dire thoughts of Milton to one side and followed my mother to the computer in the study.

I could see at once why my mother was looking so pleased with herself. Looking at those pictures, it was hard to think of Lady Jane the Snatcher of Husbands, the Wrecker of Families. Most of the photos were of her in full-on domestic-goddess mode: just one shot of her in a slinky silver number and the rest with her in soft, casual sorts of clothes. Yummy Mummy with a touch of boudoir chic. There was even a picture of her eating cookies in the kitchen complete with a smudge of flour on her nose, the implication being, of course, that she'd whipped up a batch of double-choc-chips in between having her eyelashes tweaked. As for me . . . well, the one of Mum and me on her bed was quite sweet, I suppose (they'd used a shot when we were both laughing) and the single portrait was OK. Thanks to the fake-natural make-up I looked all airbrushed and glossy and my hair was good. I didn't look obviously posed either.

Even so, I still got a sinking feeling whenever I imagined the reaction of people at school. What with all the excitements/traumas of the past couple of weeks I hadn't had much time to wonder what my classmates would think about their very own cut-out-and-keep guide to My Fabulous Life. However, I consoled myself with the thought that, when it came to guest-starring in *Stellar!*, having a Withers in the class would, for once, work to my advantage. After all, whatever the Clairbrook-Cleeves got up to in their spare time couldn't possibly compete with India's A-list looks, life and accessories. But when I mentioned this to Mum she stopped cooing over the cookie shot and looked at me anxiously. 'That's all very well, sweetheart, but don't you think it's time you stopped worrying about India quite so much? You're starting to sound just a *tiny* bit obsessive, you know.'

As the saying goes, just because you're paranoid it doesn't mean they're not out to get you. Even though India paid me little obvious attention over the next couple of days I still got the feeling I was being watched. Every so often I'd look round and find her eyeing me, or else I'd be deep in conversation with Viv or Katie or whoever, only to discover that India was suddenly much closer to us than I'd realized. If India *was* doing a low-level surveillance exercise it was most likely for the simple reason that it amused her and annoyed me, rather than being part of some grand scheme. All the same, I was very careful not to mention anything vaguely Tempest-related and kept a discreet distance from Ben for most of the school day. In fact, I began being extra nice and giggly around Will and Liam, just to throw India off the scent.

I missed my bus again on Friday morning and was hurrying to catch up with the rest of the class en route to assembly when someone reached out and grabbed my arm as I was turning into the corridor leading to the hall. I was marched round the corner and hustled into an empty classroom before I had time to catch my breath.

'Ben! What are you doing? Mr Pemberton was only just in front of me. Anyone could have seen us . . .' I went to the door of the room and peered out cautiously. The corridor seemed to be deserted, but at this time of the morning there was usually a member of staff on the prowl for late arrivals and truants from assembly. 'I thought we agreed we'd send texts before arranging to meet up.'

'*We* didn't agree so much as *you* decided.'

Uh-oh. It didn't look like he'd dragged me in here to seduce me with chocolate hearts and sweet nothings.

'Is something wrong?'

'Yes. I want to know when we can stop this stupid undercover stuff. It may only have been a couple of weeks but I've had enough.'

'Me too. But it's like I said on Monday—'

'Yeah, yeah, I haven't forgotten. Now India's back it's better safe than sorry, anything for a quiet life, low profiles all round. But I'm fed up with seeing you snuggle up to Liam and Will and the rest while you act like you can barely even remember my name.'

'I know it's been difficult and I'm sorry.' I put my hand out towards him but he moved away.

'Just as long as you still *want* people to know about us . . .'

'What's that supposed to mean?'

He shrugged, his expression unreadable. 'I want to be able to show you off. I'd like to think the feeling's

mutual, that's all. I know I'm not your usual brand of arm candy—'

'Ben! What, you think all this India business is some kind of excuse? That's crazy. I don't like hiding this any more than you do.' I reached out and took his hand and this time he didn't move away. I took a deep breath. 'And you're right, the whole situation is getting ridiculous. It's time to take a stand. Today we'll go public.'

'You don't mean—?'

'Yes,' I said, eyes resolute, jaw set. 'I think it's time we made an appearance at the Frog Pond.'

The Frog Pond is the crowning glory of what Jethro Park officially, and optimistically, calls the Nature Corner. This is unofficially, but more accurately, known as the Mating Corner, because it's the part of the school sports ground where the Jethro Park wildlife goes to smoke fags and cop off. I don't think a frog has been seen there in living memory since the pond in question is more of a scummy puddle surrounded by brambles, cigarette butts and crisp packets, but the complete absence of natural beauty doesn't seem to get in the way of True Lust. It can get quite busy down there in break and lunch, so once you've been spotted by the Frog Pond with a member of the opposite sex you can more or less guarantee the news will be round the school within the next quarter of an hour.

So as soon as the lunchtime bell had gone, Ben and I squelched across the playing field, parked ourselves on the decaying bench by the Frog Puddle, kissed briefly but enthusiastically – apparently oblivious to the other happy couples trampling around in the undergrowth – and then made our way back through the mud. Fifteen minutes later Katie ran me to ground in the girls' toilets, all agog: 'Is it true you and Ben have been having a passionate affair for the last six months?'

I've always despised lovey-dovey couples who slurp over each other in public places, but I had to admit there was a definite thrill in walking down a school corridor with Ben's arm draped round my shoulders. It was very satisfying, too, to see several people do a double take as we walked into the classroom together and even Jack tore his eyes off India for a few seconds to give Ben a thumbs up and a dirty grin. I could see Katie, who was considered something of an authority on the goings-on at the Frog Pond, was already holding forth on the gory details of our supposed six months of passion to anyone who'd listen. As Ben and I (slightly self-consciously) went to sit down together at the back of the room I heard her telling Hannah how she'd known from the start we had the hots for each other – 'All that aggro – *so* obviously sexual tension.' Hannah, of course, was in complete agreement. Meanwhile, Viv looked on fondly, like a proud parent.

India's reaction was everything that was congratulatory and insincere. After waiting a few minutes for the normal classroom buzz to start up again she sauntered over to the two of us. 'Dave! Octavia, I mean. You are a sly old thing not to tell me! When did it all start happening between you two lovebirds?'

'A couple of weeks ago,' said Ben, just as I said, 'Oh, not till this morning.' There was a slightly awkward pause as India looked from one to the other in puzzlement.

'You know, I asked Octavia straight out if there was something going on between the two of you at the beginning of the week. And she was really quite defensive, the silly girl. Kept on denying it and going all red and sweaty-looking . . .' She turned towards me. 'I realize Ben's not the type you usually go for, but if it were me, I wouldn't be embarrassed to be seen with such a lovely guy. There's no need to be ashamed about it, you know. Goodness, I would have been telling *everybody* . . . Tell me, Dave, Octavia, I mean, why *have* you been keeping it a secret for so long?'

Ben's arm was still round my shoulders, but I couldn't help remembering our conversation that morning. Of course, I'd made it absolutely clear at the time that I wasn't in the least bit embarrassed about our relationship . . . or had I? Had I made it unmistakably obvious how lucky I thought I was to be with him? I wondered if perhaps I should have made this even more explicit. Now India leaned towards Ben in a confiding sort of way.

'I'm *so* glad she's finally able to get over her fling with Alex. Just because this is her first relationship since the break-up doesn't *have* to mean she's on the rebound, you know. I think you'll make an adorable couple.' She smiled sweetly, then turned back to Tom and Vicky and the rest of the groupies, who'd all been leaning in, ears pricked, at the edge of our conversation. 'See you two sweethearts later.'

'Was that a threat?' Ben muttered in my ear.

I made a face. 'I did warn you. Ugh, she's going to have so much fun with this . . .'

'Not as much fun as I am,' said Ben with a grin. 'C'mon, if that's the worse she can do I think we'll cope. And I have to admit, it's kind of nice to be the centre of all this speculation. Next time I'd like to hold a full-on joint press conference.'

'Next time? How many times are you planning on announcing a secret relationship?'

Ben looked thoughtful. 'It depends. All these over-sexed supermodels I'm stringing along . . . I guess sooner or later something's got to give.'

Time for a repeat of my Frog Pond performance, but minus the fag packets and all that mud.

Later on, when Viv and I were reviewing the day over chocolate fudge cake, I found myself admitting that perhaps Ben had been right, in a sense, when he'd accused me of not really wanting to be open about our relationship, India or no India. I don't mean that I was ever embarrassed or unsure about the two of us or that I got some kinky thrill out of all that sneaking around. No – it wasn't the secrecy that appealed to me so much as the *privacy*. India's arrival combined with the whole Lola–Bud–Helena entanglement meant I was hypersensitive about attracting any kind of attention to myself. Hyperparanoid, even.

But now Ben and I were 'out of the closet', as Viv put it, I realized that a huge weight had lifted. My classmates were interested, gossipy even, but no more than was to be expected when two people who were supposedly at loggerheads were suddenly found to have had the hots for each other all along. It was clear Ben and I were going to be more or less left to get on with it, just like all the other lust-struck couples who'd been spotted by the Frog Pond over the past term. As for India . . . well, she'd probably find lots more opportunities to make life difficult for the two of us – but at least it was 'us' she had to deal with. That was official.

Bud came back from his trip to the States mid-morning on Saturday. Although he'd only been away for a week I'd kind of forgotten how very *large* he is, and not just in physical terms. Once Bud's in a room everything around him sort of shrinks and dims and starts looking a bit worn around the edges (though Lady Jane, of course, just looks extra dainty). Anyway, she was swooning with joy at their reunion; in normal circumstances this would have irritated the hell out of me, but as I was feeling fairly loved-up myself I made an effort to look pleased for them. I didn't even make any gagging noises while they were kissing.

Milton was not there to witness the happy scene, for all his little homilies on existential interpersonal commitment. He hadn't been around on Friday evening, either, and even if I didn't know where he was I had a pretty strong suspicion of who he was with. On Thursday night I'd gone into the study looking for a calculator and found Milton there instead, flicking through some files Bud had left behind. Bud usually kept important business papers and stuff locked in a drawer in his desk, but this was now open. When I asked Milton what he was doing he just gave me a death-ray stare and said he was looking for the telephone number of one of his psychiatrists in New York. He looked even more shifty than normal, though, and I wondered if India had got him to do a little Tempest-related snooping on her account. Later on that night, I lay in wait for him on the upstairs landing.

'So, how's Indy these days?' I asked, blocking the path to his room.

He shrugged. 'You're the one who goes to school with her.'

'Ah, but *you're* the one having fun at all these extra-curricular activities. Tell me, Milton, what do you and she get up to of an evening? Take it in turns to suck each other's blood? Swap notes on designer thumbscrews?'

'Cynicism doesn't suit you, Octavia. You're not intelligent enough to use it creatively,' he said. Then he tapped the side of his nose in a meaningful manner. I would have kicked him if I hadn't thought he'd probably get some kinky thrill out of the whole infliction-of-pain thing.

'It's about time you got over this whole gloomier-than-thou superiority complex of yours,' I told him sternly. 'I think it's pathetic – one bat of India's eye-lashes and she's already got you wrapped round her little finger.'

Milton only gave a creepy sort of smile. 'That's what you think.' Then he wriggled past me into his room and locked the door.

I decided I wouldn't raise the whole Milton–India issue with Princess and Hero until the welcome-back rapture fit had died down a bit. After all, I didn't have any proof, exactly, just a nagging suspicion. And on the subject of nagging . . . Mum had threatened to take me clothes shopping on Saturday for the Harlequin Trust bash, but I took advantage of the distraction of Bud and his hamper of duty-free loot to slip out of the house and go for lunch with Dad and Michael instead. Then I met up with Ben and Viv and Simon in the afternoon.

Viv was trying to find a special CD for her mum's birthday – a compilation of Greatest Love Themes from the Movies – so we were all supposed to meet up at one of the big music stores on Oxford Street. But it turned out that Freddie Lions was making a five-minute appearance to promote his new single, so nobody could get within half a block of the place, what with police and bodyguards and the howling mob of hysterical thirteen-year-olds and their equally frenzied mothers. Eventually we did manage to find each other and retreated to a crowded coffee shop, where Freddie Lions was crooning in the background: *I get stars in my eyes and scars on my heart, angel-faced girl, ev'ry time that we part* . . .

Viv scowled. 'Isn't it about time that moron had a breakdown or took an overdose or something and gave us all a break?'

'You know what I like about you?' said Simon. 'You're all heart.'

'It's this angel-face of mine.' Viv winked at me. 'Fools 'em every time.'

I winked back. This, I decided, was as good as it got. A group of ordinary friends sitting round a table in an ordinary coffee shop, whiling away the afternoon. I didn't even mind Freddie Lions too much, not with Ben sprawled warm and comfortable in the chair beside me.

'You know what's really sad?' Viv continued. 'I bet

Katie is out there, throwing her knickers with the best of them. I bet *lots* of people we know are part of that mob.'

'So you're completely immune to Freddie's charms, are you?' asked Ben, amused.

'Yup. Diamond nose-stud, plastic pecs, dimples and all.'

'Actually, it's not a diamond. It's a pink crystal given to him by an aged Brahman in India,' I told them. 'It has very mystical qualities.'

'I am seriously worried that you know that,' said Viv.

Ben rolled his eyes. 'Don't tell me – you went to school with him.'

'I've spent a lot of time with Katie over the last couple of weeks. And Freddie isn't a Darling – he went to one of those stage schools.'

'Oho,' said Ben mischievously. 'Do I detect a hint of snobbery? I suppose stage schools are a bit common in A-list terms. Too many leg warmers and cheesy grins.'

I was a bit annoyed with the snobbery remark but decided to play along. 'Exactly: Darlings don't grin, they simper. And leg warmers are unforgivable whatever the circumstance.'

'Er, Octavia . . .' Simon jerked his head towards a woman stalking past our table with a plate of muffins in her hand and scrunchy pink concertinas on her legs. She didn't look too happy with us.

'Though of course,' I added hastily, 'they must be very practical. When, uh, it gets cold. Or during 1980s revival nights.' In spite of myself, I started to giggle, tried desperately to suppress it, but then caught Viv's eye and the resulting hysteria nearly ended with coffee all over our laps.

The rest of the weekend was taken over by wedding plans. With the *Stellar!* article due out on Monday, my mother was feeling sufficiently on top of the Lola situation to start planning the happy day when Bud would make an honest woman of her. They'd set a provisional date for June – one month before shooting for *Gone With the Wind* was due to start – which I thought was ages away, especially as there had once been talk of doing the deed the moment Bud's divorce papers came through. I was now informed that five months was hardly enough time to choose the ribbon on the cake, let alone sort out stuff like venue, guest list and bridal wear.

It came as a big relief to find that they were still set on keeping things private. I could just about cope with welcoming *Stellar!* to our fabulous home; I didn't want it to be the guest of honour at my mother's wedding. However, it was all too clear that, since the first time my mother had said 'I do' had been a no-frills, low-impact occasion, she was determined to do things properly second time around. There was talk of getting Archimboldo to be the 'design coordinator'. There was even mention of a *Gone With the Wind* theme. I could see my mother's eyes gleam as she imagined starring in her own Southern Belle moment with Bud twirling his mustachios (specially grown for the occasion) and the bridesmaids all smirking behind their fans and saying 'fiddle de-dee' . . .

However, it soon became clear Lady Jane was a long way from making any sort of final decision and I began to have hopes of steering her away from the sprigged muslin theme before things reached the point of no return. Bud was very keen on my mother and him writing their own vows, but otherwise seemed happy to leave the 'design conceptualization' up to her. We actually had a lot of fun discussing stuff like wedding-cake ingredients (we both rejected the traditional fruit variety, but my mother wasn't persuaded by my chocolate profiterole proposal), who to invite and who to leave off the list ('Suzi Sanmartini won't be getting so much as a sugared almond from me, *that's* for sure') and whether to get a string quartet or a jazz band for the reception (we settled on both). As my mother was writing the first draft of the guest list she looked up at me a little hesitantly. 'Do you think your father would be willing to do a reading at the ceremony?'

I was touched. It wasn't so long ago that my mother could hardly mention Dad's name without going all tight-lipped and tragic-looking, but since Bud's arrival on the scene that's all changed. 'I should think he'd love to. That's a brilliant idea.'

She looked relieved. 'I'm so glad you think so. We're such a small family . . . Bud will have a lot of relatives coming over from the States, of course, but on my side . . . well, it's just you. And Hector.'

'And Michael,' I said.

She smiled at me. 'Of course. Michael too.'

I began to have quite a good feeling about this wedding.

*

Monday was the great day of our appearance in *Stellar!*. Although I didn't regret helping Mum out with her PR comeback, I found it hard to look forward to the publication date with the degree of enthusiasm shared by Euphoria and Lady Jane. The fact that I knew exactly what to expect didn't make it any easier either. The more toe-curlingly pretentious and toadying the article was, the more successful it would be. I went to bed on Sunday night with Jethro Park's howls of laughter ringing in my ears.

The Clairbrook-Cleeve-Carnaby household all got up extra early on Monday morning so we could have a preliminary read-through over breakfast. Even Milton appeared, still in the long grey shroud thing he wears to bed. Then Euphoria arrived on the dot of a quarter to eight, with a stack of hot-off-the-press copies, a big grin and a magnum of champagne. Phase One of Helena Clairbrook-Cleeve's comeback had begun.

And there she was on the front cover, looking every inch the lady in a clingy white mohair sweater and pearls, her hair tumbling around her shoulders, her smile warm but with just a hint of melancholy. The strapline read, 'Helena Clairbrook-Cleeve: Learning To Love Again.' Underneath that in even larger letters was 'EXCLUSIVE INTERVIEW AND PICTURES!' We read on, breathlessly.

Helena Clairbrook-Cleeve has become a much-loved household name on both sides of the Atlantic ever since the first episode of her award-winning sitcom *Lady Jane* was aired over ten years ago. The new face of Avilon cosmetics, Helena's delicate English beauty, wry charm and impeccable comic timing have proved a hit with critics and audiences alike. Now, however, she is returning to her roots as a 'straight' actress and is taking a break from comedy to play Ellen O'Hara in Technimax's remake of *Gone With the Wind*, a six-part, ten million dollar television adaptation of Margaret Mitchell's epic of the American Civil War.

Yet the upsurge in Helena's profile has brought with it the inevitable fascination with her private life. Her early marriage to acclaimed director Hector Clairbrook-Cleeve, son of Lord Clairbrook-Cleeve of Wornslow, ended after less than two years when Hector announced he was leaving her for another man. Since then, Helena has devoted herself to raising their daughter, Octavia. But now, nearly fourteen years after her divorce, Helena has found domestic bliss once more, in the arms of old friend Budwin 'Bud' Carnaby, the newly appointed Director of Marketing at Tempest Films UK. After a whirlwind romance, they announced their engagement just after Christmas.

And 'whirlwind' is the word. Almost overnight, Helena found herself in the midst of a media frenzy when the news broke that Budwin's then-wife – American television personality Lola Salanova – was said to be 'emotionally devastated' by the discovery of their relationship.

Helena confesses herself bewildered by Lola's response. In media circles it was commonly known that Bud and Lola had been estranged for the past couple of years; indeed, divorce proceedings had already begun when Bud and Helena embarked on their romance. Helena, however, refuses to be bitter about the situation. When she welcomed *Stellar!* into her beautiful West London home she looked the picture of happiness as she talked candidly about fame, family and learning to love again.

Helena, this is a very exciting time for you. Are you looking forward to participating in such a high-profile project as the Gone With the Wind *TV miniseries?*

Absolutely. The 1939 movie was groundbreaking cinema, but we think it's time to bring this great classic to a new generation. It's set in a quite controversial period of American history, what with the legacy of slavery and everything, so I know the producers are anxious to give the black characters in the story a much stronger voice. And, of course, doing it as a serial will allow us to dramatize more of the original book. We have a fantastic cast and a fantastic story to tell and I can't wait to get started.

You've made a name for yourself as the archetypal 'English Rose'. And now for the first time in your career you're playing an American . . .

Yes, and I've been practising a Southern accent for weeks! I think it's very sexy.

What attracted you to the role of Ellen O'Hara?

Well, in the book she's a much more complex, more passionate character than was portrayed in the film and hopefully this new adaptation will do her justice. Ellen grows up to be a society belle but then her lover dies and she gets married to someone else and becomes this saintly maternal figure instead. Her heart's broken and yet she's still loyal and loving, with this amazing moral strength. She's everything a wife and mother should be. I really admire her.

Are you feeling the pressure of tackling a 'straight' role after your years in comedy?

Not at all. Although I'm best known for *Lady Jane* I've done lots of other projects here in the UK – murder mysteries, costume dramas, and I've just finished presenting *Blue Blood and Hot Heads*, a history of the English Aristocracy for Channel Five. And, of course, I started my career in serious drama.

In fact, you made your debut in The Keeper, *which was written and directed by your ex-husband, Hector Cleeve. How does he feel about your remarriage?*

He is hugely supportive. We were very young when we got married and we've both had a certain amount of self-discovery and self-healing to do over the years. But he has always been a wonderful father to Octavia and I am looking forward to him attending the wedding. As a matter of fact, he and his partner spent Christmas with us, which was lovely. Family has always been immensely important to me, which is why I was so hurt by certain comments in the press.

Why do you think your romance with Bud has caused such a furore?

In all honesty, I can't understand it. We have always been completely open about our feelings for each other – there was never any big secret because we didn't feel we had anything to hide.

So Bud's marriage was already over when you began your relationship?

He and Lola had, sadly, become completely estranged from each other over the last few years. Not that I wish to cast any blame – we all work in a very highly pressured industry and it's tough on relationships. Divorce is always going to be difficult and painful, especially when children are involved. That's why it's so important to deal with these things in a quiet and dignified manner and that's why I've refused to trade insults or accusations. Unlike some people, I would never try to take advantage of a very sad situation for self-promotion or personal gain.

How have you coped with the strain of the last few weeks?

The support of my family and friends has been immeasurable and, of course, my fans have been wonderful too, but just being with Bud has made me a stronger and better person. Until I met him, I never believed that I would find love again. To be surrounded by so much joy is very humbling.

Helena's daughter Octavia, granddaughter of Lord Clairbrook-Cleeve of Wornslow, is a doe-eyed sixteen-year-old already in full command of the famous family charm. Known as 'Occy' to her friends, this vivacious teen is bubbling over with excitement as she shares with Stellar! *her joy at her mother's engagement.*

Octavia, you're about to get a stepfather and a step-brother [Milton, aged fourteen, who is currently staying with his father in London]. How do you feel about your mother getting married again?

I've always thought it would be nice to have a

larger family. Bud's a lovely guy and he makes Mum very happy.

Was it hard seeing your mother criticized in the press?

Of course it was upsetting, but anyone who's ever met my mother and Bud would know that all that stuff couldn't be true.

Do you find it difficult having parents who are in the public eye?

Not usually. I get on and do my own thing, and they do theirs. I'm very proud of both my parents.

Do you think you might like to follow in your mother's footsteps and become an actress one day?

No.

Are you looking forward to seeing your mother in Gone With the Wind*?*

Definitely – she'll be perfect in the role. Though I'm still getting used to the idea of her with an American accent!

'Well,' said Euphoria, when the rustling of pages and the squinting at photographs had come to a pause, 'I don't know about you, but I think it's about time we broke open the fizz. Spot of champers, anyone?'

With hindsight, two glasses of champagne on an empty stomach was not, perhaps, the most sensible start to Monday morning. I was feeling distinctly woozy when I finally tottered off to the bus stop, and during the short ride to school my insides began lurching around in an unpleasant sort of way. Though that might have had less to do with the alcohol than with Daisy's depiction of Bubbly Occy and her Famously Doe-Eyed Charm. Ugh.

Ben was waiting for me at the school bus stop, a crumpled corner of *Stellar!* poking out of his rucksack. 'Occy?' he said, eyebrow raised.

'I know, I know . . . Maybe I should just give up and start calling myself something so short and sensible nobody can do anything weird to it. Like Joan or Jan or something.'

'Or Ben.'

'I'll stick to the girls' names, thanks . . . Seriously, though, what did you think about the article? How do you think Mum came across?'

There was a slight pause. 'Well, it was an outstanding piece of spin,' he said carefully. 'She was very . . . professional.'

'Professional? But it was all about home and family stuff—'

'Yeah. That's what I mean. All that image-management with the fluffy sweaters and home-baked cookies – it was really clever. The public will lap it up. I'm sure the Salanova woman won't stand a chance.'

This wasn't what I wanted to hear. Sure, I knew that the whole article was a PR exercise, but I also knew that there was more to it than that – that something important, something *real* was at stake. I tried explaining this to Ben. 'I know it was for publicity but Mum truly meant the stuff she was saying.'

'She did?'

Now I was getting rattled. 'Of course she did. You don't understand – that's the way she and Bud are normally. It drives me up the wall sometimes, but all that sop about "learning to love again" isn't an act. She really *does* love him. And she really *is* a good mother.'

'I never said she wasn't,' he said in surprise.

'But that's what you meant. You still think it's nothing but a fake. God, Ben, how cynical do you think my family is?'

'Whoa, there.' He took me by the arm, concern in his eyes. 'I wasn't trying to have a go. I'm on your side, remember.'

I didn't know what had got into me. A year or so ago, if Asia or Tallulah or Twinkle's mum had appeared in *Stellar!* in order to justify a spot of high-profile adultery I'd have been piling on the scorn with a shovel . . . But then, a year or so ago I'd have dismissed all Bud's pronouncements on My Eternal Love for My Eternal Princess as twenty-four-carat pig poop. Things were different now. Even if Bud's little declarations still set my teeth on edge, even if my mother's Saint Helena at the Stake act still made my toes curl, I could see the fundamental honesty behind the hype. And now it was starting to matter to me that others could see this too.

Ben was looking at me anxiously. 'And did I mention that you look great in those photos? Because you do. All lovely and natural.'

I decided not to mention the forty-five-minute beauty session with the forty-five layers of make-up. Let him keep his illusions. 'Yeah, well, I was having a good face day.'

We were now nearly at 11B's form room and I braced myself for the shrieks of laughter that were probably already bouncing off the walls. It would be too much to hope that the Clairbrook-Cleeve edition of

Stellar! could somehow have escaped people's notice – for one thing, I knew Katie had been dying to spread the glad tidings ever since Viv swore her to secrecy the week before. Sure enough, I could see at least four copies of the magazine were already in circulation, each with its little huddle of goggle-eyed readers. But as far as I could tell, the majority of them weren't wetting their knickers with hilarity – if anything, they looked *impressed*. Maybe even a bit awed.

There wasn't time for more than first impressions, however, as Mr Pemberton was already hot on our heels, with India in attendance. As they came into the classroom they were laughing together like old pals; India was tossing her hair and saying, '. . . but of course, *you* know how it is,' in a confiding sort of way. Mr Pemberton's jaunty smile abruptly vanished as he took his seat, rapped his desk for attention, then realized that half his class were engrossed in *Stellar!*. He had to call out Will Adams's name three times before he got any response.

'Ahem – Mr Adams, much as I hate to deprive you of the chance to catch up on this season's lip colours, would you do me the honour of tearing yourself away from your magazine for a moment?'

'But it's Octavia, sir!'

'What do you mean?'

'She and her mum are in the magazine! Look.'

Mr Pemberton went over to Will's desk and picked up the magazine like it was a used handkerchief. A handkerchief that had just mopped the nose of a particularly grungy tramp.

'At Home With the Clairbrook-Cleeves. How perfectly delightful.'

A couple of people sniggered. He turned towards me. 'Perhaps in future, milady, you would be so kind as to give us some notice before your next audience with the press? In your scramble for the media spotlight I'm afraid you forget that the rest of the world has other priorities than your latest domestic melodrama.'

I was burning with indignation as we straggled out of the room and off to assembly. It was so *unfair*. There was India flaunting her A-list flesh, fame and fortune like every day was Oscar night, and still everyone kept exclaiming what a sweet, unpretentious girl she was. Then I made a brief appearance in one crappy interview and it was as if I'd had my photo taken while wallowing naked with Prince Richard in a vat of Red Bull vodka.

As soon as morning break arrived I was tempted to come down with an imaginary illness and sneak off home, but Ben and Viv managed to talk me out of it. 'You might as well get it over with,' Viv said, 'and if you face everybody now, they won't have as much opportunity to make snide comments behind your back.' So instead of hiding out in the computer lab or the girls' toilets I went back to our classroom where it took all of thirty seconds for the copies of *Stellar!* to be whisked out and the running commentary to begin in earnest.

'Wow, Octavia, I didn't know your grandad was a lord! Does that mean you have a title?'

'Your mum is amazing-looking. Like a princess.'

'Is this really your house? Look at that mantelpiece! You must be *loaded*.'

I didn't like how people were looking at me in this curious, respectful sort of way. It was somehow ˙
than Mr Pemberton's sarcasm or the

ridicule I'd been expecting. I knew that Darlings were full of contempt for the General Public who, poor souls, took the twaddle people said in *Stellar!* at face value and thought that browsing the gossip columns could give you any sort of insight into life 'n' times in celebsville. I also knew that the General Public were often a lot more sceptical/scornful than the Darlings gave them credit for. However, although Darlings respected high-profile spin in the same way as they savoured public pratfalls, it was considered rather bad taste to remark on either. Something as commonplace as an appearance in *Stellar!* would barely be worth even *noticing*. Which was totally hypocritical of course, but, as I was beginning to appreciate, at least it kept the embarrassment to a minimum.

I realized that maybe I'd been a bit *too* successful about playing down the more exotic elements of my home life. Of course, everyone knew that I had a glitzy mother who was on TV and in the papers a lot and that my dad made films – mostly the clever, arty kind that nobody ever sees. Everyone knew that I used to go to a super-posh school where I hung out with girls like India and made out with guys like Alex. I hadn't made a big secret out of the fact that my father lives with another man, either. But I'd always been very careful not to draw attention to myself, to fit into ordinary school life, to be included in things because people liked my jokes or shared my interests, not because they thought they'd get an invite to the Quicksilver Music Awards. As a rule, this didn't require much effort. I'm not glamorous. I don't get a huge allowance. I haven't got any famous names in my address book and very few people had actually been home with me and been introduced to Lady Jane and her marble mantelpiece. India's arrival, too, had given the class their first taste of real celebrity, the kind of celebrity I could never compete with, even if I'd wanted to. And so my sudden appearance in the glossy pages of *Stellar!* had come as something of a shock. People were looking at me almost as if they didn't know me any more.

Thank God for Viv. She saw what was happening and immediately plunged into a stream of good-humoured banter, as if the article was this tremendous joke that we'd both been looking forward to sharing. The two of us took it in turns to take the piss out of my poses, my pronouncements and my mother's mantel-piece. Instead of trying to escape ridicule, I began to encourage it. And before long, others took their cue.

'So what's "doe-eyed" mean, then?'

'Like Bambi.' I fluttered my eyelashes at Will. 'It's cos I'm such a *deer* girl.'

'Yeah, but your mum is a total babe.'

'Sorry, Jack, but she's just not interested in little boys . . . she's got her hands full with married men, remember?' Somehow I even managed to laugh as I said it.

'You look amazing in those photos, you know. Like a model.'

'Like a *super*model,' chorused Hannah.

'Well, so I bloody should after all the work that went into them.' I decided to sacrifice Ben's illusions about my natural photogenic qualities and went on to give a comically exaggerated account of the beautifying process – '. . . and then a team of dwarf stylists took it in turns to paint each of my eyelashes with a miniature toothbrush . . .' etc. People were laughing at this when India joined the conversation.

I don't know when she'd first got her hands on a copy of *Stellar!* or if the Lady Jane cover story came as a surprise to her or not, but I could tell by the chill in her eye that she was far from pleased I'd taken a turn in the spotlight. Never mind that I found the whole situation embarrassing and difficult; the fact remained that for the whole morning, a sizeable portion of Jethro Park had been preoccupied with gossiping and exclaiming over Octavia Clairbrook-Cleeve, not India Withers.

'You must be really proud of your gorgeous girl-friend,' she told Ben. 'I bet blokes all over Britain are drooling over those pics of Octavia. She looks lovely. *Oozing* with class.'

Ben had been rather quiet during my facing-up-to-*Stellar!* session. All he said now was, 'I don't need a fancy magazine shoot to realize that.'

'You know, it's funny how some men really get off on the idea of posh totty,' India mused. 'In fact, I wouldn't be surprised if Octavia hasn't won herself some new fans here at Jethro Park. Jethro Park's own cut-out-and-keep pin-up.'

'Yeah,' put in someone, 'let's hope Ben can keep Octavia in the style to which she's accustomed.'

'Or maybe Octavia will start keeping Ben in the style to which *he* isn't,' said someone else with a smirk. 'Maybe he'll suddenly turn up wearing a signet ring and a designer shirt.'

I didn't like the way this conversation was going, not one little bit. Ben was wearing an amused expression but I could see the tension in his face. I wanted him to rescue the situation with one of his sarky put-downs, but part of me worried that it would be me, not India, on the receiving end. Instead, I desperately hunted for some witty-yet-devastating remark that would stamp out this sort of thing for good. My mind, of course, was a roaring blank.

India gave one of her tinkling laughs. 'There's no shame in having expensive tastes, you know.' She turned to me again. 'For someone who's supposed to love lurking in the background you're a bit of a natural in front of the camera . . . I mean, this is hardly the first time you've appeared in one of the glossies, is it, Octavia? That portrait of you and Alexis in the *Prattler*, for example. There was a time when you were really *very* keen on life in the society pages.'

'Were you, like, one of those It-Girls?' Meera asked me breathlessly.

That did it. I thought of those years at Darlinham House, of being the awkward gangly one in the corner, then of my brief moment in the spotlight – the too-high heels, the too-tight dresses, the poisonous cocktails and all those bitchy, beautiful people waiting for me to make a fool of myself. It was time to put this behind me once and for all.

'OK, I confess – I Was A Teenage Party Poppet. For all of five minutes, and I wasn't much good at it. But while we're on the subject of people pretending to be something they aren't, why don't we talk about India for a change?'

'India is an *actress*. It's her job to pretend things,' said Vicky.

'Well, let's talk about her latest job, then. *La Dame aux Camélias* on a council estate. Only it's not much of a job, is it, Indy? Seeing how the funding's fallen through and your director's had a breakdown.'

'You don't know what you're talking about,' she said coolly. 'Jed is only a couple of days away from signing a co-production deal with Tempest. Just ask that freakish stepbrother of yours if you don't believe me.'

Hmm. Interesting. So Milton *had* been feeding India with inside information. However, I didn't have time to worry about that now.

'If there isn't going to be a film why would India be doing research stuff at Jethro Park?' put in Tom.

'Ah yes – India's research,' I said. Her eyes flashed dangerously but there was no way I was backing down now. 'We've all heard how much she loves being the girl next door and hanging out with us common folk—'

'Common folk like you, Oc-tave-ee-ah?' India asked. 'Tut tut. What would your lordly grandpapa have to say?'

I ignored her. 'The point is, your film isn't about ordinary life and you're certainly not here because you're tired of being in the celebrity spotlight. You're here because you've got as much acting credibility as a designer handbag. So you're about to proclaim to the Great Cinema-Going Public that you spent six months undercover at an inner-city sin bin, surrounded by sixteen-year-old delinquents and crack-heads. That's you, by the way,' I said, nodding at Jack and Meera and Dan and the rest with a cheery smile.

'But I thought *La – La Dam* whatsit was a love story,' said Hannah.

'Like *Pretty Woman*, but with a sad ending,' said someone else.

'Love story?' Viv was scornful. 'It's based on the life of a girl who was forced into prostitution at the age of twelve, blackmailed into leaving her lover and then dead of TB and poverty at the age of twenty-three. Very romantic, I don't think.'

'I never said it was a romance,' said India defensively. 'This project will be a radical yet stylish reinterpretation of a timeless classic—'

'It will be radical, all right,' I said. 'Have any of you lot actually seen a Jed Mosley film? Hmm?' They all stared back blankly. Except for Viv, who mouthed 'You go, girl,' and Ben, who was trying very hard not to laugh. 'Because if you had, you'd realize that Jed doesn't give a toss about bringing literary classics to a new generation or making uplifting love stories for school-girls. He's not out to help his audience pass the time – he's out to kick them in the teeth. He does cutting edge and gritty and seriously grim.'

People were looking at each other rather uncertainly. 'If that's true, why would India want to come to Jethro Park, then?' asked Dan. 'Nothing cutting edge or – or *gritty* ever happens here . . . it's just . . . normal . . .'

'India wouldn't last five minutes in a real sin bin and she knows it. This is a neat little PR stunt. For India and Jed Mosley, that is. I think Jethro Park is in for a nasty surprise.'

There was silence. An expectant sort of silence – all eyes were on India now. 'You can't prove a thing and you know it,' she said at last, with a toss of her head. 'Of course, I understand why you're doing this. One only has to look at your face to see you're *consumed* by jealousy . . . Poor old Dave. You've got used to throwing your weight around as the local celeb and then I turn up and suddenly you're yesterday's news. Sadly for you, now that these people have seen what a *real* star is made of I don't think they'll have much time for you and your D-list pretensions.' Now she widened her eyes and looked at me reproachfully as she moved in for the kill. 'Personally, I think it's very *dishonest* of you – making out you're some sort of expert on the film industry just because your dad's been responsible for couple of box-office flops nobody's even heard of. And, let's face it, your mother's just a cheap media tart who couldn't get a decent role if she slept with the entire Academy of Motion Pictures board.'

I slapped her then, hard. After all, I'd been wanting to do it if for the last five years and now seemed as good a time as any. There was a split second when she looked at me with murder in her eyes – then she began to gather herself up – her whole face was blazing – she was ready to lunge – and it was just at that moment that Mr Pemberton strode into the fray.

'WHAT in God's name is going on here?'

Caught up in the drama of our confrontation, nobody had realized that the bell had gone over ten minutes ago and that Mr Pemberton had had to fight his way through a heaving crowd of onlookers, all trying to squeeze into our classroom. Already, the chant of, 'Fight! Fight!' could be heard in the corridor outside.

India and I still stood facing each other, the mark of

my hand on her cheek, her blue eyes almost black with rage. If she'd been thinking rationally, now was the perfect opportunity to slip into her victim routine – maybe if she'd burst into tears and done the whole blonde-in-peril act people would have been a lot more quick to forget everything that had gone before. Although Mr Pemberton hadn't actually seen me hit her, one well-timed sob from Indy and he would probably have expelled me on the spot, or at the very least clapped me in irons in the school basement. But when push came to shove, India was a fighter and her blood was up. Another few seconds and I reckon we'd have both ended up going for each other tooth and nail on the classroom floor. I don't think Jack has ever got over the disappointment.

Mr Pemberton wasn't stupid; he could see that there had been a major confrontation of some sort and that major disruption to the school morning was going to follow. Unfortunately for Mr Pemberton, nobody was very forthcoming with regards what the row had been about or who had started it. Once he'd sent the rest of our audience packing he was all set to march India and me off to the Head's office, but luckily for me, although India would have loved to see my school career in ruins, she was smart enough to realize that she didn't want our whole 'debate' replayed before the headmaster. Instead, she somehow managed to soothe/cajole Mr Pemberton into agreeing that we were a couple of silly girls who got a bit overheated in debating what came top of the Ten-Most-Magical-Movie-Moments-Ever list. He didn't look entirely convinced, but in the end he settled on sending us both home for the rest of the day – so that India could 'recover' and I could 'cool off'. As a parting shot, he informed me grimly that, 'From now on, I'll be watching you very carefully, young lady, and don't you forget it.'

I didn't get to see Viv or Ben before I went. India had slipped away after giving her rescuer a tender, grateful sort of look, but Mr Pemberton escorted me all the way to the main exit, partly to formalize my disgrace and partly to ensure that I wasn't about to start another brawl on my way out.

By the time I got home and slammed the door shut behind me the adrenalin rush was well and truly over. Only Milton was in, seated at the bottom of the stairs and eating his way through a jar of cocktail olives. It looked like he'd been trying to throw the pits into the umbrella stand in the hall but, if the trail of black pellets nestling in Lady Jane's antique Persian carpet were anything to go by, his hand–eye coordination wasn't up to much.

'Are you ill?' he asked hopefully.

'Nope – just delinquent. Can I have an olive?'

'If you'll tell me what you've done.'

'Smacked your precious India in the face, actually.'

Milton was impressed. 'So you do have a dark side after all . . . was there much blood?'

'Not once they'd finished picking her teeth out of my knuckles.'

I went to call Dad on his mobile. Needless to say, he wasn't quite as impressed as Milton with my news.

'Yes, I'm sure she deserved it but that's not really the point, is it? I thought your number one priority these days was *not* to attract attention to yourself. Listen, sweetheart, I know you don't want to hear it right now, but you have to remember that this is an important year for you. Mr Pemberton—'

'Mr Pemberton thinks I'm a media floozy on the make. As far as he and the rest of Jethro Park are concerned, India's the artist with the heart of gold. Whose father just happens to be funding our new music suite.'

Now Dad sounded worried. 'I'm beginning to think that you should have a word with Michael about this. If India decides to takes this further, make an official complaint or something . . .'

'She wouldn't risk that sort of publicity, not at this stage. That's why she tried to smooth things over with Mr P.' I sighed. 'To be honest, I'm more worried about the reaction of everyone at school. India's always hated me. But these people are my friends . . . what if I've gone too far and they take India's side in this?'

'In my experience,' said Dad drily, 'hitting people who are smaller and blonder than you isn't usually the best way to win friends and influence people.'

Mum returned at around half past three, after an extended lunch party with Euphoria and some of her other media cronies. I got the impression that the flow of bubbly hadn't really been interrupted since breakfast; she was in an extremely good mood and didn't seem to notice that I was home from school early. Apparently she'd already been inundated with requests for interviews by all the major women's magazines and chat shows. 'That two-faced snake in the grass Suzi Sanmartini had the cheek to put in a call this afternoon.

She says she's been waiting for the perfect opportunity for me to set the record straight! Can you imagine?'

She was telling me this while sorting through the post in the kitchen. I had a postcard of the Grand Canyon from Jess (her mother was shooting her latest exercise video there) and a little box marked 'emergency chocolate rations' from Michael. Among my mother's usual stack of catalogues, unsolicited scripts, invitations and fan letters was a cream envelope addressed in sepia copperplate. My grandfather. She skimmed it briefly through narrowed eyes then tossed it into the bin. I managed to retrieve it later:

Dear Helen, [he has never recognized that all-transforming 'a']

Allow me to congratulate you on your forthcoming nuptials. It has, after all, been many years since your entanglement with my unfortunate son came to its inevitable conclusion.

In this respect, I confess myself perplexed by references to our erstwhile relationship that continue to crop up in certain sections of the press. Since, doubtless, you will now be assuming the surname of your latest husband, may I presume that your brief association with the Clairbrook-Cleeves can finally be put to rest?

It is still my fondest hope that this new union will bring you everything that you deserve.

Yours,

Hector

The Right Honourable the Lord Clairbrook-Cleeve, KCMG, CVO, DL

Viv telephoned me as soon as she got back from school. She told me that my showdown with India was already a school legend and she thought I had given a very 'empowering' performance. But what did everyone else think? I asked her anxiously. Did they believe the stuff I'd told them about Jed and the sin bin? Was India's cover really blown? Hadn't people thought I'd gone too far when I slapped her? She told me that while the standard-bearers of the Withers Adoration Society were still holding firm, most people – especially the girls – were starting to rebel against the idea of having India in the class. Somebody had even suggested going to the Head and asking him to investigate Jed Mosley's interest in Jethro Park.

'Thank God. I was thinking they might believe India when she said I was just jealous. And it's only her word against mine, really, when it comes to this film of Jed's. I haven't any proof.'

Viv gave a snort of exasperation. 'You just don't get it, do you?'

'Get what?'

'People *like* you, Octavia. They're not on your side because you gave them "proof" or because you argued more convincingly than India did. No, it was when India said all that stuff about you throwing your weight around and being fame-obsessed that she really blew it. Everyone knows you're not like that. And then when she started being horrible about your family . . . well, the only thing India proved was what a cow she is. Don't you see? When it comes down to it, these are *your* friends. Not India's.'

I had a lovely warm glow for the rest of the evening. I think Ben was a bit nervous when he telephoned me – like I was either going to be spitting nails or bawling my eyes out – but although we didn't talk for long it was a cheerful conversation. He said that I was very sexy when I was angry – 'Like an Avenging Angel'. I was beginning to think that maybe Milton was right and I should get in touch with my dark side more often.

India wasn't in school on Tuesday. It was too much to hope that I'd got rid of her for good, but I felt vindicated by the fact that she hadn't shown her face at Jethro Park since our row. Curiously, people didn't discuss what had gone on between us, at least not in my hearing. I guess they'd all debated it to their hearts' content after the two of us had been sent home by Mr Pemberton, but now there seemed to be an unspoken assumption that the whole topic should be laid to rest for a while. I was surprised and grateful for their tact, especially as the *Stellar!* article had now had time to circulate round the rest of the school and I had to put up with the stares and giggles and muttered comments from random faces in the playground. Ben came in for a bit of flak too. Although, as I said, my classmates were generally quite tactful in my presence, this didn't stop Jack and Tom winding Ben up with remarks about 'It-Boy Wonders' with 'stars in their eyes' and asking, 'Does social climbing count as an extreme sport?' etc., etc. Now that the tide of popular opinion was turning, I suspect they were feeling a bit foolish about falling for India so heavily, and this was their way of reasserting themselves. It was all quite good-natured on the surface, and Ben gave as good as he got, but it still made him rather prickly.

It was for this reason that I told Ben about the Harlequin Trust cocktail party that evening in vague, casual sorts of terms.

'You mean you lied,' said Viv.

'No I didn't. I just wasn't very specific. I said I was going to a work do with Mum and Bud.' Viv gave me one of her looks. 'Well, it is a *kind of* work do as far as Bud's concerned. All the top Tempest people are going. It's going to be very, er, corporate.'

'And when Ben opens up the *Daily Bellower* and finds the Clairbrook-Cleeve-Carnaby clan grinning out at him?'

'Not likely. Mum's hoping for a mention in a social diary or two and maybe a photo of her and Bud will turn up somewhere, but it's a private party, not a mega media event. That's the point. Lady Jane's relaunching herself in a low-key, er, tasteful sort of way.'

'OK.' Viv didn't look entirely convinced. 'As long as you know what you're doing.'

By the time I got home all I wanted to do was have a hot bath, a microwave supper and an evening of trash

TV. What I should have been doing, of course, was getting down to my English coursework; I could just imagine Mr Pemberton's reaction if he knew I was gadding about at cocktail parties on a school night. It may have been for a good cause ('Stage-Skills for Slum-Kids') but Mr Pemberton's heart was unlikely to be warmed by the thought of all those poor Third-World urchins learning how to leap about in leg warmers and advertise Choco-Nut Flakes for a living.

As it happened, I barely even had time for the hot bath. This was, after all, the first official function my mother and Bud were attending since the furore surrounding the not-so-ex Mrs Carnaby had started before Christmas. And so my mother, who would normally have planned every last detail of clothes, make-up and accessories at least a week before the event, was having a last-minute crisis of confidence. Since Bud thought she could wear a shirt stitched from old dishcloths and still look the pinnacle of sartorial perfection, I was drafted in as Image Consultant for the evening. What about the trouser suit in oyster silk? Or did it make her look washed out? Perhaps the black strapless number, though it was rather plain . . . What did I think about her new wrap? No, not the fur one. The pink tulle stole, with crystal beading.

My own choice of clothing was more straightforward for the simple reason that I only own one dressy outfit. Despite Lady Jane's best efforts to get me stocked up with a range of party wear, I would be wearing the same outfit I'd bought for the premiere of *Gatherings* last year: a simple oriental-style tunic dress in lilac satin, with a flower and bird motif in silvery embroidery. Not particularly spectacular, but flattering and easy to wear. It looked good with flat shoes too.

I hadn't seen any sign of Milton since I'd got back from school and assumed he'd thought better of the whole idea after all. But when I went down to join Mum and Bud in the drawing room, I found that Milton was already there, wearing a long black leather trench coat, his shoes freshly scuffed, his roots freshly dyed. That would explain the purplish-black streaks all over the bathroom.

'Well,' said Mum brightly, 'here we all are! Everyone's looking *so* nice. You know, I have a really good feeling about this evening.' She'd finally settled on the trouser suit and was having one last preen in front of the mirror above the mantelpiece.

'You and me both, Princess.' Bud was beaming fit to burst. 'Seeing us all gathered together here, well, I feel blessed. I really do. The precious warmth of fam—'

The doorbell rang.

'That'll be our driver. Octavia, darling, will you go and tell him we'll just be another minute or two?'

I made a move towards the hallway, only to find that Milton had got there first. 'Actually,' he said, 'I think it's for me.' He went out and we heard the front door open, then a silvery laugh. A moment later India was standing in our drawing room.

'Hello, everybody. Isn't this *fun*?'

Bud, Mum and I stared back at her in complete incomprehension – polite on Bud's part, apprehensive on Mum's and openly hostile on mine. Our unexpected guest was dazzling in an electric-blue sari slashed to the thigh, itsy-bitsy jewelled sandals and almost as many bangles as Euphoria. These clashed in a menacing sort of way as India advanced across the carpet towards my mother, hands outstretched.

'You know, when Octavia told me about the wedding I was simply *thrilled*. Dad sends his congratulations too, of course. He's *so* pleased for you.'

Lady Jane was nonplussed. She claims to have met Sir Rich on 'several' occasions but I suspect these were limited to a fleeting glimpse at a Darlinham House parents' evening. She opened her mouth, looked at me uncertainly, then shut it again. Now India turned to Bud. 'And Mr Carnaby too, of course. We haven't actually met before but I went out for lunch with Myron only the other week. He speaks *very* highly of you.' Myron Partlett is the Creative Director of Tempest Films UK. Then she wafted over to me. 'Darling Occy!' She moved in for the air-kiss, but caught my eye and thought better of it.

Bud was the first to recover. 'I'm pleased to meet you, India. I've, uh, heard a lot about you.' He shot a glance at Milton. 'I guess you're going to this party tonight?'

'Why, of course.' India opened her eyes very wide. 'Didn't Milton tell you?'

'No he didn't.' My mother's tone was abrupt.

'He's such a naughty boy!' India gave Milton a tender look. Throughout the introductions he'd been loitering at the doorway looking supremely bored, as if what was going on between the rest of us had nothing to do with him. I remembered how I'd caught him going through his dad's private business stuff and cursed myself for letting him off the hook so easily. *Naughty?* Treacherous two-faced weevil, more like.

'I don't know if you've realized, but there's quite a strict guest list for tonight,' said Lady Jane, glancing at me again. 'If Milton had brought this up earlier . . . as it is, I'm afraid—'

'Oh, don't worry about that. Dad's already a sponsor of the Harlequins or the Munchkins or whatever the poor mites are called.' She flashed us all a dazzling smile, then linked Milton's arm in hers. 'There's a car waiting for you outside, you know. Shall we go?'

What's more, as we were going out of the door, Milton actually had the nerve to turn round and *wink* at me.

During the ride to the party, India prattled away merrily, squashed in the back of the car with me, Mum and Milton, all of whom kept a dead silence. I could see Bud giving her puzzled looks in the front-seat mirror, although when she paused for breath he would occasionally chip in with a polite, 'Is that so?' As for me, I was preoccupied with thinking up all the ways in which I could make Milton regret his treachery for the rest of his miserable life. Unfortunately, since only a sado-masochist would invite India Withers into the bosom of his family, I came to the conclusion that the most fitting punishment would be to pamper him to death with banoffi pie and positive thinking.

I didn't have long for dreams of vengeance before the car swept through the gates of the Jericho Club, Piccadilly. I'd been here once before, at the first-night party for one of Dad's plays, and had been impressed in spite of myself. The Jericho was originally founded as a gentlemen's club by a group of nineteenth-century army officers, but had been rotting away for years until it was rescued by Cuthbert Shamrock, the media tycoon, and restored to some of its former glory. Like the building itself, most of its members are stately, discreet and just a bit old fashioned – although it does host the odd perfume launch or charity auction, it's not the sort of place where you'll find premiership footballers and their Page Three Stunnas propping up the bar.

However, as we walked into the main reception room – India leading the way, Milton and I trailing behind our respective parents – it was clear that Dame Tilda's list of invitees covered a broad social sweep. Lots of grand theatre people, of course, some of whom I recognized from things I'd gone to with Dad – designers and directors as well as actors – and quite a few society faces too. I could see Mrs Blenkinswick-Sudsbury, croaking froggily away to Grandpa Cleeve's great chum, the Duchess of Teasedale, by the fireplace. Myron Partlett's Tempest contingent was easy to spot: big, shrewd-looking business types with sharp white smiles and sharp grey suits. There was a very tall, very thin man dressed in black, smoking alone in the corner and scowling. There were a couple of minor It-Girls, sticking out their breasts and braying with laughter as if their lives depended on it. There was even a guy I knew from Darlinham House, Seth was his name, who was nibbling the ear of that Japanese model from the Blue Moon perfume ads. And wasn't that Daisy from *Stellar!* in the leopard-print camisole and ice-blue capri pants? More to the point, shouldn't I be worried that I recognized all these people?

As for the Clairbrook-Cleeve-Carnabys, it only took a moment before Lady Jane and Bud were swept up in a flurry of greetings. Little shrieks, breathy air-kisses and coos of delight filled the air. (And that was just the men.) Milton and I hung back at first, but then my mother, who had spied a photographer loitering by a potted fern, pulled us in to complete the family circle. More coos and exclamations were followed by a flash from the camera and a triumphant smile from Lady Jane. 'Oh, my darlings,' she exclaimed to no one in particular, 'I just *know* we're going to have a wonderful time!'

India, of course, had deserted our party the moment we got through the door; she was now working her way across the room towards the Tempest posse without so much as a backward glance in our direction. I turned towards Milton with my brightest smile. 'Looks like your girlfriend's decided it's time to move on.'

He gave me a Grim Reaper stare, then reached out and grabbed a champagne flute from a passing waiter, knocking back its contents in one go. Then he helped himself to another. Uh-oh.

However, I was in no mood to stay and cosset Milton, so I began to go after Bud and Mum, who were already moving deep into the throng. On the way I managed to get a drink for myself – passion-fruit Martini, a throwback to my Darling days – and made a raid on a canapé tray. They were the very small and very fiddly sort that require intense concentration if you're going to eat, talk and hold on to your glass without getting sweet-chilli clams or jalapeño-pepper chutney down you or your neighbour's front. Canapé-juggling techniques were the kind of thing that would fit right in to the Darlinham House curriculum. But then, I reasoned, real It-Girls are never seen eating in public . . . leastways, not without sticking their fingers down their throats in the toilets afterwards.

It's been a long time since I've been to one of these sorts of parties and there had been a moment or two in the evening when I'd really quite enjoyed getting dressed up and knowing I was going somewhere glamorous. However, now that I was here and right in the thick of it I remembered all the things I disliked about media and society events. As usual, I had three options. The first was to hang round my mother and her cronies, smiling witlessly and trying not to cover myself in canapés while they rehashed the same old showbiz gossip I'd been hearing for the past sixteen years. The second was to wander round by myself, pretending I'd momentarily mislaid my group of friends and admirers, but fooling nobody and getting pitying looks from all the waiters. The third was to spend the entire occasion hiding in the ladies' loos. India or no India (who I could now see was busy whispering sweet nothings into Myron Partlett's ear), it was going to be a long evening.

Somewhat to my own surprise, however, I found that I wasn't entirely without people to talk to. A lot of the theatre set came up and said hello-how-nice-to-see-you and asked whether Dad and Michael were coming later. I decided not to explain that Dad was boycotting the event because his leading lady's charity commitments had mucked up his rehearsal schedule for the entire week. The dame herself – very much the diva in a silk turban and flowing crimson robes – pinched my cheek and said what a very clever daddy I had. I exchanged frosty smiles with the Duchess of Teasedale and froggy smiles with Mrs B-S. Daisy came up – 'Well, if it isn't the delightful Occy!' – and told me that my mother and Bud had restored the nation's faith in True Romance. My old school chum Seth obviously couldn't remember my name but congratulated me on making a full recovery. 'Rehab can be hell, but you've obviously come out fighting.' Then he lowered his voice and asked me for the name of my clinic.

It was all rather exhausting, especially since the canapé supply had ground to a halt (charitable cause or no, I thought this was a bit of a cheek when you considered the cost of our tickets). I felt a brief twinge of guilt about Milton, but a quick survey of the room showed him deep in conversation with the scowling man dressed in black. A kindred spirit, clearly. Since I'd spied a small room opening out of the main reception area, I decided to take a break from the schmoozing and find somewhere I could sit down for a bit and think happy thoughts about Ben.

The room was cosy and secluded, so I wasn't surprised to find that it was already occupied. Two girls and a guy were lounging together on the sofa and all looked at me through narrowed eyes as I plumped down on the nearest chair with a sigh of relief. Not that I cared – I'd spotted a magazine rack tucked against the wall, pulled out a newspaper and settled down for a bit of peace and quiet. Rock 'n' roll!

And speaking of rock 'n' roll . . . didn't I know that

guy from somewhere? The girls looked familiar too, but that was because they were identikit arm-candy types, all legs and boobs and long glossy hair. One was a brunette and one was blonde, but even so everything about them was entirely interchangeable, from their false eyelashes to their falsetto squeals of amusement. But the bloke they were with . . . I peeped surreptitiously over the edge of my paper. He was wearing a shiny purplish blazer over a tight black shirt and jeans and had a discontented face that was nonetheless quite good-looking in a snub, puppyish sort of way. To my embarrassment, he had seen me looking at him and flashed me a smile. The smile seemed familiar too – all dimples and twinkles and insincerity – but it was only when the light caught his pink nose-stud that I realized who it was. *Gimme gold*, he'd crooned to an army of screaming thirteen-year-olds, *and I'll lose it, gimme fame, I'll abuse it, but gimme lurrrve and I won't ask for nothin' m-o-o-o-re.* Freddie Lions, in the flesh.

I buried my head in the paper again. I wouldn't have thought this sort of party was his scene but, being an ex-stage-school brat himself, his agent or record company or whoever had probably told him the Harlequin Trust would be great PR. It would make quite a touching Christmas documentary, I supposed – Freddie Lions teaching the orphans of the Third World how to spin cartwheels and warble a chorus about angel-faced girls with stars in their hearts and scars in their eyes or whatever it was. God, if Katie could see me now! I stopped trying to read about the latest tube strikes and began eavesdropping in earnest.

Not that the conversation was particularly interest-

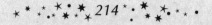

ing. From what I could make out, the two girls were called Precious and Poppet, though this was confused by Freddie saying things like, 'Poppet, precious, be a love and top up me glass, would ya?' or, 'Precious, my poppet, my poppet, how's about lighting a fag for your favourite boy?' Then everyone would giggle uproariously until the girls spilt champagne all over their cleavages. It occurred to me that Precious 'n' Poppet were exactly how Vicky 'n' Meera would be if they were four or five years older and had the looks of playboy bunnies.

After a bit more squealing and slurping, the conversation turned to those 'bloody paps'. Apparently Freddie had been trailed to the party by a couple of paparazzi on motorbikes. There was a photographer from *Stellar!* and a few society columnists at tonight's party, but Freddie was adamant he didn't want any photos taken except for the official one when he presented Dame Tilda with his cheque for the kiddies. 'And whoever it is had better make bloody sure he takes it from the proper angle. There was a picture in the *Comet* yesterday that made me look like effing Miss Piggy. Double chin an' all.' Cue vehement denials and cries of sympathy and outrage. 'Makes me wanter sue the bastards. "Defamation of looks" or somethin'. No, really I do.' He brooded over his cigarette for a while, then slurped some more booze. 'So wotcha think then, Peaches?'

It took a moment or two for me to realize that he was talking to me, and not to another Precious/Poppet clone who'd somehow appeared on the scene. 'What do I think about what?' I said uncertainly. Precious and Poppet were staring at me with murder in their eyes.

'Me, Peaches, *me*. Is this the face of a twenny-two-year-old pop idol in his prime?' He showed me his profile.

'Uh . . .'

'Or is it the face of some poor miserable sod who's bin worked like a dog for the past five years by them heartless bastards in management? Could it be the face of someone driven to the limit, the *limit* of their endurance, by a bunch of smug gits in suits who ponce around tellin' him what to do and how to do it twenty-four bloody hours a day, three hundred and sixty-five sodding days a year? Well, is it?' He seemed genuinely upset. 'Tell it to me straight now, Peaches.'

'Well,' I said cautiously, 'people say every face tells a story. And, at the end of the day, your, er, story is a very successful one.'

Freddie looked at me and nodded slowly. I even thought I saw a tear in his eye. 'Too right, Peaches. You know what, you're a luvvly girl. A very clever, very *genuine* girl. It's a rare bird, you are.' He downed another glass of champagne and belched loudly.

It was then that Milton appeared at the entrance to the room. His face was greenish-white and even more haunted-looking than normal and his eyes glittered feverishly. 'Octavia, you've got to come *now*.'

I got up in a panic. 'Whatever's happened? Has there been an accident? Is somebody ill?'

'Much worse.' He gave me the look of someone who'd just stared into the jaws of hell. 'My mother's here.'

Back in the main room there wasn't, as yet, blood on the parquet, but I could sense a cold wind blowing through the air. The dull roar of party conversation had faded to an expectant hum, the guests breaking out in a rash of raised eyebrows and discreetly craned necks as the news spread. I could see India explaining her version of the situation to Seth, then looking from Lola to Mum to Lola again with undisguised glee. The lady herself was, of course, magnificently oblivious to the effect of her entrance and was being introduced to Dame Tilda by the guy she'd come in with. I guessed he was the holistic guru Bud had told us about: a dapper, dark little man with flowing henna-tinted locks and dressed in a white linen suit. As for Lola, her face was heavily made up with glittering cosmetics, her foxy hair and bronzed bosom were both stacked perilously high, and she was resplendent in a midnight-blue catsuit in crushed velvet. The overall effect was more Black Widow than Wronged Wife, but she'd accessorized it with a smile of noble suffering.

Meanwhile, the Husband Snatcher and Love Rat were standing together at the far end of the room. It was perhaps the first time I'd ever seen any family resemblance between Bud and Milton, but now the expression of horror on their faces was one and the same. My mother was managing somewhat better, having had more practice at the art of Faking It in the course of her career. Her cheeks were a little pale and she was perhaps clutching her glass with unnecessary force, but she was chatting away to her neighbour as if she didn't have a care in the world. Since Milton and Bud had both lost the power of speech, let alone action, I decided to give the family a prod in the right direction. 'Do you think that maybe we should, er, be going soon?'

'Why ever do you say that?' My mother was wearing her battle smile. 'Aren't you enjoying yourself?'

'Oh yes . . . but it is a school night,' I said lamely. Then I lowered my voice and glanced in Lola's direction. 'I just thought it might be a good idea to leave now in case there's a, you know, er, scene.'

Lady Jane drew herself up and spoke in a clear, carrying voice. 'Don't be silly, darling. I don't see there's any reason to leave now. We're having a lovely time and we have *every right* to be here and enjoy ourselves.' She looked round the room defiantly. 'And anyway, Dame Tilda hasn't given her speech yet.'

Great. I could see we were going to be stuck here till the bitter end, Lola and Lady Jane exchanging death stares across the potted ferns until the last drop of passion-fruit Martini had been drunk. I looked at my watch and could hardly believe that we'd only been at the party for just over an hour and a half. It felt like a lifetime. After another five minutes or so of dithering, I decided that if Mum really wanted to slog it out over the sweet-chilli clams, that was up to her, but I wasn't going to hang around to cheer from the sidelines. I'd take a break from the party and go for a wander round the rest of the building instead.

So I set off through the crowd, determinedly avoiding anyone who looked like they wanted to engage me in conversation. Milton, I think, had had the same idea but was collared by his mother before he could get to the door. 'Oh sweet Lord – there's my own poor baby!' I heard Lola exclaim to the room as I slipped out. Milton gave a faint, despairing squawk as she clasped him to her bosom. 'Come to Mommy, precious boy!' Served the little toerag right.

The Jericho Club was a good place for exploring: fireplaces big enough to roast a buffalo on, oil paintings of nineteenth-century army officers with curly gilt frames, dark unexpected passageways, a cavernous central foyer and a grand central staircase leading to more club rooms upstairs. I wandered around downstairs for a while, but the sweep of the stairs looked rather inviting, and I set off up them feeling a bit like a character from a Victorian melodrama, imagining the swish of one of Lady Jane's hooped skirts trailing behind me. A couple of guests were smoking and gossiping at the foot of the stairs, but neither they nor the majestic flunkeys padding about in the shadows paid me any attention.

When I reached the top of the stairs I found myself in a long wood-panelled gallery. The first door opened to a library, crammed with book-lined shelves, stacks of magazines and deep-buttoned leather sofas. It looked quite inviting but was already occupied by a couple of producer types, who had deserted the party downstairs in favour of an impromptu seminar on the Belgian tax-shelter for film investment. I made a hasty exit and tried the next door, which led into a deserted games room filled with green baize-covered tables laid out for backgammon and bridge and the like. The final door was marked 'Smoking Room', but the room behind it was dimly lit, warm and smoke-free. Perfect. Then I heard a groan from the corner.

'Hello, is, er, anybody there?' I asked, squinting into the shadows. I was just thinking I'd imagined it when I heard a muffled sob from behind the back of an armchair.

'Nobody's here, that's who – nobody.' Snivel. 'A nobody man sittin' in his nobody land.'

'Nowhere,' I said automatically.

'What?' said the voice from behind the chair, somewhat peevishly.

'Not nobody – nowhere. As in, "He's a real nowhere man, sitting in his nowhere land." If you're quoting the Beatles song, that is . . .' I trailed off, realizing that now was probably not the best time to nit-pick over a song lyric. Here, clearly, was a soul in pain. 'Sorry. I'll, um, leave you in peace.' I began to back out the door.

'No – don't go.' A snuffly hiccup and then the chair turned round. There, clutching a magnum of champagne to his chest, his usually perky face awash with alcohol and self-pity, was Freddie Lions. He looked at me tearily. 'From the first moment I seen you, I could see you was a kind girl. A luvvly, *genuine* girl. The kinda girl who tells it to you straight.' He took a swig at the bottle. 'Not like them bloodsucking hellcats downstairs. They're only after one fing, you know. Just like them vampire leeches in management.' Hiccup. 'Ev'run in my life is out to bleed me dry, and I'm tellin' you, Peaches, I just can't take it no more.'

'Oh dear.' I was tempted to make a run for it but felt I couldn't just leave him in this state. Instead, I hovered uncertainly by the door.

'Nobody tells you. Nobody warns you.' Freddie had his head in his hands now and was swaying gently.

'Nobody warns you about what?'

He fixed me with a bloodshot eye. 'The Price of

Genius, that's what.' He took another swig. 'Think about it, Peaches. The Dutch geezer what painted them sunflowers. Elvis. Jesus bloody Christ . . . what did they all have in common?'

'Er . . .'

'Genius. First they got geniused and then they got famous. And then,' he said darkly, 'they all got royally screwed.'

There didn't seem to be much to say to this but the poor guy was obviously in a bad way. I came and sat down in the chair opposite.

'Now look,' I said firmly, 'it must be very difficult, working all this time without a proper holiday and with all these people trying to run your life for you. But think of your fans. They're not bloodsucking. Think of all the people you make happy through your music. Think of all the, er, poor Third-World orphans you're going to help, with the cheque you're presenting tonight.'

He looked up and there was a flicker of hope in his eye. I warmed to my theme. 'Music is a language in which you speak to the hearts of, well, millions. These people might not know what you suffer, but –' dramatic pause '– they can still share your pain. They feel your joy. As long as you have your music, *you will never be alone.*'

Freddie was staring at me open-mouthed. I felt the most awful fraud – if Ben could hear me now! – but managed to keep my face appropriately solemn. I gave him a moment for it all to sink in, then got up from my chair. 'Now, how about we go downstairs and get back to the party? It must be nearly time to give your cheque to Dame Tilda.'

Freddie wobbled to his feet. He looked a bit of a state, what with his mussed-up hair and his shirt half-undone and his face all blotchy, but at least the sobs and the hiccups were over. In a rare burst of efficiency, I collected his nearly empty magnum of champagne and cigarette packet on our way out. It seemed a shame to leave the room in a mess, after all. Then I opened the door and we stepped out into the corridor together –

– where there was a snap and whirr and what felt like the flash of a dozen cameras.

For a split second it didn't register. We were at a party and someone was taking a photograph. So far, so normal. But my heart had begun to pound so hard it felt as if it were about to burst out through my ears, and the sick, cold feeling in the pit of my stomach was now creeping up my entire body. Oh my God oh my God oh my God – I had just been photographed sneaking out of a private room with *Freddie Lions*. I couldn't move. My free hand had automatically gone up to shield my face and I was dimly aware of Freddie cursing behind me; the next moment he made a grab at the photographer – as it turned out, there was only one – who twisted out of his grasp with ease and made off down the stairs. Freddie fell to the floor and didn't get up. He just lay there with his hands over his head, groaning. I think at that point I shouted for help – for security, for my mother, anyone – and the door to the reading room opened and the two producers who'd been plotting inside came out to see what all the noise was about. Freddie was still slumped on the floor, I was still rooted to the spot (champagne bottle clutched to my chest), and the paparazzo was already halfway down the stairs.

This all takes time to describe but in reality it happened very quickly, a matter of seconds. 'Oh Christ, I think I'm gonna puke,' said Freddie. There was a retching sound.

I finally regained my senses and ran to the side of the gallery overlooking the foyer. Shouldn't Freddie have some minders on hand somewhere? Where had the photographer gone? Below, the rest of the party-goers were swarming into the hallway in an excited, expectant sort of way. I could hear shouting . . . somebody must have called security . . . there was Bud, trying to elbow his way to the front of the crowd . . . Something – call it sixth sense – made me turn round and it was then that I saw India, standing in the shadows a little way down the corridor. She had a funny little smile on her face. A triumphant sort of smile. But I didn't have much time to take this in, because at that moment I saw what the disturbance downstairs was about. My mother and Lola were standing nose to nose in the hall, voices raised.

'That's right – too cheap to find your own man so you had to steal mine!'

'Everyone knows you made his life a misery! You drove him away!'

'Back-stabbing little trollop!'

'Washed-up old croc!'

'Why you—'

Then they lunged at each other. I think Lola made the first move – she definitely had her hands outstretched for Mum's throat – but Lady Jane wasn't far behind. She got a good hank of Lola's hair in her fist, at any rate. And God knows what would have happened next if there hadn't been the most almighty crash as

Freddie, who'd hauled himself to his feet using the post at the top of the stairs, missed his footing and tumbled down the entire flight. All of which, of course, was accompanied by a flash and whirr and self-satisfied click from the cameras.

I don't really have the heart to go over the rest of that evening. To be honest, a lot of it remains a blur and I think it's probably better that way. I have brief, horrible flashes of lucidity: of security finally arriving and being unable to decide whether their priority was to separate Mum and Lola or chase off the paparazzo . . . of Precious – or it could have been Poppet – collapsing in a faint and one of the Tempest executives starting to give her mouth-to-mouth . . . of Daisy from *Stellar!* attempting to give Freddie Lions the same before the paramedics dragged her off and took Freddie to hospital in an ambulance . . . of Milton being sick into a potted fern . . . of Dame Tilda loudly threatening to sue the management, and the management loudly threatening to sue Dame Tilda . . . of the Duchess of Teasedale threatening to sue everyone . . . and, finally, of the four of us going home in the car, my mother's face carved from ice, her eyes two chips of burning coal, Bud and Milton both looking like extras from *Night of the Living Dead*. As for me, I got a fit of the giggles. It was hysteria, I guess, but for the whole of the journey back and even when I eventually tumbled into bed I kept breaking out in little hiccuping bursts of laughter.

I wasn't laughing in the morning.

I was woken up at about seven o'clock by someone

persistently leaning on our doorbell. The street outside my window was already seething with journalists, plus a couple of harassed police officers trying to clear the road. Several of our well-heeled neighbours were out in force, merrily chatting away to the nearest tabloid hack with a Dictaphone. I could see a TV camera crew and a little knot of people waving placards. One of the placards was heart-shaped and read, 'Marry Me, Lady Jane.' Another one said, 'Freddie is MINE so BACK OFF, bitch!' I collapsed back into bed with a groan.

I felt like staying in bed for the rest of the day, with the curtains closed and the lights off. Make that the rest of my life. But all too soon there was a knock on my door. It was Euphoria, looking even more dishevelled than usual. Presumably she'd had to fight her way through the mob outside. She informed me grimly that my presence was required in the kitchen.

The rest of the family were already there, along with the morning papers. Between the society journalists who'd been invited to cover the party and the paparazzo who certainly hadn't, the Clairbrook-Cleeve-Carnabys had made every one. Front page on all the tabloids, of course, but even the broadsheets had found room for a pithy line or three on 'High Drama at Dame's Do'.

It hadn't been so long ago that we'd all been grouped round this same table, exclaiming over the *Stellar!* article and drinking champagne. Now, instead of soft-focus shots of Lady Jane nibbling cookies in her negligee, we were looking at my wild-eyed mother about to tear a rival's hair out in a public brawl. Instead of Occy the doe-eyed ingénue there was Occy the teenage floozy, emerging from a darkened room with a trashed pop idol leering over her shoulder.

It really was the most terrible picture. I was clutching the bottle of booze and Freddie's packet of fags to my chest and had this awful expression on my face – my mouth was half-open and because the photograph was slightly out of focus I looked completely wasted. Not only that, but my dress had got a bit rucked-up from when I'd been sitting, so it appeared a lot shorter and, well, more tarty than it actually was. Freddie, of course, really *had* been wasted and, what with his shirt half-undone and his face all blotchy, the whole set-up looked spectacularly sordid. A *Comet* exclusive, no less.

All in all, the tabloids were spoilt for choice. Some had made Lady Jane's fight with Lola the highlight of their day; others gave pride of place to grainy photographs of Freddie being taken into the ambulance (it turned out that he'd only sprained his ankle, but the fall combined with the booze had knocked him out for a bit). Similarly, the headlines were either of the 'TV Babes in Brawl' sort or variations on the theme of 'Lions Hits Self-Destruct'. Even Bud didn't escape this time: most papers carried a photo of the 'high-flying film executive' at the heart of Mum and Lola's 'tug-of-love shame'. They managed to make him look like an ageing poster-boy for Hitler Youth.

As for me . . . even though the *Comet* was the only paper to show that awful photo, the 'love-struck teen' seen with Freddie before the accident still got a dishonourable mention in all the rest. I wondered how much the *Comet* had paid the paparazzo for the picture. I also wondered how he'd got into the Jericho Club in the first place and how he'd been able to make his get-away . . . It was then that I remembered India lurking in the shadows of the corridor and the little smile on her face. I didn't actually believe that she could somehow have arranged for a paparazzo to crash the party just on the off-chance that I'd get myself into a compromising position with Freddie Lions. However, I did wonder if she'd snuck after Freddie or me on a whim and then given the lucky photographer a nudge in the right direction. Certainly, there were no prizes for guessing the identity of my so-called 'close friend' who'd been so helpful to the journalist from the *Comet*.

For who was 'the sultry schoolgirl spotted enjoying an intimate moment with Freddie moments before his near-tragic fall'? The *Comet* knew. 'She might only be sweet sixteen, but posh totty Octavia Clairbrook-Cleeve ("Occy" to her friends) is already making waves on the party circuit. Occy claims to shun the spotlight but has become a familiar face in celeb magazines *Stellar!* and the *Prattler* after romping through a stormy but short-lived relationship with bad boy Alexis Withers (son of rock star Sir Rich and brother of actress India). Like mother, like daughter? Well, maybe. A close friend tells us that Occy is struggling to adjust to her showbiz mum's tempestuous personal life and in fact her encounter with Freddie might even have been a mis-guided cry for help . . .' There followed a lurid analysis of my mother's 'tempestuous personal life', followed by three pages of speculation on the mental and physical health of 'troubled' star Freddie Lions – or 'Too Much Too Young?' as those caring folks at the *Comet* put it.

For a long while we all just sat there, staring at the

papers, too depressed to say or do anything. It was a horrible feeling to be under siege in our own home: the phone had to be taken off the hook, all the curtains had to be kept drawn and people still kept pressing the bell on the front door and knocking on the windows. Even in the kitchen, which is at the back of the house, we had to keep the blinds down in case of long-lens cameras over the garden wall. I thought back to the fuss when Mum's relationship with Bud first hit the news-stands – what a storm in a teacup it seemed now! I had never seen my mother look so depressed; she had this blank, numb expression on her face and seemed past the power of speech. Bud, however, was very angry. Up until now I'd always thought of him as Captain America, all peachy-keen positivity and sunny delight. Now his face had hardened and he looked older and sterner, almost intimidating.

Somewhat to my surprise, he seemed most upset on my behalf. 'It makes me sick to my stomach that those . . . those reptile scum can do this to an innocent young girl of sixteen. At least Helena and Lola and Freddie are all adults – professionals – who have chosen to be in the public eye. Octavia's a civilian. A bystander! A schoolgirl, for Pete's sake! It's an outrage.'

'You know what really gets me?' I said. 'If I'd left Freddie to drink himself into a stupor then I wouldn't be in this mess. This all happened because I actually felt *sorry* for that stupid boozing idiot . . . Oh God, if only I hadn't been clutching that bottle!'

'If only I'd been able to talk to Lola before she started saying those terrible things—'

'If only his shirt had been properly buttoned—'

'This is all my fault,' said my mother. 'Entirely my fault. What was I *thinking* to let Lola get to me like that? She engineered the whole thing. My reputation will never be able to recover from this. And I'll never, ever be able to forgive myself for dragging the rest of the family down with me.' She put her head in her hands. 'This is the end. The end of *everything*.'

'Absolute rubbish!' said Euphoria, who'd begun to bustle about making coffee. 'Of course you'll recover from this. Every situation can be turned to an advantage, you know, as long as the right angle can be found. And don't forget, there's always the legal route to be considered, especially with regard to those disgusting insinuations in the *Comet*. Now, I would suggest—' But at this point I got up and left the kitchen. I hadn't the heart to go through all this again.

Milton followed me into the hall. He looked even paler and thinner and more shadowy than usual. 'Uh, Octavia . . .'

'What?'

'I'm sorry about last night.'

'It's not your fault.' I started to go up the stairs.

'I know, but . . . Mom . . . she always . . . do you think they'll be able to get through this? Dad and Helena I mean?'

'They'll work something out.'

'Yeah.' His face looked a bit wobbly. Then he closed his eyes and started muttering to himself:

*'Farewell happy fields
Where Joy forever dwells: hail horrors, hail
Infernal world.'*

Oh help, if Milton was about to have another break-down . . .

'Octavia?'

'Yes?'

'You and this Lions guy. When do we get to hear what *really* happened between you two?'

'Drop dead, Milton.'

I went up to my room and shut the door. Me and Freddie Lions. Freddie Lions and me. And Ben. Me and Ben. What was Ben thinking about me now?

I turned on my mobile and found that I had about twenty missed calls. Most of these were from Dad, there was a brief message from Viv ('Call me when you're ready, and only if you want to.') and the rest were from various people at school, all doubtless gagging for an exclusive on My Night of Shame with Freddie Lions. There was nothing from Ben. Hail Infernal World just about summed it up.

I was steeling myself to give Ben a ring when my phone started going off: it was Dad again. I could tell he was trying very hard to keep calm, but there was a catch in his voice.

'Octavia, thank God. How are you? How is poor Helena? I came round as soon as I heard but the whole street is under siege and I thought me turning up might only make things worse . . . Shall I come over now? Can we get you out of there somehow? My darling girl—'

'Dad, wait, you do know that picture of Freddie and me – it wasn't – I wouldn't—'

'Of course I know you wouldn't, sweetheart.' Dad was indignant. 'I have absolute faith in your judgement

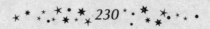

as well as your strength of character. But you know what,' he added, his voice very firm, 'even if you *had* been romping with Freddie Lions in your underwear it would still have been nobody's business but yours. These gutter journalists get away with absolute murder. Michael's made it very clear that we don't have to take this lying down and I'm sure if Lions has got any sense at all he's speaking to his lawyers at this very moment.'

In the end we decided that Dad would come over in the evening, when the mob outside should hopefully have thinned out a bit and after Mum had had more of a chance to calm down. Like Euphoria, he was full of practical encouragement about how best to handle the situation, but even as I was saying 'Yes', 'No' and 'You're so right', part of me was thinking there wasn't much point to all this talk, that it was already too late for rescue. Both mother and daughter were damaged goods.

I had the beginnings of a headache and was feeling slightly feverish, like I was coming down with something. I couldn't be bothered to get dressed and crawled back under my duvet instead; although I'd tried my hardest not to, I began to imagine the sorts of things the people I knew would be saying about me, and the kind of things they were saying to Ben. I half-wondered if Ben had decided to skip school rather than face the uproar at Jethro Park. Not that it would be like the Darlings, who'd manage to be envious and despising all at once and always in the most poisonously sweet sort of way, but it would still be bad. Poor Ben – I could just imagine how Jack would love winding him up, the gloating of Tom and Dan and the rest, Vicky 'n' Meera's greedy smiles and twitching noses . . . Ugh. I couldn't go back and face them, I just *couldn't*. After this was over – *if* it was ever over – I'd tell Mum I wanted to move to a different school. A nice country boarding school, maybe. In Australia. No, make that Outer Mongolia.

On balance, though, I didn't think Ben was the type to skulk about at home or book a flight to Mongolia, so I tried calling his mobile on school-timetable-friendly slots: registration, morning break, lunchtime and after-noon break. His phone was on but he didn't pick up. I felt that if I could just see him, explain everything face to face, I could somehow make it right, but there was no way of leaving the house without facing the cameras again. I was trapped. We all were. It was one of the longest, dullest and most depressing days of my life.

At half past five, Ben finally answered his phone.

'Hi.'

'Oh – hello. Hi. Uh – it's me, by the way,' I added inadequately. I was overwhelmed with relief at having got through to him at last but now I didn't know how or where to begin. He'd only said one word but I felt how distant he sounded. Stiff. My palms began to sweat. 'I've been trying to call you—'

'Yeah . . . How are you?' It was like he was talking to a stranger.

'Well, you know . . . pretty dreadful, actually.' I tried to laugh but it came out as a croak. 'Ben, I – I don't know what to say. I'm sorry. It was all the most horrible, horrendous mistake, you've got to believe me. I can just imagine what everyone's been saying but . . . Please. You *do* believe me, don't you?'

There was a long silence. 'And what is it that you want me to believe, exactly?'

'That I wasn't, er, you know, doing anything with Freddie.' I was so red with embarrassment it was probably just as well he couldn't see me. 'We were just, like, talking, and then we left the room and there was a photographer waiting . . . I only stayed there because Freddie was upset, you see.'

'Upset?'

'Yeah, he's been working really hard and he thinks his management are ripping him off . . .'

'Poor Freddie.'

'Yes. No, I mean. He's an idiot. He was so drunk he didn't know who he was talking to—'

'The thing is, Octavia, right now *I* don't really know who I'm talking to.' He was still speaking in that cool, formal voice, but now I could sense the anger just below the surface, ready to snap. 'Which is it today? The party animal? The reluctant princess? Or the girl next door? '

I was on the edge of tears. 'Please, Ben, you've got to believe me. You *do* know me. I'm not any different to how I was in school yesterday. Come on – you know how the media works, you know how easy it is for people to twist things. This isn't just about trust, it's common *sense*.'

'What the hell do you mean, it's not about trust?' He was half-shouting. 'You didn't even tell me you were going to that party. All day in school you sat there letting me think it was some stuffy corporate event you were being dragged along to . . . then the next morning, we're eating breakfast and my *mother* opens up the paper and says, "Goodness me, dear, isn't this one of your friends?"' Ben gave a short, angry laugh. 'What am I supposed to think?'

'You're not thinking at all!' Now exasperation had got the better of me. 'Do you honestly believe that I would go to a drinks party with my mother and step-father and a handful of journalists and then toddle off halfway through to have a quickie with some lunatic pop star?'

He was quiet for a while. I had a sudden, piercingly vivid image of him running his hands through his hair, the brightness of his eyes narrowed in concentration. 'No,' he said at last. 'No, I don't.'

I let out a huge sigh of relief. But his next words set my heart juddering all over again.

'It's not just about you and Freddie though. This mess with the *Comet* and everything – India – your mother – well, can you really, truly put your hand on your heart and say that after this is all over there won't be something else like it?' He waited, but I was silent now. 'You see? There'll always be some new showbizzy feud or fuss you'll get mixed up in . . . and there'll be other Indias and Freddies and Lolas, too. It's not your fault. It's just the way things are.'

'So you're saying you won't be able to cope with it, is that it?' It nearly killed me, but I managed to keep my voice steady.

'I'm saying that I won't ever be able to understand it. Not the way you do and not in the way you want me to, either. I'm sorry.' And he put the phone down.

For a few moments I just sat there, frozen. Then I began to cry. It was suddenly all too much, so I rolled around on the bed and pounded the pillows, swore a lot, screamed a bit, hurled my mobile across the room and

234

wailed some more. I am not proud of this, but it made me feel better. It also brought my mother bursting in through the door, Bud and Milton hot on her heels.

'Darling! Please – we can get through this! It's not that bad! Dear God, the poor girl's hysterical—'

'Waaaah! Waaaah!' I howled, pounding the pillow.

'She needs sedating,' said Milton. 'She could turn violent at any moment. You know, I have some diazepam in my room—'

'I think maybe we should try the English remedy first,' said Bud. 'Come on, son, let's go brew us up some tea.' He shot out a brawny arm and forcibly escorted Milton from the room. My mother came and sat next to me on the bed, wringing her hands.

'It just kills me to see you like this, darling. Tell me what's wrong. Please. I'll make everything better, I promise – sweetheart, talk to me—'

'There's no point to anything – my life is over – hic – and everyone I've ever known will hate me and my boyfriend's just dumped me – hic – and it's all my fault anyway and I'll probably have to be in hiding for the rest of my life,' I wailed. Then I chucked one of my shoes at the window, closely followed by two magazines and a hairbrush.

Lady Jane had at least picked up on one aspect of my rant. 'Boyfriend?' she asked, a gleam in her eye.

'Not any more. Not after Freddie. I'm going to be single forever and ever and nobody will ever love me again. Waaaah!' Like I said, not a performance to be proud of.

'My poor baby.' You could see she was struggling to balance her delight at the revelation that I had found

myself a boyfriend at last, and consternation that it all seemed to be over before the celebrations could begin. 'What a terrible thing. But is it *absolutely definite* that it's all over? Did you get to explain what happened? Surely once this boy has had a chance to calm down he'll realize that it was just a silly misunderstanding.'

'Oh, he accepts nothing happened with Freddie,' I said bitterly. 'But he still doesn't trust me. Or understand me. And he made it very clear he doesn't much want to.'

'Then,' said my mother sternly, 'I'm afraid to say, he doesn't sound worth it. Wasn't that the problem with the people at your old school? That they didn't make any effort to understand where you were coming from and that you couldn't be yourself with them? You deserve better than that, sweetheart.'

'Ben is *totally* different from the Darlings.' I was suddenly feeling very defensive. 'It's mostly my fault, anyhow. I wasn't straight with him and I handled everything the wrong way – India, my thing with her brother, being in that stupid magazine . . . he hates all that stuff. And now he hates me.' I snuffled a bit but at least the tantrum was over. 'All that time, I was so paranoid India was going to split us up somehow and wreck my life . . . ironic, really. I seem to have managed it perfectly well on my own.'

'Stop it. You haven't wrecked anything and it *most certainly* is not your fault.' My mother had been looking worn out and defeated all day, but now she was sitting up straight and wearing her battle smile again. 'It is time,' she announced, 'for this family to stop feeling sorry for itself and to put an end to this nonsense once and for all. The Clairbrook-Cleeve-Carnabys may be down, but they sure as hell aren't out.'

'Hear! hear!' said Bud, who had just appeared at the door with a tray of tea things. Behind him was Milton, carrying the chocolate biscuits, and behind Milton was Dad. I got up and wrapped my arms around him and he held me tight and I felt for the first time that day that maybe, just maybe, everything was going to be all right.

Not that life immediately burst into bloom, since the next day I came down with an evil cold which swiftly morphed into flu: hot and cold shakes, a pounding headache and a chronic inability to stay awake and focused for more than half an hour at a stretch. Mum didn't call it the flu though; as far as she was concerned, it was post-traumatic stress disorder and she was all for getting in the psychologists and the therapists and maybe a policeman or two, so we could sue for damages. She had drawn up a hit list of Freddie Lions, India Withers, Ben Harper, the editor of the *Comet* and any-one else who'd been mean to her daughter over the past month, and was in constant consultation with Malcolm as to the best way to drag them through the courts. It seemed to cheer her up.

I stayed in bed for the next three days. It was almost nice being ill; I lounged around eating nothing but soup and ice cream, watched cartoons and felt far too woozy to worry about things. As I began to recover, however, I did get regular updates on the situation. Although the house was still being staked out by the press, the main onslaught seemed to be over and now Euphoria and Mum were once again deciding whether to go for broke and put Lady Jane's side of the story to every newspaper, chat show and magazine on offer, or to concentrate on a couple of high-impact 'exclusives'. Bud was taking time off from work to offer moral support, and, presumably, keep the heat off Tempest. There had been several long calls to the producers of *Lady Jane*, and even longer calls to the folks at the *Gone With the Wind* miniseries. A charm-offensive trip to the States was planned, 'But not until poor Octavia's recovered from her ordeal.' Malcolm was in talks with Freddie's lawyers, who were considering launching a legal action against the *Comet* for defamation of character. Most surprising of all, though, was that nothing more had been seen or heard of Lola since the fateful showdown on Tuesday night. Everyone had assumed she'd be out there the moment the story broke, all heart and soul and crocodile tears, telling the world how she'd been driven to the brink by Bud and Helena's treachery and how the back-stabbing little trollop 'had it coming'. Now it appeared that people didn't even know if she was back in America or not. Bud and Mum weren't sure whether to be relieved about this or nervous.

Amongst our daily bombardment of letters, phone messages and emails was an envelope addressed to me from Grandpa Cleeve. Mum didn't want me to open it – 'The old goat's probably stuffed it with anthrax.' – but I read it anyway. It wasn't a proper letter but a pamphlet from his League for the Promotion of Christian Decency; a glossy brochure putting teenage debauchery at the root of every evil from nuclear proliferation to the decline of Latin in schools. Like they say, it's the thought that counts.

On Sunday evening I was feeling so much better that I set up camp in the drawing room with my duvet, the TV and a mound of buttered toast. I had a nice long chat with Viv who, though she was obviously dying to know the full story, understood that I wasn't yet up to reliving the whole debacle. For someone who's so blunt, Viv can be incredibly tactful. Instead, we chatted about unimportant, general things and she gave me a quick rundown on the school-work I'd missed. Towards the end of the conversation she mentioned in passing that she 'didn't think Ben was doing too well . . .'

'Glowering a lot, is he?'

'He's had a rough week.'

'Yeah, well, he's not the only one.'

'Maybe—'

'Don't, Viv. Don't start with the "maybes" and the "what ifs". It's less painful if I just accept things the way they are. I haven't got the energy for anything else right now.'

I knew Viv must be flicking her hair about and rolling her eyes down the other end of the phone, but she let it drop. Then she asked me when I was coming back to school. I didn't have the guts to say that I was thinking of, er, never, but muttered something about 'seeing what my temperature was like on Monday'. I don't think I fooled her though. 'Remember that you've got friends waiting for you. So have a little faith, OK?' she said, just before hanging up.

Five minutes later she phoned back again. 'Are you watching TV?'

'Yeah, there's this really cute documentary about penguins—'

'Switch to Channel Four.'

I pressed the remote. Four was showing *Symposium*, an arts and current affairs review that had recently been launched on Sunday evenings. 'Culturelite' as Dad calls it, with celebrity guests and a live band in the studio as well as the occasional government minister or obscure Peruvian dance group. Right now the host, a silver-haired yet improbably youthful-looking smoothie named Angus McMillan, was addressing the camera in his most velvety manner.

'Ever since Drake Montague announced he was going to spend six months farming a paddy-field in Japan as research for his role in *Warriors in the Mist*, Hollywood has seen an explosion in popularity of method acting in its most radical form. A serious artistic enterprise or just another publicity stunt? Well, this evening we'll be hearing from rising star India Withers, who was sent to attend a run-down inner-city comprehensive in preparation for her role in a new film by Jed Mosley. As the following film clip shows, what began as an exercise in character acting has turned into a personal voyage of discovery, as a young girl born into a life of privilege is forced to confront the realities of life in modern Britain's underclass.'

'Viv? I'll call you back.' I put the phone down abruptly and turned up the volume on the TV, where the scene had changed to what looked like an empty warehouse. India was lounging gracefully on a packing crate, looking every inch the kooky yet cool actress chick in an oversize corduroy cap, hooped earrings and a sort of kimono-over-skinny-jeans combo.

'. . . I wouldn't say there's much, like, overt

violence,' she was saying, 'it's more this atmosphere of, you know, intimidation. Everything's always so chaotic. So *defeatist*. I mean, I realize the teachers do their best, they really do, and I have a lot of admiration for them, but it's a constant struggle, you know?'

Somebody muttered something indistinguishable from off-camera.

'I guess you just have to keep your head down, take one day at a time . . . at the end of the day, I'm a survivor. But a lot of these kids give up before they've even begun. I mean, if you tell a kid he's a failure enough times, eventually he'll believe it, right? We like to think we live in this, you know, totally progressive society, but for a lot of people in our country, modern Britain is a harsh and ugly place.' Soulful smirk. 'The tragedy is, nobody wants to listen to their story.'

The clip ended and we were back to Angus in his studio. After a suitably statesmanlike pause, he turned to address the camera. 'We can't, of course, name the school which India has been attending, though some might argue that "naming and shaming" is exactly what institutions like this need. However, Ms Withers's experience has raised some serious questions as to why our education system is failing the very people who need it most—'

It was at this point that I switched the television off. I couldn't bear to watch any more, but when I tried to phone Viv back the line was busy. Poor Jethro Park. Poor Mr Pemberton. Poor Jack-and-Vicky-and-Tom-and-Meera and all the other credulous goons who thought India Withers had arrived to sprinkle stardust on their lives. Well, now they knew: their idol was nothing but a sweet-talking, venom-dripping snake in the grass. A velociraptor in the nursery. I'd thought I'd feel some satisfaction at being proved right at last, but I didn't. I just felt sad.

On Monday morning I definitely wasn't feeling well enough to go to school. No way. OK, so maybe I didn't have a temperature any more, but I still felt really rough and I was *sure* my glands were up. Come to think of it, my legs felt a little shaky. Look, just because I'd got my appetite back didn't mean I should rush into anything. I could overstrain myself. I could develop new symptoms. I could have a relapse.

My mother wasn't fooled. It seemed that her cosseting of 'poor dear Octavia' was well and truly over. She kept on saying heartless things like, 'This is your exam year, my girl,' and, 'You've missed a week of school as it is,' and, 'You've got to face the world sooner or later so you might as well get it over with.' Although our house was no longer under siege, she informed me that she'd organized for a car to take me to school in time for morning break and pick me up at the end of the day; if I wanted, she could also arrange for me to have a 'minder' to chase any paparazzi away. Oh, fantastic. I could just imagine the reaction in school if I walked into class with a Neanderthal bodyguard glowering at my shoulder. Right now, paparazzi were the least of my problems.

Just as I was saying, loudly, that I wasn't EVER going back to Jethro Park and that from now on I'd get home tuition and only venture outside in a burka, Bud knocked at my door. 'Uh, Octavia, you might want to have a listen to the breakfast news this morning.'

I groaned. What now? Had someone found a photo of me licking ice cream off Prince Richard's pecs? After exchanging a puzzled look with me, Lady Jane walked over to my desk and switched on the radio.

'. . . and in a few moments,' the newsreader was saying, 'we'll be going live to Jethro Park, the school at the centre of the controversial allegations made last night on the arts programme *Symposium* . . .'

It couldn't have taken long for news of the Reluctant Princess's television appearance to spread through her one-time schoolmates, so I should have known that it was only a matter of time before India's sin bin was 'named and shamed' by some enterprising journalist. It was still a shock to hear it on the news like this, though. I checked my watch: it was nearly quarter to nine and people would already be arriving at school. I could imagine the scene all too well: harassed teachers trying to shepherd everyone in for registration with a terse 'no comment', excitable students jostling to get their fifteen seconds of fame . . .

At least one good thing came out of it: there was no question of me going back to school that day and walking straight into the middle of yet another media scrum. Mum insisted that I stay in my room and spend the day working, but I took up the portable television from the study so I could keep an eye on events. The decline of educational standards combined with the adventures of a starlet-on-the-make proved to be an irresistible mix of politics and celebrity, with the result that Jethro Park was featured on most of the morning's news bulletins and chat shows. Members of the PTA were filmed marching up and down outside the school gates waving placards saying, 'PRIDE IN OUR KIDS, FAITH IN OUR SCHOOL.' The MP for the area promised that Serious Questions would be asked as to how 'such shameful slurs were cast on our community'. Several students were interviewed on local radio saying stuff like, 'India seemed really nice, we thought she liked it here,' and, 'I think our teachers are quite strict, yeah. We don't do drugs or anything like that.' For me, the crowning moment was seeing Vicky 'n' Meera appear on *Good Morning, London!*. They giggled a lot and played with their hair and talked about the kind of things India ate for lunch and what shoes she wore to lessons.

As for those Serious Questions . . . our headmaster made a statement to the press strongly rebutting India's allegations, citing Jethro Park's performance in the latest league tables and claiming that the board of governors had been 'grievously misled' as to the nature of Ms Withers's interest in the school. Of India or Jed or Angus McMillan there was no sign. *Good Morning, London!* tried to contact someone at Tempest to confirm whether or not they would be co-producing Mosley's film, but nobody was commenting from there either.

At about half past one, Mum sent Milton upstairs with a plate of sandwiches and a pile of vitamins for me. I was watching *Newsroom Southeast* at the time and trying to see if I could spot Ben or Viv lurking in the background of the latest dispatch from Jethro Park. A picture of India flashed up on the screen as the straight-faced newsreader addressed the question, 'Are Our Celebrities Out of Touch With Reality?' I laughed a hollow laugh.

'This is partly your fault, you know,' I told Milton,

who had sat down on the floor and begun eating my sandwiches.

'How do you work that out?' He sprinkled some vitamin tablets in a cheese and tomato sandwich and crunched them appreciatively. 'You should try some of this, Octavia. You're still very peaky. Personally, I find it quite attractive . . . but the Living Dead look isn't to everyone's taste.'

I felt a flash of anger – it was all right for Milton, he didn't *have* a life to be ruined. He didn't have friends to lose or a love life to screw up or a school to be wrecked. No, he was just on one long, happy holiday where he got to lounge around in a darkened room and contemplate the futility of existence all day. As far as nervous breakdowns go, Milton seemed to be having a pretty cushy time of it.

'Listen, boy genius, don't think I've forgotten about your little bit of industrial espionage. I know how you've been snooping around in your dad's papers so you could dish India the dirt on the Tempest deal. And let's not forget *you* invited her to schmooze all the bigwigs at that God-awful cocktail party.'

'Don't worry – it's not something I'll forget in a hurry.' Milton gave the most dreadful leer. 'India was always *very* grateful.'

I shuddered. 'You know what? Sneaking around, using people to get what you want . . . you and India and Jed are all as bad as each other. Of course India'll find some way of spinning this fuss to her advantage – give her a couple of days and she'll be *wallowing* in the uproar. Jed and Tempest too. This film's going to go stratospheric.'

'I wouldn't bet on it.'

'Why not?' Milton looked knowing. In fact, he looked positively smug. Hope clutched at my heart. 'Have you been snooping again? Did Bud say something to you? Milton! Are you saying that Tempest aren't going to go ahead after all? Surely . . . I thought the deal had already been signed?'

'Tempest have been ready to sign for the last week. It's Mosley who's going to pull out,' he said calmly. 'I suspect he's been dithering for the past few days, but recent developments will have given him the final push.'

'Jed?'

He nodded.

'No way! Why would Jed turn down financial backing? This film is his baby, he's put heart and soul into the project. It would be crazy to back out now.'

'You're missing the point. As usual. It's precisely *because* it's his darling baby that he's pulled out. He got wind of Tempest's plans for the film once they agreed to co-produce.'

'Plans?'

'Yeah, they want to make it more commercial. Like having an upbeat ending. Freddie Lions on the soundtrack. Introduce some comic cockneys, cut down on the nihilism, that sort of thing.'

OK, this made a kind of sense. Casting India and courting Tempest was a smart commercial move on Jed's part, but even I could see how getting Freddie Lions on the soundtrack might be an artistic compromise too far.

'But how did he – oh.' It suddenly dawned on me.

'You found some sort of report or memo in Bud's desk! *You* warned Jed what was in store for him!'

'Poor dear Dad. After all his years with Mom he really should have learned that leaving confidential papers lying around the house is *asking* for trouble.' He smiled a slow, sepulchral smile. 'And then India introduced me to Jed at that cocktail party . . .'

I remembered the guest who looked like a chain-smoking undertaker, the one Milton had spent most of the evening talking to. It was all becoming clear. 'Milton, did you plan this from the start?' I asked him sternly. He looked thoughtful.

'India,' he said, 'is a girl of many talents. Which is why it was so disappointing when she asked me point-blank to go through my dad's files. After the build-up you'd given her I was looking forward to something a little more . . . creative. Daring.' He sighed. 'To be honest, I expected the whole double-cross challenge to be a lot more fun.'

I could only stare at him in admiration. 'God, Milton, you took quite a risk. Aren't you worried Jed'll blow your cover when he turns Tempest down? And what about poor old Bud? It's his company who have lost out, after all . . .'

Milton shrugged. 'Jed's a self-righteous, left-wing ex-journalist. He'll protect his sources. And anyway, I reckon I've saved Tempest from a sure-fire flop. Dad was against the project from the start, you know – I even found a memo "voicing his concerns" to some committee or other. So you can spare me the moral hand-wringing.'

'Wow. I wonder what happens next . . . Maybe Sir Rich will come to the rescue.'

'Maybe.'

We sat there in silence for a while. I found I was nearly as relieved to discover that Milton wasn't, after all, working for the Dark Side as I was pleased that India's latest plan for world domination had been nipped in the bud.

'Milton, I – well, thank you. I owe you an apology. I really appreciate—'

Of course he looked at me with utter contempt. 'You're sounding more like my father every day.' He thought for a moment. 'However, if it will make you feel better . . .'

'Yes?'

'The thing is, I have to go and see Mom this afternoon.'

'*Lola*? She's still in London?'

'Well, I'd hardly be nipping over the Atlantic for the afternoon, would I? She's holed up in some hotel and wants me to come over. But seeing as . . . well, the way things are at the moment, I might need you to cover for me.'

'Sure.'

'Tell them I've gone to dig up bones in a graveyard or something.'

He got to his feet and trailed mournfully out of the room.

The next day the following full-page colour advertisement appeared in several US and British newspapers:

It seemed that the trauma of Bud's desertion and sub-
sequent events had sent Lola down the Highway of
Enlightenment: a painful process of rebirth and self-
discovery that had ended in the arms of Guru Abdiel-
Jones. She was therefore retiring from showbiz to
concentrate on bringing cosmic harmony to the masses
through a course of tantric sex therapies, callisthenic
beauty treatments and something called 'transcendental
vengeance-counselling'. Apparently there was already a
six-month waiting list.

Bud and Lady Jane made all the right exclamations
when Milton told us about this: 'How wonderful for
poor Lola,' and, 'What an inspiring project,' and, 'I'm
sure it will be ever so popular,' etc., etc. But when I

heard Mum on the phone to Euphoria that afternoon she was slightly less generous. She confided that you didn't need to take a spin down the Highway of Enlightenment to realize that when it came to matters of body and soul, Lola and Abdiel-J had always spent most of their time getting down and dirty with the former. She said that she didn't doubt their little cult would be a roaring success since the two of them combined 'the business ethics of a Mafia Don with the sincerity of a snake-oil salesman'. Then she added that of course she hoped Lola would be very happy.

The fact remained, however, that Lady Jane was pretty much off the hook. Now that Lola was all set to live happily ever after as a cosmic love goddess, my mother's husband-stealing/child-snatching/hair-tearing escapades suddenly seemed much more forgivable. After all, everyone knows that the next best thing to a high-profile public feud is a high-profile public reconciliation with oodles of Personal Growth and mutual gloating about how everything's turned out for the best. Lady Jane was still planning a charm offensive in the States, but the early indications were that her popularity had actually been boosted by her recent antics. That quaint English reserve had finally been broken: here was one feisty little lady, ready to Follow Her Heart and Fight for Her Man. Way to go, girlfriend!

My own PR issues weren't quite so straightforward. It was weird – a day or two ago I thought that having my face splashed all over the *Comet* was the end of life as I knew it. Right now, however, I could see that there were worse things than being caught in a so-called compromising position with some lowlife pop star. I wasn't just

Jethro Park's very own tabloid totty, I was also the girl responsible for bringing India Withers into their lives. Thanks to India's performance on Sunday night, the entire country now thought Jethro Park was a breeding ground for violent young delinquents. For all I knew, social services had already been called and taken all of Year Seven into care. The Vice Squad was probably getting ready for a raid on the boys' locker rooms. Before long, someone from the Home Office would announce that Weapons of Mass Destruction had been found in the science labs. And it would all be my fault.

My guilt trip got so bad that when I caught sight of Grandpa Cleeve's Christian Decency pamphlet stuffed down the back of the sofa I actually pulled it out for a second look – after all, if I was going to wallow in shame I might as well do it properly. And it was then that I saw something in the list of patrons that made me sit up very straight. There, in the section for 'major sponsors', was a company called Aidni Ltd.

There was no reason why this should have meant anything to me except for a conversation I'd once had, back at Darlinham House. It was during a seminar on tax evasion (of the legal kind – even the Darlings aren't *that* radical) and people were swapping stories of Mummy and Daddy's Swiss bank accounts and off-shore investment funds and the like. India's father, for example, had set up a number of private companies where he could stash his loot and save on tax. Being a proud papa, he had named two of these companies after his children – but with their names spelt backwards. Sixela Ltd was one. Aidni was another. My-oh-my.

I thought about Milton. He might be small and

skinny with suicidal tendencies but *he* hadn't let himself be pushed around by the likes of India. So perhaps it was time for me to think more creatively. Perhaps it was time for me to pay another little visit to the Dark Side.

'Hello, India.'

'Well, well, if it isn't the schoolgirl seductress herself! I must say, I didn't think you had it in you, Oc-tave-ee-ah . . . is it true that Freddie has a Teletubby tattooed on his inner thigh?'

'Sorry to disappoint, but I'm not phoning to chat about Teletubbies. This is more of a business call.'

'And what business could *I* possibly have with you?'

'Oh, Indy,' I said reproachfully, 'after everything we've been through together! And when our families have always been so close!'

'That collection of freaks you like to call a family has never—'

I pretended I hadn't heard her. 'First there was me and your brother, then you and my soon-to-be stepbrother . . . and now, of course, my grandfather and your dad . . .'

'My *dad*?'

'Sir Rich Withers himself. A good old-fashioned champion of good old-fashioned family values. Not to mention Christian morals.'

'Dave, you're babbling. Dad thinks "moral" is a dirty word.'

'Really? I think my grandpa would be very sorry to hear that, seeing as how Sir Rich is a major patron of his League for the Promotion of Christian Decency.'

There was spluttering sound down the other end of the line.

'Yes,' I continued cheerily, 'at last someone is taking a stand against sexual deviancy, drug and alcohol abuse and the decline of good manners among the nation's young . . . Heart-warming, don't you think?'

India had recovered her voice. 'You are *so* wrong. Rich Withers would never, ever betray his values for—'

'Bad luck, Indy, but I've seen the membership list.' More spluttering. 'After all these rumours that he's begun to clean up his act . . . well, it's just a shame that not all of Rich's fans are going to appreciate his new-found sense of morality. Remember those people who accused him of selling out just because he accepted a knighthood?' I was really enjoying myself now. 'I'm *sure* once the press uproar dies down they'll get used to the idea, though – especially with that "Greatest Hits" tour coming up so soon. How does that song go again? Oh yes – "Love is puke, God is dead, Sex 'n' slaughter screaming in my head . . ."'

Funnily enough, India didn't join in the chorus. Instead, there was a long silence. You could practically hear the wheels turning. Then:

'Tell me what you want.'

On Wednesday evening a spokesman on behalf of India Withers and the television company that makes *Symposium* called a press conference. He announced to the nation that a most regrettable mistake had occurred. The interview with India Withers that was broadcast on last Sunday's edition of *Symposium* was not, in fact, an interview at all. It was a video clip of Ms Withers in rehearsal, performing a piece of improvisation in the character of her latest role. Due to a series of unfortunate misunderstandings – which were being investigated with all possible diligence – this had been presented as a factual commentary on a real-life experience. This was categorically not the case. India was happy to confirm that she had been attending a West London state school for the purpose of her education, but this had no connection with any film projects she might or might not be involved in.

Ms Withers also wanted to make clear that she *loved* her time at the West London comprehensive in question and that nothing would make her happier than to settle down at such a popular and respected school. Unfortunately, constant media scrutiny had made that an impossible dream. In fact, the turmoil of the last few days had forced her to re-evaluate her current professional commitments. She felt the storm of publicity that she had unwittingly caused made her a liability to Mr Mosley's project. It was her profound respect for Jed that led her to withdraw, reluctantly, from his film.

In a separate statement, Sir Rich Withers announced that as a gesture of goodwill, he would be donating a state-of-the-art music suite to the school concerned.

I had to hand it to her – it was an outstanding piece of spin if ever I'd heard one. It looked like the guys at *Symposium* were going to take most of the blame (though it served them right for being so gullible in the first place) whereas India emerged in a rosy glow of publicity: the Bright Young Thing with an 'impossible dream'. What's more, she had the perfect excuse for

leaving Jed in the lurch now it looked like Tempest weren't pitching him into the big league after all. But when all was said and done, I was feeling pretty pleased with myself. Thanks to me, Jethro Park's reputation was saved and, thanks to Milton, India's acting career was back on the rent-a-bimbo track.

And as for Jed . . . well, now he'd got shot of India and Tempest, maybe he'd be able to make the kind of film he really wanted to. Of course, hardly anyone would ever go to see it but, hey, at least he had his integrity.

Mum and Dad joined forces on Thursday evening to insist that I went back to school the following day. It was true that the press interest in Freddie's latest fling was fading almost as fast as their interest in the school-scandal-that-never-was; in fact, now that the excitement of Freddie's suspected drugs overdose had died down it was clear that I was just another soon-to-be forgotten drop in his love-struck teen ocean. Even the girl with the 'Back Off, Bitch' banner hadn't bothered hanging round for more than a day or two. But as the glow of my victory over India began to fade, I couldn't help feeling that there wasn't much point in saving my school's reputation if my own was still in shreds.

However, although the attention of the great British public was already moving away from Jethro Park, in staffroom and classroom alike it was a completely different matter. And it was this that saved me. In fact, it's just as well I'm not of the Darling disposition, because when I finally did skulk into school on Friday morning it was (almost) as if my Night of Shame with

Freddie Lions had never been. The Great India Withers Scandal was all anyone talked, thought or cared about. That, and comparing how many camera shots they'd got their face into or how many times their sound clip was featured on local radio. (Vicky 'n' Meera were still reeling from their *Good Morning, London!* glory and were only just recovering the power of speech.) Nobody quite knew what to make of the whole business and a fine collection of conspiracy theories was in circulation, each more elaborate than the last. None of them came close to the truth, of course.

Freddie Lions's libel action against the *Comet* was also a major factor in my favour. Thanks to Viv, rumours were swirling that my name had been cited in the proceedings and that anyone who tried to press the issue could find themselves ensnared in a multimillion-pound court case. Of course, I still had to put up with a lot of nudge-nudge, wink-winking and people who burst into Freddie Lions songs whenever I appeared round a corner, but all in all I got off incredibly lightly. I didn't even have to endure any clever remarks from Mr Pemberton, as he was off on an extended sick leave brought on by the heartbreak of India's betrayal.

A week later and life wasn't back to normal exactly, but it was bearable again. I copied up the notes I'd missed, blackened India's name with the best of them, rose above the Freddie Lions wisecracks, fended off inquiries about my mother's sex life/sanity with a shrug and a smile . . . and still spent most of my time and energy pining for Ben. It was crushingly obvious that he was going out of his way to avoid me and on the rare occasions when our paths did cross he was polite but distant, as if we barely knew each other. Even worse, Katie took it upon herself to comfort me in my abandonment and I had to endure long sessions holed up in the girls' toilets with her while she reminisced about her time with Jack and drew wildly inaccurate parallels between our situations.

Then one afternoon after school I was queuing at the newsagent's for a can of Coke when two lads from the year above came in and started messing around by the magazine shelf. The shop assistant was having problems with the till, so while I waited by the counter I was treated to a loud discussion as to which tits 'n' testosterone mag they were going for this time and which of this month's Page Three Stunnas had the pertest bottom. 'Hey,' said Oaf Number One, turning from his magazine to look me up and down. 'It's Octavia, right? Look, Rob – Jethro Park's own tabloid totty!'

'Wha-hey!' said Rob, otherwise known as Oaf Number Two. 'So do we get an exclusive kiss 'n' tell on you and that Lions bloke?' He leaned towards me leerily. 'Or how about just a kiss?'

I ignored them.

'She's not going to talk to the likes of us,' said Oaf Number One. 'She's dead posh, remember. Same as that crazy mother of hers.'

'Think you're too good for Jethro Park, do you, like your best mate India?'

'She was never my mate.' I wanted to leave but that would be like running away. Besides, the shop assistant had disappeared into the back of the shop with my tenner.

'Yeah, right. You and her are just the same – acting like you want to be left alone, have your privacy, blah blah, then running off to blow kisses at the nearest camera crew. Don't try and pretend that you don't get off on all the attention.'

'All those media tarts are gagging for it.'

'Desperate for it, you are.'

'And yet you're the ones slobbering over a girlie mag,' said Ben, who had come into the shop and was standing behind Oafs One and Two. They stared at him with open hostility. 'Maybe next time you start a rant on desperation you should try to wipe the drool off your chins first.'

'Who are you, her bodyguard?'

'Just a passing fan.'

Ben might be a whole three-quarters-of-an-inch shorter than me, but he's still tall and he can also look quite mean when he wants to. He just stood there with his hands in his pockets, looking them up and down with his best sarcastic expression. Oafs One and Two sniggered together for a bit but then they slouched out of the shop, leaving their magazines crumpled on the counter.

Ben didn't say anything while I finally got my change and gathered my stuff together, but when I left the shop he came with me and we started walking down the road together. I cleared my throat uncomfortably.

'I don't need rescuing, you know.'

'I know . . . so, um, how about an apology instead?'

'Apology?'

'Yeah. For behaving like those two goons back in the shop.' He was blushing slightly.

I managed to resist the impulse to fall on my knees and cry, 'But there is nothing to forgive, my dearest one!' Because Ben was right: he did owe me an apology. 'You're not *exactly* like them,' I muttered. 'They're lecherous yobs with an IQ smaller than their shoe size.'

'Well, I don't have their excuse, then. There I was, acting all superior, mouthing off about stuff I don't really know anything about – and then when things got tough I bottled out. When you needed me.'

'Look, Ben, it wasn't only your fault, OK?' He shook his head. 'No, I mean it. I've been so self-obsessed lately I haven't been thinking straight. I should have stood up to India right from the start, been more upfront about everything . . . it's just that you were a bit, er . . .'

'Touchy and paranoid?' Now he really was blushing. 'It's all right, you can say it.' He gave me the sort of glower that if I didn't know him better would have sent me running for cover. 'It's not only girls who feel insecure, you know. And seeing you and your family in a magazine, or . . . or a paper, or hearing about this past life full of It-Boys and the rest of it . . . I know I'm being irrational and unfair, but it *does* bother me.'

I took his hand. 'Don't let it, then. Because you see,' I said gently, 'I can't guarantee that I'll always be able to keep away from that sort of stuff. I used to think I could cut myself off, stay safe in my own little bubble . . . but as long as I'm part of this family, and as long as they keep doing the things they do, it'll be part of my life, too. That's the way it is.'

He nodded, and his eyes were bright. 'I know. Because when you care about people, you can't just walk away.'

'Who said anything about walking?' Then I put my arms round him and we held each other tight.

There's a new teen chick-flick being filmed in London at the moment, about an ordinary schoolgirl who gets stuck in a lift with a famous pop star and has to cope with first love in the media spotlight. Co-produced by BBC films and Tempest UK, and starring Freddie Lions as the pop idol and India Withers as the girl-next-door, it is expected to rake it in at the box office. It appears that after the Mosley project fell through, Tempest were persuaded that India's tribulations made her the natural choice to play a publicity-shy schoolgirl caught up in the frenzy of fame.

As Katie says, it was my bad luck that the film didn't come out a couple of months ago – if it had, maybe I could have picked up some tips on life in the limelight and saved myself a lot of heartache.

People at school are talking of boycotting the film when it's released, but I expect we'll all go and see it, especially now that the uproar over the *Symposium* allegations has died a natural death. The official line from our headmaster, local MP and Parent-Teacher Association is that India was enrolled in Jethro Park in good faith and all this method acting malarkey about rundown comprehensives was a conspiracy cooked up by the press. Her former classmates have not been quite so easily appeased, but the Withers Era is still celebrated by the faithful few. In fact, Vicky 'n' Meera are convinced they'll be getting invitations to the chick-flick premiere and are already planning their outfits for the big night. What Mr Pemberton thinks about all this is anyone's guess, as his extended sick leave turned into early retirement and he hasn't been seen in school since Indy's own departure.

As for me, I've had to accept that I'll never really see the back of her. Only last week, for example, she appeared in a photo shoot with Freddie in *TeenDream* magazine. I know this because Milton has it pinned to his bedroom wall, in pride of place next to the *Scream* poster. He still thinks India is the most wonderful Harbinger of Doom he's ever met, and just remembering how he beat her at her own evil game brings a creepy little smile to his face. What's more, the creepy smile is becoming so frequent that Bud has decided that the Sunshine Project is well on its way, and is sending Milton back to school next autumn. He and Lady Jane have found a small private college for the 'gifted and sensitive' (i.e. brainy but loony) so Milton's soon going to have even more opportunity to spread gloom and suffering. His mother suggested he should come and join her own cult – sorry, School of Holistic Healing – but Milton said he'd rather stick it out in England. Apparently he prefers the weather here.

Lola and the Guru also offered to arrange for a shaman to bless Bud and Lady Jane's wedding – in a spirit of reconciliation and cosmic harmony, of course – but the lovebirds politely declined the offer.

A few months on, and the sensation of India's arrival and departure from Jethro Park had passed into the stuff of legend. 'Colourful, but not quite real,' as Viv put it one Sunday afternoon in Hyde Park, where a group of us had been playing a new ball game of Jack's invention: a high-speed cross between rugby and rounders involving lots of grass stains and adrenalin. It was May and even though exams were just around the corner there was the taste of summer and freedom in the air. Ben and I were both in a silly kind of mood as we said goodbye to the others and went to meet Dad for tea, bouncing along the street like a couple of kids and trying to stick daisies in each other's hair. Whereupon we nearly crashed into a couple of elderly gentlemen strolling down the Brompton Road. '*Octavia?*' said my grandfather in tones of pained disbelief.

It was Lord Clairbrook-Cleeve and the Earl of Morthaven. They were got up very fine in their Sunday best whereas I'm afraid to say that Ben and I probably gave the impression of being drunk or lunatic or both, what with the giggling and the unsteady feet and general dishevelment. Of grandparent and granddaughter it was difficult to tell which of the two was the most dismayed at the encounter. I decided it was too late for the usual formalities. 'Hello, Gramps!' I said, with a reckless smile.

The Earl of Morthaven shook his head sorrowfully. 'It's the actress's daughter,' he said.

'Quite,' said Lord Clairbrook-Cleeve through clenched teeth.

''Fraid so. Oh, and this is Ben.' I looked from the noble earl to my grandfather mischievously, then squeezed Ben round the waist. 'Ben, I'd like you to meet Grandpa Cleeve.' Ben gave him a cheerful nod, dislodging a daisy as he did so. 'And this is his great pal, Binkie.'

'Pleased to meet you, Binkie,' said Ben. There was an appalled silence.

'You know,' I said conversationally, 'Binkie once told me a very wise thing.' I looked at Ben solemnly. 'A true lady should only appear in the papers when she is born, when she marries and when she dies.'

Ben laughed. 'I guess you're not a lady then.'

'Guess I'm not.' And I spun free and away down the street, past the scandalized faces of the lord and earl, past Ben's outstretched arms, past the scraps of yesterday's newspaper tumbling at my feet.

ROSE WILKINS

So Super Starry

My mother can't understand why I don't devote more time and energy to looking like someone glamorous, sexy and interesting. Someone super-starry.

Despite having a mum who's a sitcom star and a dad who's a film director, Octavia has never fitted in at Darlinham House, a school for kids of the (fabulously) rich and famous.

It's hard enough for Octavia to avoid bitchy India and her 'pygmy blonde' mates, without having to deal with her mother too, who can't wait to see Octavia with the right guy, at the right party, in the right magazine.

But can a D-list disaster like Octavia ever be happy hanging with the A-team? And will the cost be worth it?

Hilarious, clever and packed with the gossipy fascination of celebrity magazines, SO SUPER STARRY delights from start to finish.

A selected list of titles available from Macmillan Children's Books

The prices shown below are correct at the time of going to press. However, Macmillan Publishers reserves the right to show new retail prices on covers which may differ from those previously advertised.

Rose Wilkins

So Super Starry	0 330 42087 9	£4.99

Jaclyn Moriarty

Feeling Sorry for Celia	0 330 39725 7	£5.99
Finding Cassie Crazy	0 330 41803 3	£5.99

Julie Burchill

Sugar Rush	0 330 41583 2	£4.99

Sarah Mlynowski

All About Rachel: Bras and Broomsticks	0 330 43280 X	£5.99

All Pan Macmillan titles can be ordered from our website, www.panmacmillan.com, or from your local bookshop and are also available by post from:

Bookpost, PO Box 29, Douglas, Isle of Man IM99 1BQ
Credit cards accepted. For details:
Telephone: 01624 677237
Fax: 01624 670923
Email: bookshop@enterprise.net
www.bookpost.co.uk

Free postage and packing in the United Kingdom